What People are Saying about
Memoirs of a Dilettante Volume One

Advance Praise for
Memoirs of a Dilettante Volume Two

"Helena Hann-Basquiat taps into what makes relationships raw, real and so destructive they can leave us ripped apart, standing alone and wondering why. Sometimes, as in this story, we find the answer..."

Sara Litchfield, author of *The Night Butterflies*

"Helena glitters, glows, and shows a depth in this book that far surpasses the first book. I love her even more. "

Katie Cross, author of *The Network Series*

"I'm thrilled I don't have to get off the Dilettante train just yet! I wasn't done with Helena and Penny, and I'm so excited I get to witness more of their journey in Memoirs Volume Two."

Beth Teliho, author of *Order of Seven*

Memoirs of a Dilettante

Volume Two

Helena Hann-Basquiat

Introduction by Lizzi Rogers

Also by Helena Hann-Basquiat

Memoirs of a Dilettante Volume One
Penelope, Countess of Arcadia

With Jex Collyer, Michelle Combs, Freya McMillan, Hayley Morgan, Lizzi Rogers & Hannah Sears

JESSICA

Writing as Jessica B. Bell

VISCERA – a collection of strange tales (coming soon)

Memoirs

of a

Dilettante

volume two

Helena Hann-Basquiat

dilettante publishing

Memoirs of a Dilettante Volume Two

Copyright © 2015, Helena Hann-Basquiat

ISBN 13: 978-0-9940419-0-6
ISBN 10: 0-9940419-0-X

Published in Canada by Dilettante Publishing

This one is for the survivors of abuse of all kinds.
May you find new life, and not spend your days like the walking dead.

Introduction

When I first 'met' Helena, we were suddenly in Paris.

The sheer elegance of her writing transported me to a chic balcony overlooking the Champs Elysees, where a tall, cool blonde leaned out over the railing, dropping swirls of smoke into the night with each perfectly enunciated word. Her throat sparkled with a creation from Tiffany's, but the polish on the fingernails holding the silver cigarette holder had chipped, and the backs of her Manolos were scuffed.

I stammered a greeting, feeling like a gawky, two-left-footed, should've-ironed-this-outfit dork in her presence. She looked over, quite languidly, transfixed me with an ice-blue gaze, and with a look of intense bemusement and a lift of one perfectly-arched eyebrow, instructed:

"Come *here*, darling…"

I've been 'there' ever since.

Since my first encounter with my absolutelyveryfavourite Dilettante, Helena has taken me from 'FanGirl At Arm's Length' to 'Trusted Friend' (with the disclaimer that I am only as certain of that as anyone *can* be, when dealing with such an unreliable (yet somehow incomparably fabulous) narrator).

Each time I read a new story, I am reminded that this is a lady who not only knows how to exit a car in high heels with her dignity intact, but that she could probably do so after having drunk most of the party under the table (as long as she stuck to Greyhounds (Grey Goose with red grapefruit juice, preferably fresh)), whilst singing, word perfect, any song by The Smiths you care to mention.

She's also a lady with a tragic past (only some of which was self-inflicted), a gorgeous (if somewhat foul-mouthed and urchin-y around the edges) niece, Penny, Countess of Arcadia, and a slew of stories which will leave you slack-jawed and wondering how on earth you're going to cope when the book ends. Or, at least, they will if you're me, because that was my response to 'Memoirs of a Dilettante: Volume One'. Once I had closed the final page and gathered myself together, I immediately sent a message to Helena nigh on *demanding* that she produce another book, because one simply *wasn't* enough.

Fortunately for me, she was in an acquiescent sort of mood.

You're welcome.

Lizzi Rogers is a blogger, writer, poet, and stick-figure artist at Considerings: Life in Silver Linings. In 2014 she collaborated with Helena and several other writers and artists on the multi-media metaphysical horror novella JESSICA.

Dramatis Personae

HELENA, Dilettante. Heroine of the tale. Pop culture aficionado.

PENNY, aka Penelope, aka The Countess, niece of HELENA, daughter to the late CHERYL and TED, unofficial Countess of the fictional land of Arcadia

CHERYL, older sister of HELENA

TED, husband to CHERYL

BROOKE, friend to HELENA

DAVID, husband to BROOKE

ROBERT, one time love interest of HELENA, in California

MAYA, friend to HELENA, in California

AMY LEFEVRE, a lost resident of Arcadia

THE BARISTA WITH NO NAME, a barista, whose name remains unknown to HELENA

THE ASSHOLE, an asshole, and a client of HELENA

ANGELA, a vice president of the student society that PENNY belongs to

CLAUDIA, the president of the same student society

SPENSER, a Jazz musician, and possible love interest

ADAM, one time love of HELENA

PAUL, friend of ADAM and, well… it's complicated.

Welcome to Arcadia – Population: Dwindling

S omewhere east of Buffalo and west of New York City, at the
crossroads of cultural stagnation and economic failure lies the
town of Arcadia, Population: Dwindling. There actually is a
real Arcadia, New York, but that's not the Arcadia I'm talking about,
darlings. No, the Arcadia I'm describing is an Arcadia of the mind,
the Arcadia of my memory, whose remaining residents press on
ploddingly like dim-witted dinosaurs denying an impending Ice Age.

Arcadia is an asylum for failed business owners and early retirees
from the nearby factory that once employed the whole town but has
since shut down; moved to some country in Southeast Asia that none
of the residents of Arcadia could point to on a map. Just a few of the
casualties of globalization, the people of Arcadia have just been
waiting for Bush, then Clinton, then Dubya, and now Obama to *do
something about it*. It is a home to shopkeepers, stationary store clerks
and druggists, who find themselves being made increasingly obsolete
by the encroaching urban sprawl of Wal-Mart, Kinko's and Rite Aid
(or Target, Staples and Walgreens – you choose).

A walk around the town of Arcadia won't give you any indication
of the history of the town – sure, there might be a plaque mounted in
the park commemorating its dedication in the name of some
prominent citizen, and there might even be a historical society at the
Chamber of Commerce where you can learn the names of the boys
who died in the Great War between the States, or pictures of the time
the governor visited, or an article about how Arcadia was the
birthplace of some not-so-prominent member of society. The
architecture around town is a mixed bag of Dutch Colonials,

Victorians, and Cape Cods, with none of the pre-fab homogeneity of suburbia. Many of the houses are decorated year-round with red, white and blue bunting that is changed regularly and with pride.

The truth is, the settling of Arcadia was likely not intentional, but rather, some settlers probably got trapped by a storm and stopped there to wait out the winter, and then in the spring, those men that survived the harsh elements found that many of their womenfolk were with child, and in no condition to travel, and so they decided to stay where they were. Maybe they set up a trading post to engage in commerce with the Haudenosaunee[1] whose territory they'd parked themselves in. Perhaps that trading post sat in the same place where there now sits a J.C. Penny as part of a tiny mall that really only features the J.C. Penny, a hair salon, a lottery booth, and Jill's Diner, home of *The Best Darn Club Sandwich You'll Ever Have.*

"The secret's in the sauce," Jill will tell you with a wink, as if everyone who's ever eaten one couldn't tell you that a teaspoon of horseradish mixed into the mayonnaise to give it zip was the secret.

The people of Arcadia do what they can to make ends meet, which isn't much, but they still manage, for the most part, to pay their mortgages to the modern corporate banks, one of the few things that have moved along with the times in Arcadia. No longer is your good standing in the community or true ability to repay taken into consideration by a shrewd but reasonable bank manager; instead, a computer calculates a credit score and makes a decision entirely based on statistics, deciding in greedy fashion that those who can least afford it pay the highest interest rates.

Main street of Arcadia features more empty storefronts every day, alongside the turnkey coffee shop, a barber shop that will likely close its doors forever when the elderly proprietor passes away, and of course, the liquor store, which does steady business whatever the state of the economy. There's a small bar that just got a karaoke machine and a textile store that won't last much longer, either. There's an old Nickelodeon style movie theatre with *Two Enormous Screens* and *A/C in the Summertime – Come in, it's Cooler in Here!* They show almost new releases and on Tuesdays, you can catch a classic

---

[1] You may have heard of them as the Iroquois. If you've seen the film *Last of the Mohicans* starring the yummy Daniel Day-Lewis, then you know who I'm talking about. They are the famous Six Nations people, comprised of Mohawk, Onondaga, Oneida, Cayuga, Seneca and Tuscarora. Don't ever say I didn't teach you anything, darlings.

for only two dollars.

Arcadia is not so much a town as it is a Norman Rockwell painting gone to seed, and those who find themselves there pray they can stay – that the winds of change don't blow too strongly across their path, forcing them to uproot and leave everything they know. If you find yourself employed in Arcadia, you'll never leave. If you find yourself unemployed, well, the population is dwindling for a reason. If Emily Dickinson was right about hope being a thing with feathers,[2] then an apt continuance of that metaphor would be to say that all the birds in Arcadia have already been shot and eaten, and closest that the folk of Arcadia get to their feathers is in their down filled pillows. It would be a romantic notion to think that perhaps these lend themselves to dreams of flight, but it is more likely that the people of Arcadia stopped dreaming a long time ago.

My parents moved to Arcadia when I was seventeen and half a world away.[3] I got the news after the fact and by post, and so Arcadia is something of a *bête noire*[4] for me. For some reason, even when my sister Cheryl and her husband left Arcadia to return to Toronto, my parents stayed behind. Arcadia had nearly destroyed my sister's marriage, and my parents only moved there in the first place to be close to Cheryl and the soon to be born Penelope, so I never understood their reasons for staying after she left, but then, I don't understand a lot of things about them. Arcadia is a spider's web, and my parents are caught in it. They live there to this day, wrapped up in the unbreakable thread of quaint, quiet, small town America, and like all the other flies in Arcadia, they have learned not to struggle, lest they draw attention to themselves and get eaten off the web; consumed by the world outside their little burg, which has moved on in ways that they can't even comprehend.

The day will come when I will get a call to tell me that one or both of them have died, and I will do my duty as their daughter to travel to that dead zone of forgotten Americana, but after that day, I will brush the dust of Arcadia off of my feet and never look back.

---

2 Emily Dickinson was an American poet 1830-1886

3 See Volume One for details. I was in the UK, and my parents moved while I was gone, expecting that I would just follow them wherever they went.

4 French, literally meaning "black beast" - something that leaves a terrible taste in your mouth, something you dread, something you hate, something that is the bane of your existence.

Countess Penelope and the
Banana Bread Debacle

I arrived home the other night to find the Countess Penelope –
you remember Penny, darlings – feisty but sweet, likes to dress
like it's Hallowe'en at Lewis Carroll's house, real knack for
neologism (that means making words up, darlings) – lounging on the
couch watching *Phineas and Ferb* [5] and laughing like it was the funniest
thing in the whole world. However, there was something peculiar
about her laugh that gave me pause. It was as if her laugh were
coming from miles away, like it was muted, somehow. I put it out of
my mind for the time being.

I'd had a long pointless day of filling out paperwork and cutting
seemingly hundreds of checks for the various clientele of the casting
agency that I work for, and all I really wanted to do was have a quick
hot shower and then sit down in front of a fan and enjoy the feeling
of the artificial breeze on my wet skin. We have A/C darlings – we're
not savages – but there's still something to be said for the old
standby of wet skin and a cool breeze to relax, refresh and
reinvigorate as it refrigerates.

Penny and I had nothing going on, and so it looked like the simple
desires of my exhausted little heart were going to be met. Little did I
know that my evening was going to get even more interesting, a trifle
more relaxing, and that the next day I would require a trip to the
massage therapist to attend to my aching appendages.

I had my shower and came back to the living room wearing one

---

[5] A children's show. A *Disney* show, no less, but it's hilarious and has amazing
music. And Richard O'Brien, who wrote The Rocky Horror Show (and was Riff Raff in the
film) does a voice in it.

towel wrapped around my head like a turban (yes, boys, we all really do know how to do that – as young girls, we are taken aside in groups of three or four and given all kinds of secret instruction when you're not paying attention) and one wrapped around my body, and sat the fan in front of my favourite chair in preparation for my big evening of doing nothing.

As is my custom, whether it be thirty below or thirty above (that's Celsius, darlings - just think "very cold or very warm") I made myself a pot of tea, and poured myself a cup.

"Penny, darling," I asked politely, "would you care for a cup of tea?"

"Oh, thawt would be luffly, dahling," the Countess of Arcadia, recent resident of Buckingham Palace replied, miming the aristocratic pinkie finger position for holding a tea cup. "Oh, and doooo help yourself to some ba-naaaah-na bread, dahling, it is simply to diiiie for. Yes. Quite. And such. Be a deah and cut me another teensy slice, would you. I'm still feeling a mite peckish don't you know. Yes. Quite."

I smiled in spite of my absolute exhaustion, and said, "Right away, Mum," adopting my own feeble attempt at Penny's cockney urchin, which the situation simply begged for. I had learned, though, that it was dangerous to start making requests of the Countess – one time she spoke like Countess Penelope the lemur Queen of Madagascar[6] for an entire week, even in public, until it started morphing, as her voices tend to after a while, back into the original Dickensian street urchin that she first launched on me all those years ago upon my return from California. Still, I had the phrase "I like to move it" stuck in my head for weeks afterward.

I found the banana bread wrapped in tinfoil on the counter, and cut a couple of slices off the already partly devoured loaf.

"How many slices have you already had?" I asked the Countess Arcade, who was laughing so hard at the antics of Perry the Platypus[7] that her face was bunched up and she had tears in her eyes. She held up two fingers, and then seemed to consider that and added a third. Her manic laughter should have clued me in, but by the time I realized what was going on, it was already far too late.

---

[6] This was Penny doing her very best King Julian, from the Madagascar franchise, originally played by Sacha Baron Cohen.

[7] Perry the Platypus is a secret agent in *Phineas and Ferb*.

"Geez, save me some, you piggie!" I teased, and oinked at her, triggering another mad bout of laughter. I reluctantly handed Penny her fourth piece of banana bread and a cup of tea and then sat down and sipped my own, enjoying the fan drying my wet skin. It felt really nice; in about an hour it would feel positively transcendent.

I wolfed down my slice, washed it down with my tea, not realizing how hungry I actually was. I was going to get myself another slice when something about the aftertaste made me stop.

"What did you put in there, Penny?" I asked, trying to place the secret ingredient. "Is that ginger or something? It's unusual."

"I know, right?" Penny said loudly, as if she couldn't control the volume of her voice. "I thought it tasted funny! I don't know what they put in it."

"Wait," I said, mildly alarmed. "You didn't make this?"

"Hell, no, bitch!" The Countess Penelope of Arcadia, late of the Bronx blurted, then slammed a hand over own mouth in embarrassment. "Omygod, Helena, I'm sorry! I don't know what's come over me."

"Oh, I think I do," I mused, aware that I had already eaten a slice myself. "Just where did you get it?"

"These boys on campus," she said, the cheer fading from her voice, "They said they were raising money for... um... I forget, Helena, but I feel funny, do I feel funny looking to you?"

"Oh, you're hysterical, darling," I said, trying hard to be a responsible adult but not having a hypocritical bone in my body, I was having a really hard time.

"I can't feel my mouth," Penny said, demonstrating this by sticking her tongue out and rolling it around her lips. "Nothing. Twenty dollars is a lot for loaf of.. uh, banana bread, don't you think?"

"Actually," I said, "that sounds about right." Then I cut myself another slice. In for a penny, in for a pound, you might say.

About an hour and a half later, the Countess had passed out and was snoring like a pug. I, however, was staring into the fan and singing *The Crystal Ship* by The Doors,[8] crooning into the wavering air and listening to my voice be transformed into something robotic and otherworldly. The song ended (and when had I turned the stereo on?

---

[8] I may or may not have stood up, opened up my towel, held my arms wide and said "I am the Lizard Queen!"

I couldn't remember doing that) and in the silence that followed, I suddenly became aware that I needed chocolate milk. It wasn't that I wanted chocolate milk, darlings, because wants we can rationalize away and ignore – no, I *needed* chocolate milk, but the kitchen seemed so far away.

"Penny," I whispered, afraid someone might hear me and realize that I was very stoned. "Penny!"

She laid still, only her rising and falling chest and the occasional unladylike snort proving that she was, indeed, still among the living.

"Penny!" I said a little louder. "Penny, I need some chocolate milk!"

It was becoming clear to me that if I was to procure the precious pasteurized potable, I was going to have to close the distance between my chair and the kitchen.

No problem. I could do that. No problem.

The problem arose when my legs refused to carry my weight, and I wobbled my way to the kitchen on trembling legs, like a newborn fawn stumbling away from its mother for the first time. I made it to the fridge and clung to the door handle like I was just learning to roller skate and had made it to a pole. At that moment I swore to myself that I was just going to stay there. I was going to sit down in front of the fridge, get some chocolate milk, and sleep right there on the kitchen floor.

That's not what happened though, because I woke up in my chair the next morning, still feeling pretty tingly and numb (or ningly and tumb, as Penny said) and clutching an empty carton of chocolate milk.

"Let's not do this again, okay?" I begged the Countess. "I'm getting too old for this shit."

The Countess nodded, and then crawled off to her bed, where she remained for, as far as I know, the rest of the day.

I, however, had to go to work, despite the fact that I felt like I'd been hit by a bus.

––––

Later that day, I scheduled a massage for myself, because my legs felt like they were two elastic bands that had been stretched until they ripped. It felt glorious, and I moaned in pleasure and relief.

"Oh my god," the magnificent masseuse remarked. "What did you do to your legs?"

I'd like to tell you that I confessed to accidentally eating some banana bread laced with weed. It would sure make me look better if I told you that I had a good laugh about it with her, and that I feigned shock and ignorance on the subject of drugs, and that we shared an After-School Special-esque moment on the dangers of marijuana. I'd like to tell you that I wasn't so embarrassed by the whole thing, and how old it made me feel, but the truth is, I was terribly embarrassed by the whole thing, and it made me feel really *old*. And that's the truth. Not like this little bit of lawn fertilizer.

"Oh, I'm training to run a marathon," I said.

"Wow!" she exclaimed. "Good for you!"

"Yeah," I said. "It's hard work, but it keeps me young."

"Well, you look great," she said, working my legs with her glorious hands.

"Why, thank you, darling."

The Disappearance of Amy LeFevre

I didn't know Amy LeFevre – not really – but I'd seen her around town, riding her bike in her short shorts and Doc Martens, bruises up and down her legs like tattoos fading in the sun. If you really pressed her about the bruises (and so few ever bothered - - I only asked her once out of polite concern) she'd offer self-deprecatory excuses of clumsiness or claim she was anemic.

She wore those Docs so proudly; she'd had to go to the city to get them, and they seemed to be her declaration that she'd gotten out once, and she would get out again. They had steel toes and Amy had gotten in trouble on more than one occasion for using them against boys who just wouldn't take no for an answer.

Amy had recently shaved her head, and the oh-so-clever boys in school and around the small-minded small town of Arcadia had taken to changing the words to that old Queen song to sing at her "I want to ride my bi-sexual, I want to ride my dyke!"[9] Amy was not a lesbian, not that it mattered to anyone. Closet homosexuality was not the secret that Amy kept, so their taunts didn't bother her.

Amy's father ran the hardware store in Arcadia, just as his father had before him, and he was a small, broken man with a broken marriage and a small house living in a small, broken town, and he was absolutely terrified of two small words: Home Depot.

By day he was congenial, and his customers all loved him and

---

[9] It's actually "I want to ride my bicycle, I want to ride my bike."

wished him well, and would join in his armchair economics lectures that he would launch into whenever the topic of the big box chains came up, which was nearly always. During business hours it was merely sympathizing and small town solidarity, and the conversations would always just be polite agreement that *the winds are changing* or some other homily. After hours, Amy's dad would park himself at the bar, and after a couple of drinks, launch into accusations at fellow townsfolk who he knew, he *just knew* were doing their shopping at the Home Depot just outside of town and *taking food right out of my mouth, goddammit!*

This is the man that Amy had to deal with every night, and if Amy wore her shorts so short, well, maybe it was so that her father would have to constantly see the bruises, and maybe, *just maybe* he'd be ashamed and leave her alone. Or maybe she hoped that the townsfolk would put two and two together and say something, do something – but her cry for help went unanswered, even, I'm ashamed to say, by me. Maybe the reason why she shaved her head was so her father couldn't grab her hair when she tried to scramble away from him when he came into her room at night stinking of Johnny Walker and the sickly sweet tobacco of those cheap cigars he liked to smoke.

One day, Amy just disappeared.

By the time they discovered her father's body at the bottom of his basement stairs, Amy was long gone.

They found her bike at the Amtrak station in the next town ten miles away.

They never found Amy.

The Great and Terrible Countess of Oz

"It's a twistah! It's a twistah!" exclaimed the Countess Penelope of Arcadia, which is, in this instance, a county in Kansas by way of Oz.[10] It wouldn't be the last Oz reference made this weekend. The sky swelled black like a bruise, and the wind howled and threw things around in a poltergeist tantrum.

The cat-like but never cowardly Countess and I had driven through it, swerving to avoid minor debris like small tree branches, and once, a stray shopping cart blowing across the road. I kept my white-knuckled hands tight on the wheel, while Penny twisted and turned in the passenger seat, looking this way and that to see where the storm was coming from; where it was going. We drove right through the middle of it and came out the other side, like we'd gone through a car wash. The rain beat and battered us but did not best us.

When we made it safely home, I made sure to park far away from any trees, and when I saw the debris the next morning, I knew I'd made the right decision. We got out of the car and ran to our door, both of us getting soaked to the bone just crossing the street, and then locked ourselves in for the night, lighting candles and huddling on the floor in the living room, just watching our big bay window in terror as shingles blew off our roof and tree branches broke and fell.

---

[10] *The Wizard of Oz.* C'mon, it's a cultural phenomenon. If you have never seen *The Wizard of Oz* or read the books or are not at least aware of the reference I'm making, darlings, then please, put this book down immediately and correct this grievous oversight.

The next morning, we woke up *sans* power, which means *sans* air conditioning, and neither Penelope nor I woke up with the cheery disposition of a member of the Lullaby League. I told Penny I was heading out, and asked if she wanted anything. She buried her head in her pillow and told me to go away and come back tomorrow.

"Why don't you get your lazy butt out of bed and come with me?" I suggested.

"Pay no attention to the girl beneath the blanket! I am the great and powerful..."

"Okay, get up," I said, pulling the blanket off of her. "If you've got the energy for snark, you can come to the store with me."

"Oh, have a heart, Helena! Can't you see the circles under my eyes? I didn't sleep all night!" And then she gave me the most pathetic, pitiable look – which she knows full well I am helpless against.

"You know, I shouldn't let your puppy dog face get to me! I should be on my mettle, and yet, I'm torn apart. Okay, darling, you win. What do you want me to bring you?"

"Bring me the broomstick of the Wicked Witch of the West!" She demanded weakly, still trying to sleep, before the humidity began to rise again, making sleep impossible. "Oh, and coffee. For the love of Oz, the great and terrible, bring me some coffee. I don't care how many curly toed Munchkins you have to kill, fa la la la la, blah blah blah, just bring me some coffee."

"Uh, *bring me some coffee...* what?"

"Now, bitches!" The Countess demanded mock-indignantly.

"That's more like it," I replied.

I went out to try to acquire coffee for the Countess and myself (as no one wants to live with an under-caffeinated Countess, darlings) and was confronted with debris the likes of which I've never seen. Tree branches had broken and fallen all over the place, and entire streets had been blocked off with yellow police tape. I had to navigate around a labyrinth of newly altered landscape, taking twists and turns, and more than once running into a dead end and having to turn around. There was one rather straw-headed guy trying to direct traffic, but when I asked him which way to go, it became rather clear that he didn't know any more than anyone else.

"This way seems to be clear," he said, pointing left, but before I could drive away, he pointed right and added, "but then I haven't seen too much debris down this way, either."

"Then again, people do go both ways," I replied, and was given a confused look by the accidental scarecrow, who just waved me on, unappreciative of my witticisms.

As of this memoir missive, we are still without Internet (oh boo hoo, what a tragedy – do you want us to start an emergency fund, Helena?) and while your sarcasm is always appreciated, there is no need to be concerned for your favourite dilettante and her aristocratic accomplice – we are just fine, thank you very much.

Oh, but anyway, darlings, we're home – *home!* And these are my memoirs – and you're all here – and I'm not going to leave here ever, ever again, because I love you all! And... oh, darlings, there's no place like home!

Return of the Son of the Bride of the Barista With No Name

"So," the Countess Penelope of Arcadia said, sipping her sarsaparilla slowly, "you managed to avoid the hoosegow."

"Spoilers, Penny," I replied, wrapping my hands around a hot cuppa Joe. "I reckon I'll spin that yarn another day. These folks are achin' to know how yours truly managed to stay a free woman and all, but I reckon that story'll keep a while. You know, let it simmer and gain some flavour. Like my momma always said, you don't drink the 'shine afore its time. I reckon."

"You know, you said *I reckon*, like, a dozen times there," Penny pointed out with a presence most persnickety. "And also, grandma's a teetotaler."

"I counted three at most," I replied, "and your face is a teetotaler."

The Countess Penelope of Arcadia, late of the City Formerly Known As York,[11] once worked as a barista herself, until she was fired for spitting in someone's coffee (or rather, I should say, for getting *caught* spitting in someone's coffee. Who knows how many times she did it before getting caught)? During her short stint as a grinder monkey (as they are known in the trade), she coined the phrase "Your face is..." It all started on a shift where things started getting busy and tempers started rising, and someone kept calling out drinks. They'd call *Grande Americano, no room*, and the barista would call the order back. Well, I guess this day, Penny had so many people

---

11 That would be Toronto, darlings, whose original name was York. Well, you know, original after it was named by the English, who just loved naming things in the New World after their own cities back home.

calling drinks at her that she couldn't keep up, and when the order of *Tall Hot Chocolate* came, Penny, without thinking, yelled back "Your face is a tall hot chocolate!"

As you may already know, Penny is quite fond of making up insults that mean nothing and therefore cause no offense,[12] and so this affectation has become very popular, not only in Casa de Hann-Basquiat, but also among friends and acquaintances. I think the happiest I've ever seen Penny is when she overheard a total stranger using this faux-insult.

"Well, uh..." Penny had no comeback yet for the *Your face is...* maneuver, but give it time.

"Yeah, that's what I thought," I said smugly and slurped my coffee in most un-ladylike fashion. "Anyway, it's all formulating in my head. Don't worry, I'll give my readers a story they'll enjoy."

"I don't know how you sleep at night, Helena," the Countess deadpanned, "keeping thousands of faithful readers who hang on your every word waiting to hear the tale of your near-miss with incarceration."

"Now you're just being mean," I pouted. "People will read this and enjoy it."

"Well, there is that cowgirl bird,"[13] Penny said, slipping easily into the Dickensian urchin persona she affected so effortlessly. "She'll want to know wot's wot, roit? Ennit, an' such?"

"I'm sure," I said, "but there are all kinds of people who read the memoirs."

"Well, criminy! Why don't you bloody well make a public service announcement, loik?"

"Hi, I'm Helena Hann-Basquiat. You may remember me from such tales as Sister, I'm a Poet, or Something, or, more recently, LAID (A Halesowen Adventure).[14] Please enjoy this slight diversion as I cook up the next serialized tale "Return to Arcadia" where you'll learn about the years post-Halesowen but pre-California, as well as my recent forays into the world of traffic court. You'll laugh, you'll cry, you'll pee your pants. Chocolate milk may shoot out your nose whether you're drinking any or not. For those of you who

---

[12] Couche Tard, for example.

[13] That would be Hannah, late of Texas, currently of the Greater Boston Area, whom Penny likes to refer to in Wild West terms, because, well, Texas.

[14] See Memoirs of a Dilettante Vol One

are lactose intolerant, an alternate beverage will be provided. You'll learn the dangers of walking away and how the past comes back to bite you in the ass. You'll..."

Suddenly a hush fell over the coffee shop (we were sitting in a coffee shop, darlings, in case you hadn't surmised that already), and the bat-wing doors burst open, allowing for the Barista With No Name to enter with a flourish of his serape. Twin blue sapphires sparkled out of his squinted eyes as he gazed my way and gave me a nod, while touching one hand to the brim of his worn cowboy hat.

My heart stopped its beat, and I felt my cheeks flush with warmth.

"Oh mah stars," said the Countess Penelope of Arcadia (which was evidently somewhere in Arkansas). "That there's a tall drink o' water, I do declare."

It was not the first time that the very sight of this man, who I maintain looks like a young Clint Eastwood, had affected me so. He was the fastest draw in town, and never burned my espresso once since the Countess and I had started coming here a few months back. Plus, he shared my elder hipster sensibilities and disdain for the younger generation of clueless hipsters. If I recall correctly (and my recollection is beyond reproach, darlings) we had a shared moment one day not too long ago that said that he'd noticed me, too.

So when the Barista With No Name was followed through the bat-wing doors[15] by a woman carrying an unruly toddler, my previously swelling and exploding heart stilled and sunk into my stomach. I felt Penny's hand on mine and knew she'd seen it, too.

"Wow," the Countess Arcade sighed, slipping back into the street urchin voice I adored "that Alanis Morissette bird was roit. Iss loik meetin' the man o' your dreams, and then, loik, meeting 'is beautifow woif, ennit? I mean, iss just pathetic, ennit?"

"Don't you mean ironic?" I asked, recognizing the angry pop-anthem lyric at once.[16]

"Well, thass wot *she* says, but it's not irony, it's bloody pathos, ennit?" The Countess smirked, and I couldn't help but laugh.

I can only hope that somewhere, Alanis Morissette is reading this nearly twenty years on and realizing, that "Holy shit! It is pathos, not

---

[15] The establishment in question may or may not truly have batwing doors, darlings – but for the sake of the narrative, let's say it does.

[16] Alanis Morissette's song *Ironic*, whose lyrics describe situations that are either coincidences or descriptions of pathos, is infamous in its misuse of the word ironic.

irony! Well, I can't bloody well sing "Isn't it pathetic? Don't you think?"

I'm not sure why I suddenly made Alanis Morissette British, darlings, but work with me here.

"It is pathetic," I said after a moment, feeling sorry for myself. "I mean, look at her – she's beautiful, and she's given him a baby, and – do you think she's prettier than me?"

The Countess Penelope carefully considered this. She looked at the BWNN's[17] wife, then back at me, and then back at her, and then back at me.

"Maybe from the front," she said, dropping the urchin bit, "but from behind, you've got her beat hands down. I mean, seriously – have you seen your ass lately? It's like two dogs fighting under a blanket!"

"What does that even mean?" I asked, perplexed.

"I don't know," Penny admitted. "But I heard two frat boys say that about a girls boobs one time and I figured that as cleavage is simply ass-by-proxy that the analogy would apply to butts as well. Is it not flattering?"

"No, not very," I sighed.

"You want to get out of here?" Penny asked, realizing that I was upset.

"Yes, please."

Together, we rode off into the sunset, wiping the dust from our clothes. There would be other towns, other baristas. For now, it was just the Countess and I, alone against the world. That would have to be enough.

---

[17] That would be the Barista With No Name in case you've forgotten.

Return to Arcadia Prologue – The Burrito of Doom

*L*ike almost no story ever (or at least, none that I can recollect), it all began with a burrito. It was a Monday not too long ago, and all afternoon, I had been craving a burrito – I could almost taste the tangy lime and fresh cilantro, the creamy guacamole, the pleasant burn of jalapeño on my lips. Mexican food – really good Mexican food (well, California/Mexican food) was one of the things I really missed after I left California, and it's been a long time coming, but I finally found a couple of places that make a pretty decent burrito. I like burritos and Mexican food in general, because it's pretty simple food using real ingredients, which is important to me, not because I'm part of some natural foods movement, but rather, because I have, over the last few years, developed a severe intolerance and sensitivity to MSG. While I could go into details, darlings, suffice it to say that unfortunately, that shit is in *everything*, and so it is very hard for me to avoid it altogether, no matter how hard I try. Even so, at least once a week, I wake up with a sinus headache so bad that the pain makes my hands tremble and it's everything I can do not to throw up. So you can imagine that I really want to avoid this.

Such was my craving for a burrito, however, that when I arrived home that night after work, and the Countess Penelope of Arcadia greeted me at the door with the news that she'd discovered a new Mexican place (I may have sent her a half dozen text messages on the subject of my burrito fixation), it never once occurred to me that this new place would use some sort of pre-seasoned chicken breast, or that they didn't actually make their guacamole fresh.

I'd love to tell you that I avoided an MSG headache the next morning, and that I didn't wake up feeling like someone had driven a knitting needle up my nose and into my brain. I'd like to be able to say that I didn't dry heave in the car all the way to work, nibbling a bagel and sipping a Lemonade Monster (energy drinks, with their dangerously high levels of caffeine and taurine are the only things that seem to counter the MSG reaction), and it would certainly be preferable not to have to depict your favourite dilettante holding her hair out of her face and kneeling by the toilet, all because some tiny little hole in the wall taco joint decided that lime, cilantro and natural salt weren't flavourful enough. But in this case I'm afraid I'm going to have to own up to all those things, because that is exactly what happened.

Oh, and one more thing I wish I could say, darlings, but can't because it's just not true – I wish I could say that waking up with an MSG headache was the worst thing that happened to me that Tuesday, or even that week. Sadly, there were things coming that I had no warning for, and by that weekend, I would look back on the Day of the Burrito of Doom as a golden age. Looking back now, I realize that it all began with that burrito – an awful week that would end with a return to Arcadia – which is not exactly on my top ten vacation destinations, to say the least – and a headache over a fifteen-year-old speeding ticket that no amount of energy drinks could clear away.

Post-Civic Holiday Blues

*W*ell, darlings, it's that time of year again – the day after Civic Holiday,[18] a sacred time in Ontario, Canada, when we celebrate the blessed occasion when Al Gore invented the Honda Civic. For weeks before, we prepare, decking the halls with decorations featuring that revered of all symbols, the Honda "H". Throughout the neighbourhood (with a 'U') children can be heard singing their favourite Civic Holiday carols, like Rudolph, the Alcoholic Red-Nosed Used Car Salesman, or, my personal favourite, It Came Upon a Midnight Clearance Sale.

But now that the day is over, and all the Civic Holiday presents have been unwrapped, and all the Sangria has been consumed (or as we like to call it, Summer Eggnog), what is left but the inevitable post-holiday crash, where we fall into that depression, berating ourselves for falling prey to consumerism, having forgotten the true meaning of Civic Holiday. I always get a little weepy, myself, whenever I watch the Charlie Brown Civic Holiday special. Especially when Linus gives that little monologue on the true meaning of Civic Holiday: "And lo, there were some bankers in their offices, guarding their flocks of cash by day, and an angel from Parliament appeared to them, saying 'Do not be afraid, but instead, take great joy! For today, in the city of Toronto (and all across the province of Ontario) it is declared that all banks and government offices shall be closed, and that other businesses will have the option of being closed, and yea,

---

[18] This would have been August 5th. It's always the first Monday in August. There's nothing sacred about it, darlings, and no, Al Gore didn't really invent the Honda Civic.

verily I say unto thee, that if said business decides to stay open, they will not have to pay their employees holiday pay, for this is a banking holiday, not a statutory one.' And the bankers responded with great joy, and began singing hymns of praise to the angel from Parliament, singing 'I don't want to work, I just want to bang on me drum all day', and there was great rejoicing."

And so it is with heavy hearts and empty wallets we return to our places of employment, having taken down our Civic Holiday tree and put away all the little silver "H"s until next year. There's a collective sigh among the parents as they are finished Civic Holiday shopping for another year. The children have had their fill of gingerbread cookies cut to resemble either "H"s or the smiling, benevolent face of Al Gore, or Gingergores, as the kids call them, and now they look forward to Labour Day, the time of year when everyone in town dresses up like a nine-months pregnant woman and goes door to door moaning and groaning and asking for pain medication, ("Drugs or Water!" is the phrase they yell, and how I do look forward to this hilarious ritual!) and if the person has none to offer, then the proper response is to splash the person with water. The really clever costumed Labourers incorporate a water balloon under their belly so they can make the breaking water re-enactment more authentic.

Well, I guess that's something to look forward to.

Return to Arcadia - The Asshole

When I came in to work Tuesday morning, suffering from an MSG headache at the hands of the Burrito of Doom, the last thing I expected (or needed, darlings) was to be assaulted via e-mail. But if experience has taught me anything, it's that expectations rarely match up with reality.

The fact that the email was sent by The Asshole was no surprise, but this was out of line, even by his standards.

The Asshole is that one client – everyone has one – who cannot be satisfied, who plays by his own rules, and who is never, ever wrong, even when he quite frequently is. The whole world revolves around The Asshole, and his needs supersede those of everyone else.

Mine just happens to also be old college buddies with the owner of the production company that is also one of our biggest clients, and so he pretty much has free reign to do and say whatever he wants to whomever he wants, and nobody is going to say too much about it.

So when I came into work on Tuesday and opened my email, what I had to read that morning both hurt and frustrated me, because I knew nothing was going to be done about it.

"I quit," I said to Candace, my co-worker. I was fighting back tears, both of rage and embarrassment as I stormed through the office with a shopping bag, throwing any and all of my personal papers or whatnot into it. I had printed out the email and written I QUIT at the bottom in pink highlighter (not only because it added a touch of femininity, but because it was the closest thing at hand) and pinned it to my boss' door. He wouldn't be in for another half hour, but I planned on being gone by then, darlings – long gone and likely four sheets to the wind before noon, but for Candace's timely intervention. (Later I would have time to reflect in shame that The Asshole nearly drove me to drinking in anger, which I don't condone and cannot recommend).

"What is this?" Candace asked, honestly concerned. Candace had been in earshot during many of my near-screaming matches with The Asshole, and had talked me down off the ledge more than a few times before, so she recognized the signs. But even Candace hadn't been prepared for that morning's email. She pulled it down off of Steve's door and scanned it, her lips moving and then suddenly stopping, her eyes widening as her fingers began crumpling the edges of the paper.

"That fucking *asshole!*" she yelled, and the couple of people who weren't already secret spectators to my little tantrum poked their heads out of their offices or from behind cubicle walls.

"What are you looking at?" Candace snapped. Apparently my anger was contagious.

"I've had enough," I said to Candace, hanging my head and biting my lip. I refused to cry in front of the whole office.

"Come on," Candace said, and tugged me by the arm out to the back yard. Our office was actually just a big old Victorian that had been converted to office space, and the back door opened on what was once the back yard, but had now been paved for parking. We all still referred to it as the back yard, and it's where Candace slipped off for a smoke whenever she could. She lit up a DuMaurier and offered me one.

"You know how hard I'm trying to stay quit, darling," I said without much conviction, and took the offered smoke.

"You know what this is all about, right?" Candace asked, and I nodded.

Of course I did. A couple of weeks earlier, I had given The Asshole (whose real name is Peter, but I only call him that via telephone or email – any other time, it's The Asshole, capital T, capital A implied and understood by my emphasis when saying them – usually through clenched teeth) a verbal dressing down, which apparently his boss happened to overhear.

I had been calling The Asshole to confirm some information on a request that he had made – in most basic terms, think of it as a purchase order. The Asshole had put in an order for something, but, as is his fashion, the order was so incredibly vague and non-specific that there was no way that I could fill it. This is his M.O. – he'll make a request that I can't possibly fulfill without more information, but then when I go back to him for more information, he tells me that he can't possibly go back to his client to request more information, and can't I just do my job and figure out what it is he needs and provide it.

I hate to bring sexual politics into the mix, darlings, but it has been my experience that a man cannot handle having his balls handed to him by a woman. I have watched a man be yelled at by another man – screamed at, even, with the screaming man's face turning purple with rage – and watched him take it. But then I've seen that same man laugh at a woman who tries to assert herself, or else try to intimidate her by coming back with chest puffed out in a display of physical domination.

So I should have known that there was some sort of retribution coming for the telephone conversation that I'd had with The Asshole not that long ago, trying to gather more information with which to fill his order.

Now, just to clarify – I don't work for The Asshole. It's not my job to make The Asshole happy. It is my job to fill his order to the specifications he provides. But if he doesn't provide specifications, then I can't fill his order.

Okay – is everything clear?

One more piece of information before we move on, and this is very important – Steve – my boss – and Bill – Steve's boss – have my back. They share my frustration with The Asshole, and have, in fact, instructed me on numerous occasions to hold up orders until The Asshole clarifies what it is he needs, exactly. We really aren't in the business of guessing what our clients' needs are – mostly because when we have done so in the past and guessed wrong, it cost us a lot of money.

During my time in Halesowen as a would-be evangelist, and then in my short lived career in telemarketing, I had learned how to overcome objections using a simple model: listen, express sympathy, then empathize with the problem the person has, and then suggest how you can solve their problem. So I had tried being patient with The Asshole's insistence that he couldn't possibly give me the answers that I needed (oh, and just a side note – The Asshole isn't the only salesperson in his office – there are several – and I never seem to have any problem getting complete information from any of them), but no matter how patient I was being, or how many times I told him that I understood his frustration, or suggested that maybe he could get the information from his clients *before* he placed his order with us, and that might save both him and me a lot of frustration, he just kept coming back with the same answer.

"I can't possibly go back to the client at this point – do you know how unprofessional that will look?"

"Well, it can't be more unprofessional than not delivering because you couldn't procure the order," I said, trying my best to remain professional myself.

"But I can procure the order," he said smugly. "You are just holding it up for no reason."

"Not for no reason," I replied, temperature rising. "I need details. I can't fill this order without them. And it's not me holding the order up. Bill and Steve have already audited the order, and it's on hold pending your revision."

"Do you have any idea what I'd have to do to get what you're asking for?"

And here it is, darlings. Here's what I said to deserve the email that I received that morning – the vicious and humiliating email that I would have quit over – I surely would have quit over had I been ten years younger – but for Candace's cool head.

"I don't give a rat's ass what you have to do to get that information! That's *your* job. My job is to fill orders based on the client's specifications – and your order has no bloody specifications, so I can't fill it. If you want to talk to Steve or Bill about it, that's fine by me!" And then I put him on hold and stormed into Bill's office.

"Asshole on line three!" I spat, and stormed out back and smoked and fumed with Candace.

Which is where I found myself again that Tuesday morning, reading and re-reading the email of retaliation that crossed the line between professional frustration and personal attack.

"You know, if you or I said something like that, we'd be fired," Candace said, commiserating with me.

I nodded and took another drag, feeling the smoke burn my throat and make my head go light in the old familiar way. By the end of the week I would be buying them again, and would be up to a half a pack a day by the weekend. But I didn't know that then. Then, it was just one — just falling off the wagon a little bit — one little cigarette and nobody had to know.

"Read it again," I said, needing to hear it one more time, to be sure I wasn't just having a bad dream, and that I might wake up at any moment, angry and bothered, but with the satisfaction of knowing that it was all just a dream, likely caused by residual anger from some episode of butting heads with The Asshole at work the day before.

"Are you sure?" Candace asked. "Helena, c'mon…"

I looked at her with cold eyes and nodded at the paper she held in her fists.

"Alright," she sighed, and read the e-mail aloud.

Helen,

You miserable, interfering cunt.

I don't know why you are being deliberately difficult, but you are costing both my company, and by extension, yours, a lot of money because of your obstinate refusal to fill my orders as requested. You are the joke of the office here — we say that it's easier to get a contract sold than it is to get it filled by Helen the Bitch. (We also think you seriously need to get laid, but that's besides the point).[19]

It really shouldn't be so difficult to fill orders — a monkey could do it. So do your fucking job, and fill my order, or I'll find someone else to take my business to.

Peter

P.S. I've attached a note from the client with the specifications you bitched about needing so badly.

Candace finished reading and was quiet for a moment.

"You don't deserve that," she said finally, as if I didn't already know that. "But hey — at least he sent you the specifications."

I coughed a weak laugh, which turned into an unexpected breakdown. I thought I had it under control, but there I was, sobbing and hyperventilating in powerless anger. Through my sobbing I tried to articulate what bothered me most.

"The worst part," I started, and then wailed in frustration. "The worst part is that he copied Steve and Bill."

Candace didn't seem to understand. "So? It's not like you weren't going to show them."

---

[19] It goes without saying that I hate people who say besides the point. Also, he calls me Helen, when he knows damn well it's Helena.

I shook my head, my mascara turning my eyes into something ugly and pathetic. Why is it men seem to be able to hurt us so much, and we are so powerless against them? How is it they can reduce us to a shuddering, blubbering mess like this?

"Don't you see?" I yelled, but not really at Candace. "He doesn't care! He said those... those *things*, and he doesn't care! He knows that nobody's going to say anything, and they're certainly not going to do anything! He's completely fucking untouchable!"

It would be a few more days before my suspicions would be confirmed, but in the end, I was right.

I usually am.

Return to Arcadia - The Windfall

The Countess of Arcadia picked at her salad unenthusiastically, pouting at the greens as if they'd been responsible for some great slight against her. In fact, it wasn't the spring mix that had her in a snit, but rather some girl in one of her summer classes who had asked if she'd put on weight. Penny, for some reason, took this as an accusation rather than a question, and had been in a foul mood since she'd walked in the door that night.

"Did anyone call you a cunt this week?" I asked bitterly, not wanting to be so self-absorbed, darlings, but I'd had a really bad week by that point.

The Countess cringed at my use of the C-word and looked at me sympathetically.

"No," she said, and then added: "Not *this* week."

"Well, then, there you go," I said cheerily. "You're having a better week than me."

Penny continued pouting and pushing the leafy greens around her plate. The phone rang, and I left her to her to ruminate over her radicchio.

"Hello?" I answered wearily.

"Yes, this is she," I admitted with dread. It was a collection agency – I usually manage to dodge them, but for some reason I picked up without looking at the call display this time.

"Uh huh," I said, acknowledging their standard line of identity confirmation. And then the person on the other line said something quite unexpected, and I had to ask her to repeat it.

"You're kidding!" I said, and started laughing with joy. "How much?"

The woman repeated what she'd already told me, but I just had to hear it again.

"Oh my god, you have no idea how amazing that is, darling!"

"What? Oh, I call everyone darling – but you, my dear, are a true darling! Oh, I could just kiss you through the phone."

The lady from the collection agency laughed as I made kissing noises through the phone – not obscene kissing noises, you understand – I reserve those for telemarketers who just won't take the hint.

"This is just wonderful news, darling! Thank you so much. Oh! I had such a shitty day yesterday, you have no idea! This just couldn't have come at a better time.

"Thank you. Oh, and you have a wonderful day, too, darling. Mwah!" I blew the debt collector a final goodbye kiss and then hung up the phone and gave a long, loud cry of triumph.

"Thank you, universe! You owed me one, you crazy bitch!"

Penny was looking at me with anticipation, and because of her previously petulant posturing, I decided to tease her a bit.

"I'm going out now," I announced. "Do enjoy your salad, darling."

Penny's face morphed into a perplexed frown.

"Oh, Helena," the Countess said sweetly. "dooo be a deah and commence with the exposition, would you? Yes. Cheerio, tut tut. For if you do not, well, we shall not be amooooosed."

"You won't be a moose?" I asked, purposely ignoring her Countess of Arcadia by way of Windsor Castle routine.

Penelope rolled her eyes and dropped her phony accent.

"Where ya goin'?"

"Hmm," I said, trying to draw it out as long as I could. "I thought maybe I'd go treat myself to a nice, thick, juicy steak. Yes. Yes, I think that's what I shall do."

"Steak?" The Countess asked, intrigued. "Penny want steak. Penny *love* steak. Penny om-nom-nomnivore, but like steak best of all!"

I laughed at her cavewoman speak and told her to get her shoes on, then.

"So what gives?" she asked. "Isn't money too tight for steak?"

"Apparently not," I said, and told her how the collection agency I'd been paying an old debt to had actually settled with the company I owed, and how I'd overpaid them by almost $1500. The fact that they'd actually contacted me about the refund was something of a miracle. (Though certainly more lucrative than finding the weeping face of the Virgin Mary in your cornflakes or some other nonsense).

"Woo hoo!" the Countess Arcade exclaimed, her former funk fading fast. "So we're going shopping then?"

I glowered at her, only five percent – okay, maybe ten percent – actual annoyance. Penny hadn't yet reacquired a part-time job since she'd been fired for dumping a plate of pasta on a deeply discourteous and disrespectful diner, and so we were a little tight when it came to money for the little extra things that make life more enjoyable – such as steak, for example.

"Sadly, no, darling," I said with honest regret. "But I will treat you to a steak dinner."

Penny grunted and grinned a silly grin that made her look ten years younger.

"Penny like steak," she said and mimed a Homer Simpson-esque drool, tongue lolling lazily out the side of her mouth.

"But the rest we should pack away, okay?" I said, trying to convince myself of the wisdom of this almost as much as Penny.

"Fair enough," Penny agreed with a shrug. "It's your money, Helena."

In retrospect, I couldn't have possibly known how smart I was being. By the end of the week, I would be very thankful indeed that I didn't just decide to blow the windfall on a shopping spree for the Countess and me. If I had, well, darlings, I might be sitting and writing this amusing missive from the cold comfort of an Arcadia jail cell.

Nobody, least of all your favourite dilettante, wants that, darlings. I look so bloody awful in orange – it washes me right out, makes me look like an under-ripe peach.

Ghastly, indeed!

Return to Arcadia - Aggravation, Operation, Masturbation, Defenestration

B y the time Friday rolled around that week, I was in a state of severe aggravation. If you have no idea what I'm talking about, darlings, well, *mea culpa* – I haven't been as timely in telling this tale as perhaps I should have been,[20] and if I have lost your interest, well, I hope that I can recapture the magic, as if we were some old married couple who decides to try role playing in order to rekindle the passion.

I'll be the naughty nurse, and you can be a battle dwarf, and we can test your resistance to the power of my magical saline enema. (Or insert your incredibly unsexy fantasy here, darlings – whatever floats your boat). I just rolled a six, which gives me +5 against verbally abusive clients, which would have been incredibly useful earlier in the week, when I had been called that most vile of all names (I'll give you a hint – it's a four letter word that rhymes incredibly well with cunt), which was only the opening salvo in a letter that attacked my intelligence, my character, and made inappropriate (if not entirely inaccurate, but that's beside the point) assumptions about my sex life or lack thereof.

My boss was conveniently away for a couple of days having some minor operation, so he hadn't actually been in to address the email I'd received earlier in the week, and it has been my unfortunate

---

[20] Of course, you have the benefit of just having read about this week, without having to wait for me to write it. Aren't you lucky?

experience that the longer things go unanswered, the more likely they are to just fade away or be swept under the carpet. I mean, it's not as if you can respond a week later and say *Oh hey, remember that email you sent Helena a week ago?*

If it had been an urgent priority, it would have been addressed immediately, and as it wasn't, well – message received loud and clear. All I could do was just push through, and thicken my skin.

I was looking forward to a quiet, uneventful weekend. As much as I would have loved to be heading for a vacation destination, I would gladly without hesitation take a day or two of relaxation with sweet and potent liquid libation that warms the skin and dulls sensations; of long hot baths and masturbation, to wash away with sweet elation the week that brought such aggravation.[21] But right near the end of the day – when the clock was ticking away the last few seconds of my work week – the telephone rang, and all my sweet, pleasurable thoughts of soothing solitude were stolen away, not only by the ringing cacophony of the phone, but by the voice on the other end, and what it had to say.

It was a phone call from Arcadia, which seemed an entire galaxy away at that point – my mind was somewhere else entirely – but which brought me back to earth in a harsh, unwelcome way that nonetheless defenestrated all my previous plans for a do-nothing weekend.

An old friend called to ask for a favour, and while I am many things, darlings – a dilettante, a dreamer, a dallier and sometime doer of dastardly deeds – the one thing I am not is a bad friend. A friend in need is friend indeed, as the saying goes, and so when one of the few people that I have kept contact with in that black hole known as Arcadia called to tell me that she needed my help, well, I couldn't say no.

Brooke had grown up in Arcadia, and had never managed to escape – at least not physically – but her mind had somehow managed to expand to horizons outside of the suffocating borders of Arcadia nonetheless, which is why she and I still got on well. There was none of the small-minded bigotry or ignorance that so broadly characterized the people of Arcadia. I always called her my bird in a gilded cage after that old song that Hitchcock used in *The Birds*. I

---

[21] Yeah, you can go back and read that again if you like. You're smiling, aren't you?

never understood why she never left before it was too late – but then, you can't live others' lives for them.

Brooke ended up caught in the same web as everyone else in Arcadia, marrying the captain of the football team or some other cliché nonsense, and moved into a two bedroom split level with a garage and a white picket fence, where she spent the best ten years of her youth trying to give him kids and the last three or four trying to avoid the back of his hand on a Saturday night after he came home from the bar.

I'd offered a number of times to take her in – to rescue her, and aren't I just the Damsel in Shining Armour responding to a 911 distress call – but she wouldn't hear it. Any time the phone rang and I heard Brooke's voice on the other end, I secretly hoped that she was going to tell me that she was leaving the bastard – and finally, that time had come – and in spades.

"I'm kicking him out," the tired but triumphant voice of my old friend told me. "The house is in my name, and anyway, he's got some girlfriend up in Syracuse, so he's shacking up with her, apparently. But he wants to come by this weekend to move his shit out and... well... I don't... Helena, I don't..."

"You don't want to be alone," I finished for her, knowing what she was afraid of.

"No," she agreed. "No, I don't want to be alone in the house with him ever again."

So I told her that of course I could come down, in fact, I'd drive down right after work, and we'd spend the weekend together – maybe go for a drive to the big city – we'd do a whole Girls On The Town thing – I'd only ever been to New York City once before, and it was a disaster (but that's a tale for another day, darlings) and so maybe it was time to give it another go.

I never made it to Arcadia, though. I was pulled over about half way there, and while the officer was filling out my speeding ticket, something else completely unexpected popped up on his computer that threw all my plans for that weekend out the window in one swift and heartless act of defenestration.

Return to Arcadia - Aggravation (Slight Return)

I sat in my car, squinting at the glare of the repeated red and blue of the police truck behind me, having been pulled over for speeding on my way to see an old friend in Arcadia. She had called me for help, and so I tossed my weekend plans aside and set out to rescue her from having to face her good-for-nothing soon-to-be ex-husband as he came by to collect his shit.

I'd missed my exit, and the GPS said that I was completely off the map, which is never comforting. On top of that, I was running out of gas – the light had been on for at least fifteen minutes and I was starting to get nervous, so yes, I'd been speeding, trying to find a gas station.

I looked at myself in the mirror and tried to judge whether I was still cute enough to flirt my way out of a ticket, when the knock on the window startled me. I put the window down, and the cop looked at me and then back to my driver's license, and then back at me again.

"Have you ever lived in New York State?" he asked, and at first I had no idea how to answer that question. Nervously, my brain spat out the first thing that popped into my head.

"Oh my god," I said stupidly. "They've found the bodies, haven't they?"

"Excuse me?" the officer asked, as if he hadn't heard me.

"It was a joke," I said smiling my best *please don't take me to jail* grin.

"It's not very funny, miss," he said, and repeated his original question.

"It was a *little funny*," I muttered under my breath. He continued to stare at me, so I answered his question.

"Not exactly," I said, knowing that sounded incredibly vague. "My parents live in Arcadia, and my sister lived there for a while. I came out and lived with my sister for about a year or so, but I never had my own place or anything."

He recited an address to me that I recognized as Cheryl's old address in Arcadia.

"Yeah," I said, "But that was… god, that was, like, fifteen years ago. What's this got to do with anything?"

"I'll be right back," he said, and nothing else. He walked back to his truck, leaving me confused, and, I'll admit, a little alarmed. What could…?

Then it came to me – after I'd been in Arcadia for about six months or so, Cheryl insisted that I get my New York State driver's license, just so I didn't get in trouble if I ever got pulled over driving her car. I'd forgotten all about that – I only had it for about another six months or so before I moved back to Canada and tossed it in the trash.

When the officer appeared back in my open window, he was carrying two large pieces of paper with him, and started reading me the details of my speeding ticket, which I ignored and waited for him to hand it to me and go away.

"And this is a charge for Aggravated Operation of a Motor Vehicle without a license," he said, and suddenly I was paying attention. "This is a very serious offence, Miss. It's a third degree misdemeanour. I am doing you a huge favour by not bringing you in right now for arraignment. But you need to appear in court next Thursday, or else a bench warrant will be issued for your arrest. Do you understand me?"

I felt like I'd just been punched in the stomach.

"No," I finally said after a moment. "Aggravated what?"

"Unlicensed operation of a motor vehicle, miss." the officer replied.

"But I don't understand," I repeated. I was bouncing back and forth inside between panic and anger. "I have a valid driver's license and insurance."

"Your New York State driver's license was suspended in November of 2000 for non-payment of a speeding ticket."

I honestly couldn't even remember getting a speeding ticket, and I told him so. He told me what county it was in, and told me that I could contact them for the details and make payment.

"Okay," I said, "I can do that. But I still don't understand. I have a valid Canadian driver's license – I'm not operating a motor vehicle without a license." Though I was getting aggravated, but I kept my mouth shut on that account, thank whoever for small mercies.

"Your driving privileges in the state of New York have been revoked," he told me, and then explained about something called Scoffield Law, which grants the Department of Motor Vehicles the ability to suspend a person's driving privileges in that state in the event of non-payment of fines. And here's the kicker, darlings – it doesn't matter where your license is issued. Drive there as much as you want, but get caught driving in a state where your privileges have been suspended, and you could face a fine of no less than $200 up to $500, and/or thirty days in prison.

The officer was kind enough to explain all of this to me as I felt all the blood drain out of my face and my bladder suddenly scream to be relieved.

"But I was never notified of any suspension," I said weakly – all the smartass and wit had dried up, just like the spit in my mouth.

"I'm sure they sent it to your sister's address," he said. "I'm sure she got a notice for you there. It's quite a while ago, but maybe she's got some of your stuff packed away?"

"My sister died," I said in almost a whisper.

"Gosh, I'm sorry, Miss," the cop said, and when I looked up at him, I was surprised to see that he wasn't much older than Penny. *If it had been Penny*, I thought, *maybe he would have just given her a warning.*

No, if it had been the Countess who got pulled over, she would have been in handcuffs by now, screaming about police brutality, or *Free Mandela! Free Tibet! Free Willy!* Or some other outrageous nonsense.

"Again, I'm doing you a big favour by not towing your car and bringing you in for arraignment now." he said, and I tried my hardest to feel grateful. "But you need to turn your car around right now and drive back home, and come back on Thursday for court. You can't drive yourself, though – if you're caught driving again in New York before this is cleared up, well, I can't guarantee another officer would be as nice as I am."

I smiled at him to show him I appreciated it.

"Of course, Officer," I said as demurely as I could manage. Inside I was seething and swirling with anger at the stupidity of it all. A thirteen-year-old speeding ticket that I don't even remember and he said I could go to jail.

I'm too pretty to go to jail, darlings!

"I got lost," I said before he walked away. "And I'm running out of gas. Could you...?"

"Yeah, a lot of people miss the new exit a couple miles back," he said. "If you just turn around, you'll find gas and restaurants and such right past the highway."

"Thank you, Officer," I said, and started my car back up. Before I drove away, I sent Brooke a text message and told her that I had to turn around, and that I'd call her when I got back home.

I AM SO SORRY, I wrote, CAN'T BE HELPED XO XO.

Then I called Penny and told her to make sure we had vodka and grapefruit juice.

"I'm coming home," I told her, defeated, "and I plan on getting very drunk when I get there."

The Countess Penelope of Arcadia laughed, and when I didn't join her, she got suddenly quiet.

"Is something wrong?" she asked. "Is it bad?"

"It's not good," I sighed. "See you soon, okay?"

I hung up the phone and sighed, and allowed myself a few tears of frustration before turning on my signal and turning across the empty country road and back the way I came.

I stopped only for gas and a pack of Marlboro Lights – the first pack of cigarettes I'd bought in years, but I smoked half of them by the time I got home, and the other half before the night was over.

Saturday morning, the remorse set in.

Return to Arcadia - Countess Penelope and the Great Prison Break of '13

"**Y**our honour, I object!" the Countess Penelope of Arcadia declared, shaking her tiny fist in the judge's direction. "My client is guilty, and you *know* she's guilty! I say lock her up for her own good and for the good of *these* fine people, who don't need to be subjected to…"

"Out of order!" the judge interrupted, pounding his gavel. "You're out of order!"

"I'm out of order?" the Countess of Penelope of Arcadia (which is apparently somewhere near Baltimore, circa 1979)[22] exclaimed. "You're out of order! This whole trial is out of order! Attica! Attica! Fredo!"[23]

"Tell me the truth, darling," I said, tugging on her hand to try to get her to sit down. "You've never actually seen *And Justice For All*… have you?"

"The truth?" she asked, perplexed. "The truth? You want the truth? You can't handle the truth!"[24]

"Out of order!" the Countess repeated, and I felt her shaking me out of my dream. "Helena, the stupid thing is out of order. What

---

[22] Setting of the classic Al Pacino film *And Justice for All*, which contains the iconic scene where Al Pacino declares that everything is out of order.

[23] Penny seems to be confusing her Al Pacino movies. Fredo is a reference to *The Godfather* movies.

[24] And now she's confusing her courtroom dramas, borrowing from *A Few Good Men*, starring Jack Nicholson.

should I do?"

I had only nodded off for a few minutes, or so I hoped. I woke up that morning with a headache, and had to be rid of it before that night, when I had to appear in traffic court to face a misdemeanor charge which was the result of not paying a speeding ticket nearly fifteen years earlier.

"What's out of order?" I asked, and immediately regretted it.

"You're out of order!" she yelled in her best Al Pacino voice. "I'm out of order! That deck of cards over there is out of order! My pop machine at school is out of order! My collection of Stephen King books is out of order! This whole damn trial is out of order! Oh, and also, the gas pump is out of order."

I stumbled out of the passenger seat (as I was forbidden to drive in the state of New York until I cleared all this up) and looked at the sign on the gas pump.

"It's just the pay-at-the pump part that's out of order, Penny. I'll go pre-pay and you pump."

I returned a few minutes later with a couple of energy drinks, and got back in the car and stared Penny down.

"Seriously," I said in my sternest voice, "none of that when we get to court. This is very serious, and I don't want to end up in jail because you caused some kind of disturbance."

I had seen way too many court scenes in various television shows and movies, and so I had a certain picture in my mind as to what this whole experience was going to be like.

"Oh, but I was already planning your daring escape! I had the twenty metres of tinfoil, the duct tape, a roll of chicken wire, a bathtub full of papier-mâché, forty five rubber chickens and the giant tub of Old El Paso thick and chunky salsa. All I needed was a Tesla coil, an 8-track player and a copy of *Breakfast in America*[25] on 8-Track, and the cast of *Game of Thrones* and my brilliant plan would be complete!"

I couldn't help but be curious, darlings

"Please explain," I prodded.

"Explain what?" Penny asked, driving away.

"Explain how all that stuff fits into your plan to break me out of prison."

I was expecting her to brush me off and tell me that she was just

---

[25] Seminal album by Supertramp.

naming a bunch of random things, but instead she surprised me with this:

"I'd think it's rather obvious, don't you? It's all about misdirection, Helena. I'm planning on creating a scene in the parking lot of the prison by creating a giant electric rubber chicken monster that sings *The Logical Song* and spews forth chunky salsa while the cast and crew of *Game of Thrones* perform scenes from the beloved Broadway musical *Les Misérables*.

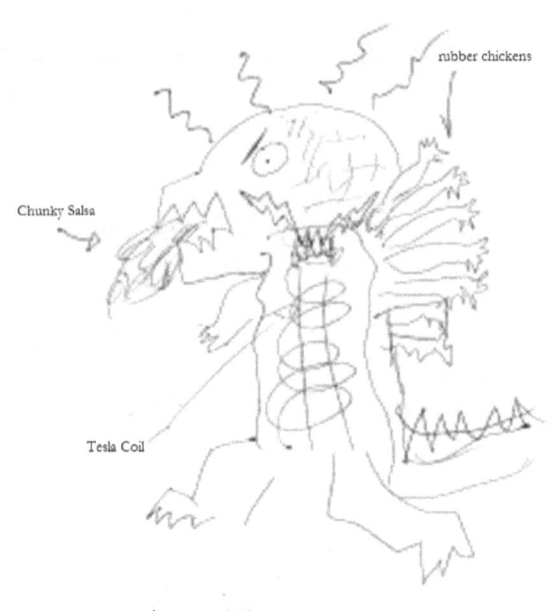

Artist's Rendition

I figure Jaime Lannister as Jean Valjean and Daenerys Targaryen as Fantine. Ned Stark would have to play someone that dies, I suppose – Sean Bean dies in everything, doesn't he?"

"And Cosette?" I asked, not having any idea why I was playing along with her, other than that we had nothing better to do on the drive to traffic court.

"Oh, that's a tough one, right?" Penny replied. "Do you think Arya Stark is too young?"

"I think you're insane," I said, popping the top on the first of my Monster energy drinks. "I think I still have no idea how you're breaking me out of prison."

"I told you – I'm creating a diversion in the parking lot..."

"Yes, yes, with a salsa breathing Supertramp fan dragon made of papier-mâché, rubber chickens, tin foil and duct tape." I agreed.

"And don't forget the Starks and Lannisters singing *Do You Hear the People Sing?* You know, the official anthem of the oppressed, Helena. There won't be a dry eye in the prison." the Countess Arcade replied without a touch of irony.

"And that's all well and good, darling," I said, impressed by her indomitable imagination, "but how exactly are you getting into the prison to break me out?"

"Oh," the Countess replied, deflated. "Well, I hadn't got that part all worked out just yet. I spent all my time thinking up the diversion, I forgot to come up with the actual escape! Well, you'll just have to take advantage of the chaos, and, I dunno, muscle up to the bars and VOOM! Make your escape."[26]

I laughed until chocolate milk came flying out my nose, despite the fact that I was drinking an energy drink and not, in fact, chocolate milk.

"You just keep thinking, Countess," I said, catching my breath, "that's what you're good at."[27]

---

[26] The Countess Arcade is intentionally, if subtly referencing the famous Dead Parrot sketch from Monty Python.

[27] I may or may not be cribbing a line from *Butch Cassidy and the Sundance Kid* here. But stealing from Robert Redford is just too delicious not to do.

Wild Thing (An Arcadia Flashback)

I must have been around nineteen years old or so when I decided that I was never going to have sex again. Certainly not with a boy, though I've never had the inclination to go with women, so it appeared that chastity was my only guarantee that I would never have a tiny little monster of my own.

My monstrous niece, the Countess Penelope of Arcadia (which is populated by a fellow named Max and a colourful consortium of clamorous creatures all drawn by Maurice Sendak)[28] had soured me on the very thought of procreation.

It wasn't just the screaming – I could handle the screaming.

It wasn't just the slamming of doors, or the throwing of her little monkey (whom she affectionately and creatively named 'Ooh Ooh Ah Ah', *'cause that's what monkeys say, Auntie 'elna!)* nor was it her frequent and proficient use of the word *no* whenever I asked her to do... well... *anything.*

All of these things I could have coped with, darlings, as the actions of a willful and stubborn two-year-old without the language skills to express herself adequately.

But when she came to me with a big grin on her face and said, "Poo poo, 'Elna," and then proceeded to present me with the promised poo poo, which she'd removed from her diaper by hand, that's when I began to wonder about my capacity to cope with such a

---

[28] Arcadia, it would seem, is *Where the Wild Things Are*

capricious creature as the Countess.

The first time it happened, darlings, I admit that I was calm and smiling, and that I did my best not to show the revulsion that I was feeling. I merely took her to the bathroom, put the poo in the toilet, washed her hands and cleaned her up. I couldn't be angry with her; she looked so proud of herself.

So I explained that she couldn't do that, and that it was dirty, and that she'd get sick by playing with her poo, and I spoke to her in a calm cheery voice, and I thought everything would be understood and wow, was I ever wrong.

See, I thought that if I got her to look at me and listen to me that she would actually hear me and understand me, and that she would learn something from my years of experience not playing with my own fecal matter.

Instead, it seems that the words coming out of my mouth were magically transformed into *Blah blah blah, blah blah blah blah, blah blah blah Penny*. She smiled at me and giggled and kissed my face so hard I think she gave me a hickey, but then when all was said and done, she went on her merry way completely oblivious that I'd said anything of importance.

A couple of hours later, when I tried to put her down for a nap, she fussed and cried and screamed and then I put her in bed and closed the door, and she fussed and screamed some more, throwing toys around her room, yelling *Let the wild rumpus start!* or something approximating that sentiment. By this time I was thoroughly frustrated and exhausted, and was very tempted to either slip her some Gravol,[29] or else play the whole *Does this cloth smell like Chloroform to you?* game, when suddenly, the screaming stopped.

I thought that I had finally won.

I started the water running for a bath and added some bubbles. As I slipped into the gloriously relaxing water, I felt like everything was going to be okay. The first few bars of Tori Amos' *Under the Pink* album were playing in my headphones, promising that it would be a *Pretty Good Year*, and I realized that some of the problem I was having with little Penny was probably caused by the fact that I was wound up myself, and that my frustration was probably stressing her out as well. A pretty mature and Zen-like attitude, if I do say so

---

[29] Gravol is a name brand of Dimenhydrinate – also known as Dramamine – an anti-nausea medicine with the nice side effect of drowsiness.

myself, and I was feeling pretty good about myself, until I felt something poke my elbow, and nearly jumped out of the tub in equal parts fright and irritation.

"What the fuck?!" I yelled, immediately regretting my cursing in front of the impressionable young Countess.

"Uck!" the juvenile Countess Arcade repeated. "Poo, 'Elna! Uck poo!"

Now, I would love to tell you that I am not responsible for the Countess' predilection for this particular piece of profanity, but I probably am, darlings. *Mea culpa. Mea maxima culpa.*

I would also like to tell you that when she presented me with a parcel of poo the second time around, that I was patient and understanding. I would love to tell you that I didn't yell things like *What are you thinking?* or *Are you trying to drive me insane?* Furthermore, I wish that I could, without perjuring myself, craft a version of this tale where I, a grown ass adult, did not scream in frustration at a helpless toddler and make her scream and cry in return.

Sadly, I did do all those things, and then proceeded to feel a right horrible monster about it afterwards.

I picked up the little Countess Arcade and cleaned her up by throwing her in the tub and scrubbing her clean. Then, wet, naked and covered in bubbles, I ran around the house until I found the portable phone, and proceeded to call my sister Cheryl and beg her to come home to rescue me.

"She pulled her shit out of her diaper and was playing with it like marbles!" I screamed over the phone. "Crazy people do that, Cheryl! Crazy people! What the fuck?!"

Cheryl said that she'd come home as soon as she could, and I wrapped a towel around myself and pulled Penny out of the tub and sat her on my lap. I was crying in frustration, and little Penny looked up at me and smiled. Then she kissed my face a dozen times, grabbing fistfuls of my hair as she did so. I just kept crying, feeling defeated and guilty for losing my temper.

"Elna?" Penny asked.

"Yes, Penny Arcade?" I said, nearly choking on my tears.

"Are 'ou all 'ight?" she asked. Penny's always been a sweetheart.

I smiled at her and gave her the biggest squishy hug I could.

"I am now, darling."

The King Is Dead
(Long Live the Queen)

I had the occasion, recently, to have an unusual experience. As I am a collector of unusual experiences (I have a first edition of Get Stuck in an Elevator with a Ventriloquist and His Hermaphrodite Dummy still wrapped in plastic, but that's a tale for another day) I didn't hesitate when I received the bizarre invitation. A friend of mine had lost her elderly uncle (great-uncle, actually) and had called me up and asked if I'd like to come to the wake with her. A strange request, perhaps, but then, as you may have already gathered, I'm a strange person. I have been accused of being an unreliable narrator, and I have never denied that, and I have been charged with outright fabrication, and while I do not take offense at that, I maintain that going through life with a highly attuned sense for the surreal has benefited me greatly, darlings, and if you have the means of picking one up, I highly recommend it. I believe that if you scour eBay, you may be able to find one for a good price.

So it is that I, on occasion, find myself in situations that lend themselves with great ease to — not satire — satire's not the right word — but rather, *illumination.* Such was the case when I found myself at the wake of my friend's uncle, who was, in the later years of his life, a professional Elvis impersonator.

Was it Jean Paul Sartre, or Bruce Wayne who once said: "The things we do define us, darlings"?[30]

If that is true, then, by definition, my friend's uncle was a king among men. And, as is befitting of a king, his wake was an opulent

---

[30] It may have even been Jane Austen in *Sense and Sensibility:* "It isn't what we say or think that defines us, but what we do." Take that, Batman.

event filled with singing, dancing, and rhinestones. Lots and lots of rhinestones.

As I walked into the hall with my friend on my arm, I was assaulted by a barrage of sequins, sideburns, and wraparound sunglasses.

There were Elvises (Elvii?) of all ages and races. There was an Elvis in a wheelchair decked out in a blue jumpsuit, while his nurse pushed him around so he could dance to *Jailhouse Rock*. There was an Elvis dressed up all in black leather, looking like '68 Comeback Elvis, doing karate kicks and talking about his little Lisa Marie. There was even a Sikh Elvis, who incorporated his turban into Aloha from Hawaii Elvis, complete with white sequined jumpsuit, which he had apparently Bedazzled[31] himself, complete with that famous gold eagle. He sang something with such a heavy Indian accent that it was either *A Little Less Conversation* or else *In The Ghetto* — I'm still not sure.

There was a young Elvis, who got up and sang *Heartbreak Hotel*, and there was gospel Elvis who gave a heartfelt rendition of *Just a Closer Walk With Thee*, and in the corner of the hall that they'd decked out as The Jungle Room, a freshly lei'd Elvis sang *Blue Hawaii* for a group of older ladies who looked as if they'd like nothing better than to pluck his ukulele, if you know what I mean.

I marveled in the utter lack of irony in the performances, and found myself a little humbled and ashamed at my own cynicism as one by one, friends and loved ones paid sincere tribute to the man they knew in the best way that they knew how. In life, he had loved Elvis, they said, but he loved his family, his friends, and his Lord even more. (This coming from gospel Elvis, of course, right before launching into *How Great Thou Art*, the song that won Elvis his last Grammy.)

But the highlight of the afternoon was when a female impersonating Elvis impersonator got up with tears in his/her eyes and sang *Love Me Tender*, dressed as old, fat, white sequined jumpsuit 1977 Elvis.

I'd never seen a man dressed as a woman dressed as Elvis before, but I have to say, darlings, it was not something I'll soon forget.

---

[31] How do I explain the BeDazzler by RonCo? Think As Seen on TV. A do it yourself rhinestone applicator, huge in 1974.

My Mood Swings
(Arcadius Interruptus)

"**S**nap out of it, Helena!" Penny said, not unkindly. "Have some beans."

"Beans?" I asked. "What are you talking about?"

"Have some beans, Helena," she repeated. "They're from Baaah ston. They're wicked aaaah-some."

The Countess Penelope of Arcadia had learned that my friend Hannah had recently relocated to the New England city most famous for its baked beans, Bo-Sox, loud Irish, and for its charming accent. Ergo, Arcadia had suddenly relocated there as well. Ever since we'd stopped at Red Lobster on our way back from traffic court (and yes, that tale is forthcoming darlings – stay a while; I will be faithful) where Penny ordered the Bar Harbor Lobster Bake, she'd been slipping into a Boston baseball hooligan voice, sounding like an extra from *Good Will Hunting*[32] or anything based on a Dennis Lehane novel.[33]

"I'll have the Baaa Haaabaaa Laahbstaaah Bake, doll," the Countess Penelope of Arcadia (which is a little known neighbourhood in South Boston) ordered.

The waitress looked at her and tried not to laugh.

"Right," she said, "one Bar Harbor. And you?"

Before I could answer, the Countess cut me off.

"No, no, no, dollface," she said, totally deadpan. "Repeat aftuh me: Baaaah Haaa Baaa."

---

[32] The film that made Matt Damon and Ben Affleck household names, and won the late Robin Williams an Oscar for Best Supporting Actor.

[33] *Mystic River*, or *Gone Baby Gone*, to name a couple you'd be familiar with.

"Bar Harbor," the waitress attempted feebly, starting to grin. I got the feeling that if we'd been cute college boys (or if she'd been into Penny), she might have at least feigned more amusement.

"Baaah," Penny O'Arcadia repeated sternly, "Haaa. Baaaaaah."

Something in the way that Penny looked at the waitress must have cracked her up, because suddenly she turned bright red and nearly dropped her notepad, breaking into a chuckle that quickly became a chortle, which led to a most unladylike snort.

"Say it!" the Terror of Southie[34] demanded, and the waitress began hyperventilating and had to sit down next to Penny, who immediately put her in a friendly headlock and repeated: "Say it, me foine scullery-maid, or I'll have yer guts fer garters!"

The waitress suddenly stopped laughing, and both she and I looked at Penny quizzically.

"Sorry about that," Penny said, dropping her eyes. "Did I just slip into 17th Century pirate? Sorry, the Southie thing is all fairly new. But it's wicked good, huh? How'd you like them apples?"[35]

I just looked at Penny, and then at the waitress, who had regained her composure for the most part, and was looking at Penny like one might look at a strange dish in a foreign restaurant that was unidentifiable.

"Bah Hah Bah?" Penny tried once more, but more gently.

"Bah Hah Bah," the waitress complied, as if placating a cute child.

It was this Red Sox cheering, chowdah munching, baked bean loving Penny O'Arcadia that was now trying to snap me out of the righteous funk that I'd been in for several days, due in part to a bout of depression and part feeling sorry for myself for one reason or another.

"Baked beans are ahhh-some!" she repeated. "Wicked ahhh-some."

"You need to get more material," I said, grinning despite my rotten mood. "Go watch some Denis Leary[36] standup – you'll love it. He's got almost as foul a mouth as you do."

"Hey! I've been cutting back on the fucking swearing, I'll have

[34] A nickname for South Boston, a notoriously rough neighbourhood.
[35] Penny cribbing a line from *Good Will Hunting.*
[36] American comedian/actor with a biting, caustic style, with frequent use of profanity.

you know. Goddammit, Helena! It's like you don't know shit about me!"

"Really?" I said, unimpressed. I motioned to her T-shirt, which she'd immediately gone out and had printed after seeing Rooney Mara wear a similar one in *The Girl with the Dragon Tattoo*. It read: *FUCK YOU, YOU FUCKING FUCK*.

Penny looked at her shirt and shot me a lop-sided grin.

"Well, it certainly illustrates the diversity of the word," she said in a singsong Irish lilt.

"And no cribbing lines from *Boondock Saints*, either, darling – you can do better than that." I replied, my mood swinging back toward loving life and all of its absurd ups and downs.

"You'll never get me Lucky Charms?" she tried, going for the old stand-by.

"Now that's more like it!" I said jovially. "So what are we going to do tonight, then?"

"Beans," she stated plainly.

"No, I'm serious," I said. "What do you want to do tonight?"

"Um, beans," she repeated. "They're wicked..."

"Yeah, I know," I said, getting mildly irritated. "They're wicked awesome."

"Ahhhh-some," Penny O'Arcadia corrected.

"Ahhhh-some," I relented. "But what do you want to do tonight? And don't say beans."

The Countess went into the kitchen and came back with a pot of baked beans and hot dogs in one hand, and a copy of *Good Will Hunting* in the other.

"Beans," the Countess repeated, ignoring my request. "Baaah-ston baked beans. They're wicked good. And theah's some cold beahs in the fridge, too."

"I see," I said, trying my best to conceal my blossoming smile. "So that's your plan? Boston baked beans and Matt Damon?"

"And beahs," the Countess O'Arcadia reminded me. "I figure one of us will get aaahhf some wicked good faaahts, and the othah will go runnin' from the room!"

At this, I lost my proverbial shit, and laughed until tears of chocolate milk were pouring from my eyes.

"Oh, you're rotten!" I cried. "You're just absolutely rotten!"

"Wicked good," the Countess beamed.

Almost Like Coffee

"You know, if you put enough sugar and cream in this shit it tastes almost like coffee," the Countess Penelope of Arcadia (which is somewhere in the hills of Columbia) remarked, making an awful look of distaste.

We had decided to try a new place to get our coffee this morning, and we were regretting it. We couldn't go to our old favourite place, because of a certain Barista With No Name and his lovely wife and baby. I mean, of course we *could* go there, but then the Countess would accuse me of making goo goo eyes at a married (or at least very attached) man, and we'd have to have a showdown, and I am a much quicker draw than the Countess, and so I'd be forced to kill her and then I'd be consumed by grief and I would stop eating and my stomach would start eating itself and I'd lose a dangerous amount of weight and get an eating disorder and as you can see, it's just better for all parties involved if we just find a new place to buy our coffee.

"I can't even drink this, Helena," the Countess complained. "Let's go somewhere else. And I am *not* going to fucking Tim Hortons. I'm not sure exactly what it is that they serve there, but it's not coffee."

"I know, right?" I concurred. "It doesn't smell like coffee; it doesn't taste like coffee, and yet it's like the official non-alcoholic drink of Canada."

"Sure, it's *almost* like coffee, but then, so's Sanka or Ovaltine."

"Their hot chocolate's okay," I admitted. "Do you want to get some hot chocolate with me? I need to wash the taste of this...

whatever this was... out of my mouth."

And so we ended up at a Tim Hortons. We didn't have far to go – Tim Hortons are the noxious weeds of any city. They pop up wherever there's a crack, are impossible to get rid of, and they choke out every other business so that nothing else can grow. It's not uncommon for Tim Hortons to build a new store right beside a Mom & Pop coffee shop, that's just the kind of business model they follow. Six months later, the Mom & Pop coffee shop will be gone, and Tim Hortons will be building another store *right across the street*.

In front of us in line was a very European looking man studying the menu and trying to figure out exactly what a mochaccino is, and asking if their croissants were fresh.

The look on his face when he received his espresso (which the counterperson – I will *not* call a Tim Hortons employee a Barista, and you can't make me, darlings – called an *expresso*,[37] whatever that is) in a paper cup almost made me feel better about the horrible coffee I'd been subjected to earlier. But the string of curses that came out of his mouth (along with a piece of the dry, crumbling culinary crime masquerading as a croissant) after he'd tasted what Tim Hortons was passing off as espresso was easily worth the price of our hot chocolates.

"What the hell is this shit?" the man asked with an accent I couldn't quite place. It could have been French, it could have been Dutch, but it was neither. "How can you serve this... this..."

"Shit?" the Countess offered, and waved at the distraught man. She handed him a bunch of sugar packets and smiled at him madly. She'd slipped seamlessly into the lovable Dickensian street urchin. "Iss bloody awful, that is. 'Ere you go, gov'ner. If you put enough o' that in there, it tastes almost like coffee, it does!"

---

[37] There is <u>no fucking X in espresso.</u>

Countess Penelope
and the Cowboy Mystic

A friend of a friend told Penny about a new psychic in town, and wouldn't stop talking about it until the Countess agreed to go see him.

"Apparently he had some sort of near death experience," Countess Penelope told me afterwards. "He was this cowboy down in Texas, and..."

"Do they still have cowboys?" I asked doubtfully.

"Oh, yes," the Countess confirmed casually, "they do. And occasionally they're even on horseback, which is where this guy had his terrible accident."

"Do tell," I prodded. But, you know, not with a cattle prod.

"Well, Bill – that's his name – the Lonesome Cowboy Bill," the Countess Penelope of Arcadia (which was apparently at the intersection of Gullible and Naive) explained.

"Uh huh," I nodded dubiously, appreciative, at least, of the Velvet Underground reference.[38]

"Bill was riding in a rodeo," she continued.

"Of course he was," I laughed.

The Countess glared at me. "Can I continue?"

"Please," I insisted.

"Thank you," she said coldly. "Bill was riding his horse, roping calves and doing tricks with his lasso and whatnot, when suddenly, a group of rodeo clowns came running out onto the grounds, and spooked Cowboy Bill's horse. His horse..."

"What was his horse's name?" I asked, biting my cheek to stop

---

[38] Lonesome Cowbow Bill is a song from *Loaded* by The Velvet Underground, which is one of my favourite albums, by the way. Lonesome Cowboy Bill rides the rodeo, according to the song.

from laughing at the image I had in my head of rodeo clowns running amok.

"I don't know," the Countess Arcade replied in annoyance. "It had no name."

"A horse with no name, huh?" I remarked with a grin.

"Yes, Helena, a horse with no name." Penny sighed. "Maybe it's the same one that dude from that hippie seventies band[39] rode through the desert – are you done being clever now?"

Nothing makes you feel old like having a girl whose diapers you changed suddenly all grown up and chastising you.

"Okay," I mumbled, pouting. "Tell your story."

"Where was I?" Penny asked.

"Spooked horse," I offered.

"Yes," Penny said. "His horse was spooked, and started trying to toss Bill, but he hung on as tight as he could for as long as he could, but that horse was just too wild and threw Bill off, where he was nearly trampled to death by the troupe of rodeo clowns."

"Wow," I said, trying not to laugh, "that's awful."

"Oh, he was okay," Penny replied, continuing with her tale. "He got up and brushed himself off and gave the rodeo clowns a few choice words, but then a bull got loose, and Bill had to take it down before it hurt somebody."

"Oh my god," I said, alarmed. "Did he seriously take a bull down by hand? Did he get gored or something?"

"Nah," Penny laughed. "He shot it. What kind of nut do you think this guy is?"

"But then, how did he sustain his horrible injuries?" I asked, both intrigued and impatiently annoyed.

"If you'll let me finish and stop asking questions, I'll tell you," the Countess snapped.

"Fine," I said, raising my hands in surrender.

"After the show was over, he was leaving, and was turning to wave to some fans, and didn't see where he was going, and he walked in front of a bus."

I didn't say anything for a moment. I wanted to laugh. I wanted to choke Penny.

---

[39] That would be the band America, and even if you don't think you've heard this song, if you've *ever* even listened to AM radio for five minutes, trust me, you've heard *A Horse With No Name.*

"So," I said, shaking my head. "Let me get this straight. You told me this whole story about his rodeo show only to tell me he got hit by a bus?"

"Hey, that's what happened," Penny shrugged. "I didn't make the story up, I'm just recounting it to you."

"Uh huh," I said, annoyed. "So now what?"

"Well, he was busted up pretty bad, and while he was in a coma, he claims to have gone to heaven and come back, and that he still has a link to the great beyond. But he travels in a full body cast wheelchair, and only has limited motion. He can't even talk – his trachea got all crushed or something, so he has to write out his replies to your questions."

"Okay, then," I said. "So what did you ask him? And did you get any answer?"

The Countess handed me a piece of paper filled with nearly illegible handwriting. I could make out words, but the spelling was so horrible I had to translate rather than just read it.

"Wow," I remarked, "that super fragile cowboy mystic's spelling is atrocious!"

Seriously, Helena? All that set up for a lame Mary Poppins joke?[40]

"Yeah, Helena," the Countess Penelope of Arcadia agreed. "What the hell?"

"That's all the time we have, folks!" I said, addressing the non-existent studio audience. "Thanks for coming! Uh... I'd like to thank the Velvet Underground, and the rodeo clowns, and Julie Andrews for being such a good sport! Tune in next time when you'll hear the Countess sing the entire score from Pirates of Penzance![41] Good night everybody!"

---

[40] They say that if you have to explain a joke, it's not funny, but I would be remiss if I didn't at least try to explain to some of you who may be culturally impaired that this is a reference to a song with the wonderful neologism *supercalifragilisticexpialidocious*, from the Disney film *Mary Poppins*, starring the always delightful Julie Andrews and Dick Van Dyke, sporting an impossibly impossible pseudo-English accent that defies belief and makes my snort chocolate milk out my nose every time I hear it. On a related note, The Countess Penelope's Dickensian street-urchin voice owes more than a little to this chimney sweep accent of Dick Van Dyke's.

[41] *Pirates of Penzance* is a Gilbert & Sullivan musical, containing the fantastic tune *I Am the Very Model of a Modern Major General*, among others.

The People vs Helena Hann-Basquiat Part One

This is the story of how my comely compatriot, the incorrigible Countess Penelope of Arcadia (you remember Penny, darlings – Alice in Wonderland aficionado, short-tempered; swears a lot) and I faced off against the tyrannical terror of the New York State judicial system and emerged mostly unscathed.

As a quick synopsis for those of you with short memories:

I was pulled over for speeding a while back, only to be informed that, due to a speeding ticket I'd received thirteen years earlier but had forgotten to pay, my driving privileges had been suspended in the state of New York, and I was being charged with something called Aggravated Operation of a Motor Vehicle. I was very aggravated indeed, darlings, especially since I now had to appear in traffic court in a tiny little town in upstate New York.

The first thing you need to know about this tiny little town, darlings, is that I'd never seen it before in daylight. I had received my speeding ticket in the middle of the night, and so had no reference for this town. I had to find it by using my GPS, and as I wasn't allowed to drive, Penny had agreed to drive me down, more to laugh at me than any other reason, to be honest.

And so it was that we drove right through the town the first time around, with me looking at the GPS with a look of bewilderment.

"Pull over, Penny," I said, confused. Penny complied, and then looked at me for an explanation.

"Well?" she asked, tapping her fingers on the steering wheel.

"I don't understand," I said, looking first at the GPS, and then out the window at the nothingness that presented itself. "It says we're here."

"We're where?" the Countess replied, scanning the horizon for signs of civilization.

"Here," I answered. "It says this is Mill Hollow. But there's nothing here. Certainly nothing resembling a Mill Hollow Community Center."

"Let me look at that," Penny said, snatching the device out of my hands. She looked at the GPS, then out the window, and then back at the GPS.

"Well, fuck me sideways," she swore, and then tossed the GPS back into my lap.

"Right?" I said, incredulous. I looked out the window at the sun lowering toward the horizon, and figured we only had a few hours of daylight left before the wolves came out of the woods and picked what was left of our emaciated bodies after we starved to death in the wilderness.

"You know, I think there was an intersection a few miles back. I think it even had a flashing yellow light. Do you think that was it?" Penny suggested.

It was, dear readers, and when we arrived in the threatening metropolis of Mill Hollow (fake name cough cough) we realized that we'd missed so much when we drove through before. Why, how could we have possibly missed the community center, a tiny square building that looked like over-zealous kids could have constructed it with an abundance of cardboard boxes? And directly adjacent to that, a church transplanted from the set of Little House on the Prairie, complete with a bell that rang out the hours. But the real draw of Mill Hollow was the authentic, old-timey saloon, a few hundred feet down from the center of the town proper, where the Countess and I decided to stop and ask for directions, which went a little like this:

"Hello," I called to the empty bar. Televisions in the corners were the only sound, and when I heard the creak of movement, I assumed that the noise came from a wooden chair or something, and not from the ancient man who twisted his dusty frame out from behind the bar to greet us.

"Ah, hello," he replied, voice sounding like sandpaper on stucco. "You must be here for Traffic Court, yeah?"

I nodded, transfixed. Did the old man have psychic powers? Did I have the look of a criminal or something?

The old man chuckled dryly.

"How could you tell?" I asked.

"It's Thursday, ain't it?" the man said plainly. "You should stick around. We've got some mighty fine dinner specials Thursday nights."[42]

"Uh huh," I said, taking in the rustic ambiance of the bar.

"Oh, can we, Helena?" Penny begged, looking wide eyed with wonder. I could tell that any moment she would slip into her Dickensian urchin voice and I'd be forced to comply or suffer great embarrassment.

"We'll see," I said to her as if she were two and not twenty-something.

"Oh please, gov'ner," she pleaded, slipping, as I feared, into a voice resembling that of a cockney street kid circa 1870. "I 'aven't nevah eaten fresh possum before, I 'aven't. Blimey I bet that's good eatin'!"

"Something wrong with your friend?" the old man (who we would later learn actually responded to the name Pops) asked, cocking his head to the side like a dog.

"Her parents were first cousins," I said off-handedly, and the old man shrugged and nodded, as if that didn't faze or surprise him at all. "Anyhow, I'm looking for the community center. Any idea where that might be?"

"Yup," the man said and laughed again. "Just turn right out ma door and head toward that there yella light. Community center'd be on yer left."

"Thank you," I said as kindly as I could, and grabbed Penny before we ended up on the menu.

By that point, I had drafted in my mind two different scenarios for the court. Either it was going to be a shining beacon of civility and order, with a well-spoken judge in full robes and a powdered wig (I realize that this isn't the way they do things in America, but I've always thought that if I had to go to court, I'd want the judge and the

---

[42] Penny and I theorized that the town's entire economy was based on this Traffic Court, and that in fact, the cops might just have some sort of deal with the local businesses, few as they were, to bring in outsiders. That line of thinking only led us down darker, more pagan paths, and it wasn't long before we found ourselves cast in a horror story of human sacrifice like Stephen King's *Children of the Corn* or Thomas Tryon's *Harvest Home*.

barristers to be all British style, or at least, what I perceived from movies as British style, and to speak like the judge from Pink Floyd's *The Wall*)[43] and I was going to be relieved, or else it was going to be like something out of an old western, with a barefoot judge in overalls, chewing tobacco and spitting it into a brass spittoon while a hooded man stood behind him practicing tying a noose.

Neither of which would have surprised me, darlings.

---

[43] Incidentally, the judge in Pink Floyd's *The Wall* is a giant animated ass.

The People vs Helena Hann-Basquiat Part Two

*I*n which the Countess Penelope of Arcadia swears to tell the truth, the whole truth, and nothing but the truth

"I object, your Honour with a U!" the Countess objected, although the man who looked like he'd be more at home swinging a hoe at some cow patties (or whatever it is farmers do) hadn't actually said anything yet.

The man dressed in the judge's robes had been walking around earlier in shorts and cowboy boots, and had the distinct features of someone whose parents shared common ancestry. That is to say that some of the same people show up at both his mother's and father's family reunions. I'm not saying he was inbred, darlings, but.... oh wait, no... yes. Yes, that's exactly what I'm suggesting.

When it came time for my case to be read, and the judge called out my name, Penny popped to her feet and shouted that *she* was Spartacus.[44] The judge looked at her and asked her to please sit down.

"I swear to tell the truth, the whole truth, and nothing but the truth!" she Countess Penelope exclaimed, and then, for some reason, saluted.

"Miss, that won't be necessary..." the judge began, but was interrupted by more truth than he probably needed to hear.

---

[44] In the 1960 film by the late genius Stanley Kubrick, Spartacus, played by Kirk Douglas, leads a slave revolt, and when the slaves are recaptured, they're offered leniency if they'll identify Spartacus, who was the ringleader. In a show of solidarity that some have said was really about the Communist Witch Hunt led by Senator McCarthy, the slaves all identify themselves as Spartacus.

"I like soup," the Countess Arcade began. "Chicken noodle is my X-Factor. Sometimes I wear mismatched socks on purpose to appear absentminded in order to give my enemies a false sense of security. When I'm all by myself I watch Supernatural in my underwear and pretend that I'm on a date with Sam Winchester and it's... you know... going *well*. I don't like eggs. Nasty things. I practice my voices out loud in the car and if someone catches me I pretend I'm talking on the phone. I've never been to Dallas, but I sometimes have recurring dreams about a grassy knoll, so, you know, maybe in a past life I shot JFK – that's not an admission of guilt, your honour with a U, I'm just, you know, open to discussion. I love ice cream more than is probably healthy, and once I let Brian McDonald lick a bit of chocolate ice cream off of my nipple. I told him it was erotic but afterwards I just felt silly and embarrassed. My hair is not naturally pink, and I'm not a real Countess! Oh please don't send me to the chair, your honour with a U – I'll never do whatever it is I'm accused of ever again. Well, actually, that's not true – I probably will – I'm incorrigible. The jury is advised to disregard that last statement. Uh... let's see... what else? Oh, I know! I've never actually read Alice in Wonderland *or* Through the Looking Glass – well, you know – not without skipping some bits. But I have seen the Disney movie. My favourite bit is the Walrus and the Carpenter, and..."

At this point, the judge stood up and had somehow transformed into a great big fat woman that looked remarkably like the Queen of Hearts, and she just kept yelling "Off with her head!" over and over again.

Did that all happen? You know, as I wasn't actually in the courtroom, such as it was, at the time, I can neither confirm or deny the accuracy of this account, which Penny provided for me after I'd returned from my meeting with the woman from the District Attorney's office, though I can think of no reason why the Countess would make such outrageous claims.

While all that was going on, I was meeting with the D.A. – a woman who would have been about 10 when I got the speeding ticket that caused all this mess in the first place. She explained the particulars of what they were willing to drop the charges to – I wasn't going to be charged with a misdemeanour, and they even knocked my speeding ticket down to a parking ticket (???) and while I wasn't going to have any problems with my license or insurance, I was going to walk away with fines in the amount of around $500.

Later, in the car ride home, when I explained to Penny that they'd cut me a deal, she looked at me suspiciously.

"What'd you give them, Helena?" she asked, squinting her eyes at me. "Huh? Who'd you roll on? You're a marked woman, Helena! Marked for life! Everyone will know what you did. You'll be walking down the street, and you'll see people watching you out of the corner of their eyes. Children will point at you and ask their mothers who you are and their mothers will tell them not to stare at the nasty lady. Why, you won't be able to get service anywhere. You might as well get thousands of dollars of plastic surgery, assume a new name and move to Quebec."

"Quebec?" I asked, perplexed. "Why Quebec?"

"Well, it worked for Karla Homolka,[45] didn't it?" Penny asked.

"Wow," I replied, unable to come up with a witty rejoinder. "Inappropriate, darling."

"Withdrawn, your honour with a U," the Countess said agreeably.

"Thank you."

"So," Penny said after a few moments of rare silence. "What'd you give them, stoolie?"

"Oh, shut up and drive!" I laughed.

---

[45] Karla Homolka and her then husband Paul Bernardo kidnapped and killed at least three teenage girls (including Karla's own sister) in the Niagara Region of Ontario, Canada in the early 1990s. I remember when it happened. I didn't know either of the two other girls personally, but I had friends that did. Karla agreed to testify against her husband in exchange for a reduced sentence. Paul Bernardo is in Kingston Penitentiary for the rest of his life, while Karla got out in 2005, changed her name, got plastic surgery, book deals, and is in hiding somewhere tropical. She's the most notorious woman I can think of.

Snow Blind and Starless

The Countess Penelope of Arcadia had been up for two hours already, watching *Scooby Doo* and eating Cocoa Cheerios in chocolate milk as if she were six years old and not twenty-something.

I crawled up the stairs. Sleepless and only barely awake, and certainly too tired to either care or adequately defend or explain the contradiction inherent in that statement, I followed my nose (*it always knows!*)[46] to the coffee pot, and poured myself a cup.

I rubbed my eyes, pushing them into my head with my fists, and when I took my hands away, everything looked bright and white – I was snow blind, and I closed my eyes and wished for darkness, but the bright corona wouldn't fade – I'd just have to wait it out.

"You ever notice that there are never any stars?" the Countess asked me, and I wasn't even sure what to make of that question.

"In *Scooby Doo*," she explained. "There's always a big full moon, and clouds and fog and whatever, but there's never any stars. It's like they live in an entirely starless universe."

"Huh," I said, sipping my coffee, holding it with both hands so the warmth permeated my skin. "Well that's depressing."

"I know, right?" the Countess Arcade agreed, crunching her double chocolate concoction.

I kept blinking, trying to get my eyes to clear, but everything still looked bright and washed out, like an overexposed photograph.

---

[46] A reference to Toucan Sam, the cartoon spokesperson for Fruit Loops. Follow your nose to artificial fruit flavours.

Outside, it was still dark and equally as dully coloured and starless as a *Scooby Doo* cartoon from the 1970s.

"Do you think that was an artistic choice or a limitation of the animation budget?" the inquisitive Countess queried.

I mumbled something unintelligible and non-committal. Then I tried pressing my fingers over my eyes to make the snow-blindness go away.

"It makes you wonder if maybe they were making a statement about the existential dread of being all alone in the universe – the decline in faith, the crucial end of childhood belief in magic. No stars to gaze upon, ergo, quid pro quo, e pluribus unum, no stargazing, no dreaming." the Countess Penelope of Arcadia (which was, apparently, somewhere near Vienna in the late 19th Century)[47] proposed.

I must have grunted or made some other noise that signalled my agreement or approval, though I don't recall doing either, so Penny continued.

"I mean, the entire crux of the show is the disproving of the supernatural. It's all about destroying children's illusions that there's something magical out there to inspire awe and wonder. It's never a real ghost, or ghoul, or vampire – it's old man Withers in a rubber mask! How utterly..."

"Depressing?" I suggested.

"...Disillusioning." Penny finished.

"It's a cartoon, Penny," I said blandly, and without any inflection in my voice. I sounded washed out and drowned. "It's teaching kids that there are no such things as monsters."

"Huh," Penny snorted. "Really? John Wayne Gacy, Charles Manson, Ed Gein, Jeffrey Dahmer, Paul Bernardo..."[48]

"Well, this is turning into a cheery breakfast conversation," I sighed and rubbed my eyes again, trying to make my vision clear, but to no avail.

Penny kept talking, something about Velma and Shaggy making a cute couple; or maybe it was Daphne, I don't know. I think I heard her say something about Rob Ford[49] being like a *Scooby Doo* villain, and that someone was going to pull his mask off and underneath was

---

[47] A reference to Sigmund Freud, darlings.

[48] Serial killers all.

[49] Notorious Mayor of Toronto who somehow kept his job, despite being captured on film smoking crack, public drunkenness, and a host of other lewd behaviour.

going to be Bill Clinton, smiling a big *Ah shucks* grin and reiterating that not only did he not smoke crack, but that he also did not have sexual relations with *that woman*. Her train of thought moved through rhythms I couldn't keep up with. From *Scooby Doo* to Rob Ford to Bill Clinton back to *Scooby Doo* and Shaggy's perpetual munchies back to Rob Ford's appetites and whether or not he had enough to eat at home.[50] Everything felt blurred around the edges, and nothing made sense. Words sounded like they were coming from far away, like I was underwater, and everything drifted... drifted... faded...

This would become a metaphor for the rest of my day, darlings. Everything washed out and unintelligible, with no stars to guide me; sailing through frozen waters, snow blind and starless.

---

[50] Further, he was accused of telling one of his staff that he wanted to "Eat her pussy." He denied saying this, on national TV, saying that he had enough to eat at home.

Helena Says

With my return to Arcadia interrupted by a speeding ticket that turned into a Kafka-esque fiasco (only, you know, with less metamorphosis)...

You know, Helena, Kafka wrote other stories. In fact, he wrote a novel called The Trial, *which is perhaps what you were referring to?*

Yes, yes, you're very clever, darlings, but who's telling this story? That's right, I am.

And now you've interrupted my train of thought.

Speaking of trains, I remember taking the train to Arcadia to visit my sister and the wee Countess, who would have been about three at the time, and was a right terror. Things were not going well for Cheryl and Ted, not because he was beating her, or because she was sleeping around, but because Arcadia was sucking the life out of them. Ted had been working for a company in Toronto that had been bought up by some giant American company that, despite promises to preserve jobs, decided to shut down the Canadian operation altogether, leaving about 3500 people out of a job. Ted was lucky that his particular skill set was required, and when he got an offer to relocate to upstate New York; an offer that came with a large bonus, well, how could he refuse? The bonus would be enough to move them, and put a down payment on a house in Arcadia, the small community only a thirty-minute drive from the city where he'd be working. Ted and Cheryl thought they were making the smart decision to live in Arcadia rather than the city – they could afford twice as much. A house that went for $200,000 in the city was a mere $95,000 in Arcadia, and there were houses for almost half that for sale in the small, idyllic town that reminded Cheryl of turn of the century post cards.

So they moved down to Arcadia, and I went to England, where I later found out that Cheryl was pregnant, and that my parents had moved down to Arcadia to be close to Cheryl and Ted and the newly born Penelope.

But Cheryl was not made for small town living.

"We've made *no* friends," she cried to me on the phone one night. "And Mum and Dad are here all the time! It's like they never moved out!"

Our parents had moved down to Arcadia – I've told you that much – but what I didn't tell you was that they moved down and in with my sister and her husband. It would be nearly eighteen months of hell for Cheryl and Ted. I finally had to go down, find them a place and make them move out. Cheryl was just too... *nice* to be confrontational.

"I can't get a job – not anything that would make enough money to be worthwhile – I'd have to take Penny to daycare in the city, and then we'd need another car, and... and Ted's gone all the time, and when he's here, we fight all the time, and Penny just... fucking cries *all the time*."

I gasped. Cheryl never swore. Not if her hair was on fire.

"Oh Helena," she sobbed, "I *hate* it here. I want to come home. I want subways and cafes and pubs and traffic. I want noise and industry and people, no matter how rude. I want to see unfamiliar faces. You have no idea how quickly you run out of faces here! I see the same ten people *every fucking day*."

"Hey," I laughed, "easy, sailor! Don't hurt yourself. You gotta pace yourself with that kind of language."

Cheryl laughed back. "I miss you, Helena."

"Oh, you're just sayin' that 'cause you're drunk," I teased. Cheryl wasn't one to get drunk. "If I were there you'd be sick to death of me. Remember when I came back from England? You couldn't wait to be rid of me."

"Come down for a visit, will you? Please?" Cheryl pleaded.

"You don't have to beg, Cheryl," I laughed. "Of course I will. You, Brooke and me will go out. We'll leave Penny with Mum, and the three of us will go into the city, and..."

Cheryl coughed.

"What?" I asked. Cheryl wasn't the type to interrupt you by talking over you, but if she wanted to stop you, she'd cough.

"Brooke won't be allowed to go," Cheryl said awkwardly.

"Allowed?" I asked. "What do you mean *allowed?*"

"That bastard she's married to – it's like he keeps her a prisoner. Ever since the last time you were here and we went out for drinks, I haven't seen her. I mean, I've seen her, but not, you know, *socially.*"

"I remember that night," I said. "That guy was in there shooting his mouth off about Home Depot and shit, right?"

"That was that girl's dad, you know," Cheryl said solemnly. "Amy LeFevre."

Cheryl had called me the day they found the old man at the bottom of his basement stairs to tell me all about it. At first I hadn't even remembered Amy at all – I'd only seen her around a few times, riding her bike around town in short cut off shorts and Doc Martens, bruises all up and down her legs like leopard spots.

"I think he hits her," Cheryl said, breaking the silence that followed Amy LeFevre's name.

I knew immediately what was going through Cheryl's head, because it was going through mine as well. People saw Amy LeFevre every day, covered with bruises and angry all the time, and they did nothing about it. If Cheryl thought that Brooke was getting hit by her husband and did nothing about it, she couldn't live with herself.

"Have you tried talking to her about it?" I asked.

"I tried," Cheryl sighed. "But she made excuses, or she was busy, and then eventually she got mad at me and told me to mind my own business. I haven't even talked to her in months. I see her around, but she usually tries to avoid me, or just smiles and nods, you know."

I did know. I spent most of my high school years avoiding people's gazes or smiling and nodding. I made my own share of excuses for bruises, and cried all the time. People thought that I was crazy, or that I was upset about some boy. I sat at the back of the bus, crying into my jacket, trying not to draw attention to myself, and even succeeding once in a while. Listening to Lou Reed's *Berlin* and crying to the lyrics of Caroline Says II : *Caroline says, as she gets up off the floor, 'You can hit me all that you want to but I don't love you anymore'.* [51] It

---

[51] I wrote this chapter shortly after Lou Reed died, and it got me thinking about when I'd first fallen in love with his music. Was it *Transformer*, with its David Bowie glam

got to the point that Helena crying was no longer a matter of interest. I kept my secrets, not knowing that I shouldn't have had to. I was angry all the time, and I scared my teachers with the horrible stories and poems that I wrote. And all the while, what I really wanted was for someone to save me. But no one did.

I should have said more to Amy. I should have done something. Now Cheryl needed me, and Brooke might be in trouble. I had to go. I had to save someone, even if it was only myself.

And so I ended up on a train bound for Arcadia.

---

production, or was it *Berlin*? I think I flirted with Lou Reed with The Velvet Underground and Transformer, but I really fell in love with him with *Berlin*.

The Return of the Thin White Duchess, or, Rather, Countess

I arrived at the Amtrak station in Arcadia the next day by late afternoon, having listened to nothing but *Changesbowie* over and over again on cassette. I had left in a hurry, taking my Sony Walkman with me but no cassettes – in my world, something of a tragedy, darlings. Helena with no music is like a fish without a cracker, or a bird with a broken record, or a writer at a loss for a cliché metaphor. So when we stopped at one of the train depots, I had gone to the lunch counter to get something to drink, and to my delight, noticed that they had a small selection of cassettes. I perused the paltry pickings, rejecting Patsy Cline, Merle Haggard and Hank Williams Jr. in favour of the Thin White Duke's[52] greatest hits package which may or may not contain the title track to *Station to Station*, but for the sake of narrative, let's say it does, reality be damned.

I had taken the train to Arcadia, because it's a more romantic way to travel, thank you very much, and I was twenty and broke, but my sister had asked me to come down for a visit. Cheryl and her husband had been in Arcadia for just about three years, moving there while Cheryl was still pregnant with Penny, and it hadn't been the easiest three years for them. Partly because my parents, who may just be the two most useless people in the world, had followed them to Arcadia under the guise of being near them and their grandchild, and had, in fact, moved in with Cheryl and Ted for nearly a year and a

---

[52] It occurs to me to note here that David Bowie has gone through a number of stylistic periods in his career, and at one point (*Station to Station* era mid to late '70s) he was known as the Thin White Duke.

half. I confess I made myself scarce – I had come back from England and visited my family for a little over three months, but after three mind-numbing months of recovery in Arcadia, home of... well, absolutely *nothing*, I headed back to Toronto to make my way in the cruel, cruel world on my own. I'd go back to visit my sister and my wee little niece now and again, even moving down there for nearly a year when Penny was five and Cheryl had finally decided to go back to college or else go insane in Arcadia. (It was during this stay that I received a speeding ticket which would impact my life almost fifteen years later, if you can but believe it, darlings.)

But this particular trip was brought on by a cry for help from Cheryl who was losing her mind in small town America, unable to make friends, unable to get out of the house, and caring by herself for the very young Countess Penelope, who was not quite three years old but already endowed with more personality than one person should possess.

I was greeted at the train station by a pixie with a mane of wild blond hair and chocolate smeared across her smiling face like lipstick applied by a blind woman during an bout of epilepsy.

"Elna! Elna!" she shrieked with joy, and I admit, I teared up a little bit, darlings. It was the first time I'd heard her say my name. I didn't even know she could. I squatted and held out my arms for her, squeezing her back as tightly as she gave.

"Come here, you little hellion!" I said, and got a look from Cheryl.

"Careful, Helena," she said, looking exhausted. "She repeats everything these days."

I gave my big sister a hug and promised I'd watch my mouth, and got into the car.

We hadn't been in the car two minutes when the first demand came from the back seat.

"Want ice cream." Penny stated, not bossily, but rather, just casually. Like you or I might say *Nice day, isn't it?*

"No ice cream before dinner, honey," Cheryl said unconvincingly, as if it were the first futile salvo in a battle she knew she was destined to lose.

"Want ice cream," the little Countess repeated cheerfully, ignoring her mother. "Want ice cream, Elna!"

I looked at my sister and shrugged.

"You wanted to get out of the house, right?" I said. "Maybe she'll fall asleep on the way home."

"There's a Dairy Queen about twenty minutes from here," she said, and I smiled at her.

"What?" she asked, confused.

"Do people give you sh... uh... do people still give you a hard time about being Canadian?" I asked.

"Sometimes," she said, still looking at me like I had a rat's tail hanging out of the corner of my mouth. "Why? What'd I say?"

"How far away is the Dairy Queen?" I asked her.

"About twenty minutes from here. Why?"

I laughed at her. I'd always teased her that she was going to become a damn Yankee if she lived in Arcadia long enough, but evidently she was still Canadian enough to give distances in terms of how long a drive it was.

"So what's that in miles, darling?" I teased.

"Oh, shut up!" she laughed, and put her hand over my face.

Penny giggled madly from the back seat.

"Ut up!" she parroted. "Ut up, Elna!"

I shot Cheryl a look of mock disappointment, and crossed my arms over my chest.

"That one's all on you, babe," I said smugly, and pulled out my Walkman, popping out the David Bowie cassette and pushing it into Cheryl's stereo.

"Penny loves music," Cheryl said, "Don't you, honey?"

Penny banged her head up and down, wild hair just *everywhere* and giggled and shrieked with pleasure as the music came on.

"Of course she does," I said, and started twisting and shaking my head exaggeratedly to the music, dancing with my wee little niece. To this day, this is how we dance together.

We got our ice cream and listened to more Bowie on the ride home. Penny particularly enjoyed *China Girl*, and so I had to keep rewinding it for her to listen again and again.[53]

That night, as I was trying to put her to bed, I sang it to her as a lullaby, but it may have backfired on me – Cheryl certainly wasn't amused at what Aunt Helena had taught her.

And when I get excited, my little china girl says...

---

[53] I had to explain to Penny where this tradition comes from, but whenever she and I are in foul moods, we quite often go for ice cream and listen to David Bowie.

After that night, every time anyone tried to shush the little Countess, she responded with a totally deadpan:

"Ooh baby, just you shut your mouth!"

Scary Story

"Tell me a scary story, Helena," the Countess Penelope demanded with a demonic grin. "Something to keep me awake."

I looked at my niece with mild interest, as that is all I seem capable of these days.

"And why would you want that, darling?" I inquired.

The Countess sighed and yawned. "Because it's only 7:30 and I want to go to sleep and it's *way* too early for me to go to sleep."

"You're weird," I remarked.

"What's weird is the fact that it's pitch black at 7:30. It messes with my arcadian rhythm. I blame Al Gore."[54]

"That's *circadian* rhythm, and I think you give Al Gore way too much credit."

"Whatever," she said with a wave of her hand. "Tell me a story. And make it a scary one."

"Okay," I relented. I had all kinds of scary stories tumbling around my head, though none of them featured vampires, or ghosts, or a homicidal, axe-wielding maniac wearing a hockey mask. My stories were much more frightening.

"Lately," I began, "I've been thinking that what I'd really like to do is draw a nice hot bath, turn on something soothing, like Brian Eno's *Discreet Music*, pour myself a nice tall vodka and grapefruit juice,

---

[54] Penny often insists that Al Gore invented all sorts of things that he clearly didn't. This is a riff on his supposed claim that he invented the Internet. In this case, Daylight Savings Time.

and swallow handfuls of sleeping pills like they were M&Ms until I just fall asleep and never wake up again. The end."

Penny looked at me with weariness – she was way past concern at this point.

"Well, congratulations," she said, "I'm not going to sleep now."

"You're welcome," I said with a mock curtsey.

"That's not what people want to read, Helena," the Countess Penelope of Arcadia chided. "You're going to completely alienate your audience. People want fun; people want funny; people want light, zany adventures."

"I tried that," I moped. "Every day for months, I tried that."

"So do it again!" Penny demanded. "You were having such fun then!"

"No," I sighed. "Can't. Besides, I think I've lost my sense of humour."

"Well, did you check in the couch cushions?" the Countess deadpanned. "You would not believe the shit I lose in there."

I winced at Penny's attempt at humour, and shook my head.

"It doesn't matter," I mumbled. "I think I've figured some things out now."

"What's that?" Penny asked. She moved to sit beside me on the couch now, forcing me to face her as I spoke.

"You know that old riddle about the tree falling in the forest with no one around to hear it?" I asked rhetorically and she nodded. "Well, I think it does make a sound. I think it screams. I think it screams the most horrible scream possible; a scream so full of despair and loneliness – but it doesn't matter – because nobody hears it."

Penny said nothing, but began stroking my hair.

"And do you know why it was screaming? Because up to that point, it had been singing. I don't know if it was the most beautiful song, or what (if any) words it was singing. But it was singing, because it wanted to be heard – because it needed to be heard – because the songs inside it were so strong and so powerful that if it didn't sing them then they would just rot the tree out from the inside. But again, it doesn't matter, because this tree – this tree that is not content to just be a tree and stand and grow and be lost in a forest of trees – goes on unheard. And after so long singing and no one hearing it, the tree kills itself, and that's why it falls. And that's why it's screaming unheard, horrible screams."

"Okay, now you're scaring me," Penny whispered.

"I'm scaring myself," I admitted.

"I think you need some help," Penny suggested.

"I think so, too."

The Countess Penelope of Arcadia Wishes You A Happy Thanksgiving

'*K*ayso, it's Thanksgiving time for all you lovely Americans, and Helena said I could share some pumpkin-related humour with y'all (see – me speakee your dialect) in honour of it being Turkey-time.

'Kayso, Cinderella's all bummed out 'cause she can't go to the ball, and she's got a real lady hard-on for the prince, who apparently looks like Sam Winchester[55] or something, and she wants to break off a piece of that and just, you know, go to town... you know what I'm sayin'...

AnyWHOOO, she's stuck cooking and cleaning up after her evil stepmum and her two wicked stepbitches, but out of the blue, POOF! David Bowie shows up dressed as the Goblin King (or is it Goblin Queen – I can never tell with Bowie) from *Labyrinth*, and tells her that he's her fairy godmother... er... godfather... whatever... and that he's going to make it so that she can go to the ball.

(Oh stop it... I'm telling the story, and everything goes better with Bowie... I've been a fan since I was two, what can I say?)

So Bowie, the Goblin King, changes a pumpkin into a carriage, and rats into drivers and horses and whatever... yada yada yada... you know this part. He's dancing around singing *Ch-ch-ch-changes* and turning Cinderella's rags into a beautiful Versace gown and glass slippers, the whole shebang.

---

[55] A character from the TV show *Supernatural*, played by Jared Padalecki.

But then Cinderella, she kind of looks at Bowie all sheepishly and whispers something in his ear.

"Well, that is distressing, Sarah,"[56] he purrs like only Bowie can purr.

"My name's Ella," Cinderella corrects.

"Well, that is distressing, Ella," Bowie amends.

Then he takes a pumpkin and magically transforms it into a tampon, which Cinderella was in terrible need of.

"But remember, Sarah..."

"Ella,"

"Remember, Ella," Bowie warned, "You must be back by the stroke of midnight, or that beautiful dress of yours will turn back into rags, and so will everything else turn back into rats and pumpkins..."

Ella promised that she'd heed the Thin White Duke... er... Goblin King's advice, and went off to the ball to throw herself desperately at the prince, despite the all the rumours she'd heard about him and his page boys.

Well, Bowie waited around for her, listening to Lou Reed's *Transformer* and delighting in his handiwork, which is, I admit, kind of couche tardy, but I mean, if I'd produced an amazing album, I think I might just listen to it now and again – I know, I know... it's like masturbation, but come on, we all enjoy that, right?

AAAAANYWHO... midnight comes and goes, and no Cinderella. Bowie's getting a bit nervous, and by the time Cinderella finally strolls in at a quarter past three, he's ramped up higher than he was during the cocaine years of the late '70s (seriously, listen to his live album *Stages* and hear how fast and frantic everything was!)

Cinderella comes in looking absotively splattered – her dress has returned to rags, and it's all torn up and she's practically hanging out all over the place.

Bowie looks concerned but confused – the girl's got a giant grin on her face.

"What happened to you?" Bowie demanded. "How did it go with the prince?"

"Oh never mind the prince," Cinderella said with a wicked grin, "I met me the greatest guy! I think his name was Peter... I dunno, but he just fucking LOVED eating pumpkins!"

A WAKA WAKA WAKA!!!!!

---

[56] Sarah was the name of the character played by Jennifer Connelly in *Labyrinth*.

Happy Thanksgiving, all you lovely Yankees! (You horrid ones can get sweet potato poisoning, y'hear!)

Nah, I'm just fucking with you! MWAH!

Penny

You Want the Truth? Part One: It's Just a Jump to the Left

T he truth is that everyone, once in their lives, if not more than once, succumbs to the madness, and dresses up like the cast of *Rocky Horror* for Hallowe'en. If you have already capitulated to this craze, then you know just what I'm talking about. If you have not yet given in to the passion, then let this be a cautionary tale – mind your purse, darlings.

Seven of us set out that evening to take home the prize for best group costume at our local watering hole, where we met once or twice a month to sing karaoke, bitch about our jobs, get drunk and express our undying love for one another, and generally make asses of ourselves. And what better way to make an ass of yourself than to dress up in corset and stockings, or, in my case, gold hot pants and fishnets, and parade around in public singing songs from a campy 1970s musical? Seven of us set out that evening, but only six of us would make it home with their dignity more or less intact.

I admit that in the past, I may have said that we were dressed as strippers – because the two could be easily confused. And to be totally honest, my costume was mostly in the *spirit* of *Rocky Horror*. I had really wanted to find something to be Little Nell but in the end, I couldn't find a gold lamé jacket or top hat, but I *did* have some shiny gold hot pants that I'd kept as a souvenir from my misadventures in Cheyenne, Wyoming,[57] and I figured that as long as fishnets and general trashiness was involved, that I would fill out my part of the sordid ensemble.

---

[57] See Volume One: Cheyenne Wyoming and the Accidental Plagiarist.

So we showed up, outlandishly attired, to our karaoke bar, and of course we took home the prize (I don't play if I can't win, darlings) which was just free bar food. Nothing spectacular, perhaps, but it's not about the prize, it's about the bragging rights.

As the evening moved along and the novelty had worn off, a couple of the boys started trying to convince us to go to the strip club. Because that's what boys do, darlings, surprisingly, even when they are dressed in drag, shaved legs and all.

Even though my experience in Wyoming was a couple of years behind me at that point, I still had no desire to relive that moment. Like the warning on the side view mirror says, objects may be closer than they appear – the same is true with memory, I've found. Unpleasant memories in particular tend to linger. But I also didn't want to be the proverbial wet blanket, and so I went along, in the spirit of debauchery and libertinism and everything else that *Rocky Horror* embraces – besides, it was Hallowe'en, I told myself. When was I ever going to get a chance to see my best guy friends make absolute fools of themselves by dancing around a stripper pole dressed in corsets and stockings?

We all packed into two cars, and the last part of the evening was everything you'd expect, culminating to the, ahem, climax of the evening, when the guys found themselves up on the stage gyrating to Aerosmith's *Dude (Looks Like a Lady)* to the applause and cat-calls of the club's dancers and the disgust and angry, hateful, homophobic jeers of the club's classiest customers.

Then two o'clock rolled around, as it is known to do on occasion, and the bouncers started kicking everybody out.

I would like to preface the next bit by telling you that I was absolutely stone sober at this point. I really had learned my lesson vis–à–vis me + excessive amounts of alcohol + strip clubs, and so I had resolved, not only because I was driving (it wouldn't have been the first time that I'd driven somewhere only to have to abandon my car in favour of public transportation) but because I was not going to find myself a debauched participant in the evening's carnality – no, darlings, that night I was there merely as an observer. So wipe away any visions of me shaking my delicious dilettante derriere under the glow of pink neon. My time on the stage, brief and regrettable, was firmly (as firm as my fine fanny) in the past. And yes, now I'm just being a tease, darlings. I hope I haven't given anyone a heart attack (you know who you are, I won't call you out).

Sober as I was, however, I still managed to lose my purse somehow. Sadly, it was not until the club was closing that this panic-inducing circumstance presented itself so unexpectedly.

Now, I don't know if you've ever been the sober one in your group of drunken friends, but if you have, then kudos to you. You are a hero, and you know full well that your friends are all assholes, even more so when they're drunk. Trying to wrangle your drunken friends out of the bar and safely home is akin to trying to get a toddler who's just had an entire bag of Skittles and a sippy cup full of chocolate milk out of a Toys 'R' Us. The behaviour is uncannily similar, now that I think about it. Screams of *I don't wanna!* coupled with the flailing of arms and total loss of body control in an attempt to make moving them nigh impossible. Gandhi called that move "passive resistance", but I think it was just a leftover from his pub-crawling days in the streets of London.

So when my asshole friends were being corralled out of the club by our other sober friend, (who, incidentally, had made a wonderful Dr. Frankenfurter - not as good as Tim Curry, of course, but then, no one is, darlings) I was left behind in the chaos, still frantically searching for my purse. At some point, I told them to just go, that I'd be all right, because I am horrible at asking for help and I always have been. So I got left on my own again. A couple of the waitresses were sympathetic and really tried to help me find my purse, but at the end of the night, they needed to close down, and for that to happen, I needed to leave.

I left the club, walking out into the cold night with no keys, no wallet, no money, no cell phone, exhausted, frustrated and a little bit pissed off with my friends who had left me without making sure that I was okay. In retrospect, I guess they figured that as I was sober, I was the least of their worries. Still...

Without a dime to my name, and it being three in the morning by that point, I decided that the quickest, safest thing for me to do was to sleep in my car, which the fates had generously left unlocked for me.

And then you were arrested for prostitution, Helena?

No, darlings, not yet – but don't fret, I'm getting there.

A few hours later, after restlessly tossing and turning and shivering in the skimpy outfit I was wearing, I decided to try to find some help. I got out of my car, careful not to lock it on habit, and went out to the road to try to flag down some help.

I confess that at the time, I didn't even think about my appearance. I was cold, I was tired, I was hungry, and I was angry. If you've ever lost your wallet or keys, you know what an incredible pain in the ass that is. Compound that by being locked out of your car, locked out of your house, and stranded in the parking lot of a strip club in hot pants, fishnets and a corset top (did I mention the corset top? Thing One and Thing Two looked *amazing* that night, but I digress) freezing your ass off in a part of town that you generally don't want to be alone in if you can avoid it, and maybe you can imagine the kind of panic/fear/anger I was feeling. I comforted myself by uttering that horrible phrase that no one should ever think, let alone speak, because doing so is like spitting in the eye of the universe and yelling *bring it on, bitch!*

"Things couldn't possibly get any worse," I told myself. I was going to figure this out, and everything would be okay, and this would just be a funny story that I told someday.

Only that last part was true.

You Want the Truth? Part Two: And Then a Step to the Right

*T*he car that pulled over was an avocado green Eldorado – I'll never forget it, because the rest of this scene played out like something out of a movie – *Sin City*,[58] perhaps – and the details are forever playing in the blooper reel of my memory. The driver pulled over and rolled down the passenger side window, and I had to bend down to poke my head in. Now, I don't know if you've ever worn stiletto heels, darlings, but they are pretty much engineered to make you look like a hooker. Bending over in them makes you thrust your ass in the air, and you can practically hear David Attenborough narrating your life like something out of a BBC special on the mating habits of the wild dilettante: *Thrusting her magnificent hindquarters into the air and bending over to give full display of her ample cleavage, the dilettante signals to any male in the area her availability for mating.*

They say if it walks like a duck and quacks like a duck and waddles like a duck, then it must be a duck, and so apparently this guy thought that's what I was – a working girl, that is – not a duck. So when he asked me if I wanted a ride, I reached for the handle cautiously, but when he followed the question up with a mention of not having much money, and *how much for just a blowjob*, I quickly backed away and shook my head and laughed nervously.

Apparently I hadn't backed away fast enough, though, because we'd drawn the attention of the kind of car with blue and red lights on top. The green Eldorado pulled away with a screech of rubber on

---

[58] An over-the-top film noir/exploitation film based on the comics of the same name by Frank Miller. Sin City itself is full of vice like drugs and prostitution.

asphalt, leaving me shivering in the dust while a police officer approached me with a smirk and an unfriendly hello.

Shivering so badly my teeth were chattering, I tried to say hello, to ask for help, to explain what had happened, but instead, was told that I knew the routine, and to face the hood of the car and put my hands on it.

I wasn't sure exactly what routine he thought I was so familiar with, but I recognized this from every vice cop show I'd ever seen, and I realized that I was about to be handcuffed. Usually it was about at this point in the show that the greasy cop would lean over while he was putting on the cuffs and whisper something suggestive into the hooker's ear, like *I bet you like that, huh?*

Thankfully, I got no such treatment, and afterward I would have occasion to reflect on the details of my near incarceration and be a little disappointed, if you want to know the truth (and clearly you do, darlings, or you wouldn't be reading this). I mean, really – wasn't I worthy of a little bit of creepy, inappropriate leering and lust?

Once I was in the back of the patrol car, I tried earnestly but politely to explain what I was doing On The Strip at seven o'clock in the morning, dressed the way I was, and what my business was with Mr. Howmuchforjustablowjob. (I wonder if there was a Mrs. Howmuchforjustablowjob? Maybe even little Howmuchforjustablowjobs. God, what an embarrassing surname. I'd change it if I were them. But I digress, darlings – it's what I do, so sue me). Considering that I'd been crying some, had slept in my car, and had been wearing far too much make up to begin with, I must have looked like I'd been up all night turning tricks, so I really couldn't blame them.

They asked me for ID, and I reminded them firmly but politely (no, I'm being serious) that I had lost everything, but that if they would just be so kind to let me make a phone call, I could clear everything up.

They informed me firmly and perhaps a little less politely than I would have liked that I was being cited for solicitation, and that I would be allowed a phone call once I reached the station.

And then I started to cry, darlings. I'm not proud.

"Oh, come on," Officer One sighed. "I'm sure this isn't your first time, honey."

Maybe it was his patronizing tone, maybe it was just the *honey*, but something inside me snapped.

"Stop the car!" I yelled. "Stop the car, or so help me god I will tell your partner what you whispered in my ear when you were putting these cuffs on me, you sick fuck!"

"Settle down, Miss," Officer Two said sternly, and I shut up.

"Yeah, sorry about that," I said, retracting my previous bout of melodrama and smiling a sheepish, disarming grin. I was exhausted to the point of mania, I now realize in retrospect. "That kind of thing usually works on TV, though, you know?"

Officer One started laughing. "What's your name, honey?"

I sighed. "If I tell you, will you stop calling me honey? I fucking *hate* that."

"Fair enough," Officer One sighed.

"It's Helena," I said tiredly.

"Well, you seem like a smart girl, Helena," Officer One said in his best patronizing tone. "What are you doing turning tricks out here. Are you on drugs?"

I wanted to spit back that I was hardly a girl, and that if was going to peddle my flesh, it certainly wouldn't be in this neighbourhood, and certainly not for drugs. Instead, I sighed and laughed.

"No good deed...." I began, and sighed again, and then tried to explain once more. "I was the designated driver! Do you understand? That means I wasn't even *drunk!* I'm not supposed to be the one that ends up in the back of a police car at the end of the night – or, well, the next morning – you know what I mean!"

Officer One looked at me in the rear view mirror, and then at his partner, and began to laugh heartily and not without sympathy.

"What do you think?" Officer One asked his partner, who just shook his head in pity.

"Look, Miss..." Officer Two began.

"Helena," I said indignantly, not enjoying being laughed at.

"Helena," Officer Two amended. "We'd like to help you out – sounds like you've had a hell of a time..."

"You realize that you two are sort of *part* of that hell of a time, right?" I asked, pushed past the point of perturbance.

Officer Two blushed – I swear to god – and Officer One coughed and pulled the car over. For a brief instant I had visions of being pulled out of the car and violated like something out of a misogynistic porno – it had just been that kind of 24 hours – but instead, Officer One opened the door and asked me to hold out my hands so he could remove my handcuffs, and then apologized sincerely and asked if there was anything they could do to help.

"Well, my car is sitting back in that parking lot, but without my keys, I can't do any of the things that I'm going to have to do today, like – well, I'd really like to put some actual clothes on, you know? So I'd say, if you could take me to my car dealership, not only can they confirm my identity for you, but they can give me a spare key – I lease, so, I'm sure they have a backup."

And that's just what they did, darlings. Those two nice boys in blue drove me to the administration office of the dealership I got my car from, all the while apologizing over and over again until I finally laughed at them and told them to shut up about it, and to just keep my name out of any reports, though I'm sure that I was the subject of much ridicule between them after I left their care. By the time we got to the leasing office, we were old friends, and I think Officer Two had even taken something of a shine to me, which I would have probably felt better about had I not been dressed like a fancy call girl.

"So, what *did* he whisper in your ear when he was putting the cuffs on?" Officer Two asked me, eliciting a dirty look from his partner.

"Hey, I never..." Officer One protested, and I laughed and winked at him.

"Don't worry, darling," I said cheekily. "It'll be our little secret."

They even laughed as I had some fun with the high school boys hanging outside the convenience store that was beside the leasing office. They happened to notice what was quite clearly a coked out hooker in the back of a police car, and began staring and leering.

I've never been one to miss out on an opportunity to vamp, darlings, and so I began blowing kisses and making obscene gestures, eliciting a response from the boys that almost made everything that had happened up to that point seem worth it. I nearly lost my head in the moment and went so far as to lick the glass, but then I remembered where I was, and reconsidered, as that would not only be unwise, but possibly dangerously unhygienic.

I could tell you the rest of the day, but really, the worst of it was over. I got my keys and several looks ranging from disgust to lust from the office staff at the leasing office, and I played it all cool, laughing my way through the questions about the police presence and my choice of wardrobe. It didn't hurt that it was Hallowe'en, which, like love, covers a multitude of sins, apparently.

Once I got back to my car (to which the officers so obligingly drove me back) I drove to my sister Cheryl's house to regroup and take care of what I needed to – calling my landlord, cancelling my credit cards – boring business stuff that you don't want to read about, darlings.

It wasn't the first time I'd shown up on Cheryl's doorstep, not even the first time I'd shown up with a story that involved the police, but it was the first time I'd shown up in gold hot pants and fishnets. There's a first time for everything, I suppose.

Cheryl didn't even bat an eye. She just took me in and made me breakfast. I remember Penny was there, too. The three of us sat around Cheryl and Ted's table and ate banana and chocolate chip pancakes with mounds of butter and rivers of maple syrup, washing it down with gallons of strong coffee, the two of them laughing at me and making suggestions and insinuations of how I really got the cops to let me go. Cheryl was wearing this great terry and satin housecoat and had her hair up like she was some kind of Japanese geisha. She looked beautiful, and it's how I'll always remember her. Penny had rolled out of bed when she heard me come in, and looked like a female Robert Smith[59] – her hair was standing up every which way, and I smiled, knowing that she hadn't an ounce of self-consciousness. If she wanted to, she'd just leave it like that all day and call it her style.

I'll always remember that morning. It was the last time the three of us sat around a table together. Not long after that, Ted and Cheryl had their accident and Penny came to live with me, and everything changed.

But for that moment – we were beautiful, and not yet broken.

---

[59] Lead singer of The Cure, famous for morose lyrics and wild hair, among other things.

Cummerbund Bandersnatch and the Desolation of Smog

There is a place, a dark place, just outside of the GTA (that's the Greater Toronto Area, if you're interested, darlings) where darkness dwells. A place where the smog hangs over Lake Ontario like a malignant force — for the Dwarves that lived there burned the fires of steel refining day and night, pumping their smoke into the sky, leaving a desolation usually reserved for such detestable places as Pittsburgh or (*shudder*) Cleveland. In the long dead language of the people who once dwelt there, it is called *Khazad-dûm,* but people today refer to it as Hamilton, and its name is spoken in hushed, fearful tones. Children are warned never to venture north of King Street in the dark, and in particular to avoid the dreaded Barton Street, where all manner of twisted creatures dwell, seeking to prey on any weak straggler who might venture into their path. It is a place of horror, where...

"Seriously, Helena?" Penny interjected.

"What?" I asked, standing firmly by my assessment.

"Well, iss not very noice, issit?" the Countess Penelope of Arcadia accused. You remember Penny, darlings. Tends to talk like a Dickensian street urchin from time to time, fancies herself something of a fashion trendsetter because of a incomparable collection of stripey socks, and is not, by any stretch of the imagination, a fan of the writing of one Mr. J.R.R. Tolkien.

"No, Penny, Hamilton isn't very nice," I agreed, knowing full well that's not what she meant.

"You know full well thass not wot I meant, ya daft cow!" Penny protested passionately.

A couple of months ago, Penny and I had moved into her grandmother's house in Hamilton in order to help look after her, and it had been an adjustment for everyone.

"Besides," the Countess of Arcadia continued, "I fought you loiked West-day-oh."

"*Westdale?* Oh yes. Three coffee shops, a bakery, a shitty pub, a Pita Pit and a TCBY. What's not to love?" I held my hand over my heart, all a-flutter.

"Hmm," the Countess of Arcadia said, tapping a finger to her lips and looking pensive. "Interesting. How *very* interesting."

I wasn't going to bite. I had an inkling as to where this was going, having just sat through *Star Trek: Into Darkness*, *Tinker Tailor Soldier Spy*, and two seasons of the BBC's *Sherlock* on the weekend. Neither of us were feeling well, and so we loaded up on junk food and bundled our bacteria-besieged bodies in blankets and binged on Bandersnatch. Cummerbund Bandersnatch, that is, and if you want some back story on that silly sounding bit of schizophasia, it's simple, darlings. One night, after one too many vodka and cranberries, the Countess declared her undying love for the star of *Sherlock*, one Benedict Cumberbatch, only in her drunkified state (drunkified is a good, fine, strong word, thank you very much, and seeing as it's referring to a state in which one slurs one's speech and engages in such dreadful activities as neologism, I'm standing by my use of it) she insisted (quite insistently, if I recall correctly, and I always do, darlings) that his name was Cummerbund Bandersnatch. It took, and that will forever be how we refer to the man in Casa de Hann-Basquiat.

"Fascinating," the Countess continued, caressing her mouth as if deep in deductive thought.

"Okay," I sighed. "What's so fucking fascinating?"

"You seriously just swore for the sake of alliteration, didn't you?" the Countess queried capriciously.

"You're one to talk with your capricious queries," I quipped.

"You need help," the Countess Penelope of Arcadia accused, not unkindly.

"Yes, I thought we determined that," I grinned. "Now go on, then. What do you find fascinating?"

"Ah yes," the Countess of Arcadia (which is somewhere in the vicinity of 221B Baker Street, it would seem) resumed. "I find it fascinating that you claim to know so much about the village of Westdale, and claim to find it disagreeable and pedantic, and yet the true story of how you feel about it can be found in what you deliberately neglected to mention."

I was driving Penny to the train station. One of the adjustments that we both had to make when we moved to Hamilton was a longer commute, and while neither of us enjoyed that very much, we tried to make the best of it.

"I'm sure I don't know what you're talking about," I deflected, and then tried a different tact. "So are you going to go see the Desolation of Smaug this weekend?"

"You're pronouncing that wrong, Helena, and you know you're pronouncing that wrong." the Countess Penelope of Arcadia (which is somewhere in the Misty Mountains) accused.

"How can you tell?" I asked, amused.

"Well, iss all in the bloody title, ennit?" the Dickensian street urchin that contrarily fancies herself a Countess replied. "You're sayin' it to rhyme with fog, but it don't go loik that, does it? And Smaug don't live in the Misty Mountains, neither. 'E lives in the *Lonely* Mountain. And don't fink I 'aven't noticed that you've, loik, changed the bleeding subject, you devious dilettante!"

I snickered into my coffee, nearly spilling it and driving us off the road.

"I thought you hated Tolkien," I reminded her.

"I do," Penny admitted. "Horrible writing. Archaic, laughable plot devices and in terrible need of an editor – but that man's voice..."

"Cummerbund Bandersnatch," I volunteered.

"Thass the one, 'Elena, my love, my sweet," she agreed with a lusty grin. "That beautiful man's glorious voice melts my knickers, it does. And 'e's voicing the dragon Smaug, so..."

"I see," I said plainly.

"Now," the Countess resumed, composing herself. She may or may not have wiped a string of drool from her lips. "Back to the matter at hand. You deliberately neglected to mention the following bits of information concerning the village of Westdale, which you claim to find boring and uninteresting. One - Westdale has a charming little theatre, which I happen to know that you *love*, because you have chosen to see not one but *three* films there lately as opposed to seeing them at the giant cineplexes. Two - Westdale has not one but *two* comic book stores, and I can't help but notice that you are not behind in reading *Saga* or *Unwritten* – so tell me, Helena – where have you been buying your comics, huh?"

"Well, I..." I began, but was immediately interrupted.

"Three!" The Countess continued presenting her damning evidence against me. "Adjacent to one of these comic book stores is a wonderful little used book store that has the TARDIS-like quality of being much larger on the inside than it appears from the outside. Why, you could get lost in there for days perusing all those wonderful books."

"Okay, okay, so what's your point?" I asked, and she ignored me.

"Four!" Penny persisted. "You *love* one of those coffee shops you so surreptitiously dismissed. Any time we're even in the vicinity, you're all *Hey, Penny, you wanna go to My Dog Joe?* I submit that you are over-compensating, my dear. I have used my highly tuned powers of deduction to see through your ruse!"

"Have you, now?" I replied, amused at her amusement.

"Indeed." Penny insisted.

"Indubitably." I agreed.

"Yes. Quite." The Countess Penelope of Arcadia counted, affecting a posher, more Windsor Castle-like accent. "And we are *not* amused."

I laughed. "Oh, you are *so* amused, darling – admit it."

Penny smiled at me. "Well, perhaps we are a *touch* amused. That does not mean I won't call for your head if you do not agree to accompany me to the film this weekend!"

"So now I have to go with you?" I asked.

"But of course," the Countess Arcade stated regally. "Who will protect me from the rabid Tolkienites?"

I sighed, "You're going to wear your *FUCK TOLKIEN* t-shirt, aren't you?"

"Well, yes, but only because my *TOLKIEN WAS A LAZY, UNIMAGINATIVE PRAT* shirt got destroyed during that melee at the Role Playing Gamer's convention, and I thought you promised you'd never bring that up again, thank you very much for re-opening those old wounds."

"I'm terribly sorry," I said, completely deadpan.

"Apology accepted, Captain Needa,"[60] the Countess replied in her best Darth Vader (which wasn't very good, and to be honest, still had a trace of the cockney street urchin in it, if you can imagine that). "But just for that, you're paying for the tickets."

"Very well," I complied.

"And popcorn," Penny amended.

"Okay," I agreed.

"And ice cream after the show," the Countess demanded.

"We'll see," I said, as if she were four and not twenty-something.

"And then can we go mini-golfing?" Penny asked, deliberately upping the ante. "Or on pony rides?"

"You just keep pushing it, young lady," I said in mock parental tones, "and we'll be spending the weekend giving sponge baths at the old folk's home."

The Countess threw me a pathetic looking pout, and we both broke out laughing.

All things considered, it was good to be young and insane.

---

[60] To complete the trifecta, a *Star Wars* reference. After Darth Vader kills Captain Needa, he then accepts the man's apology. You didn't see that kind of badassery in those horrible prequels.

The Exorcism of
Hann-Basquiat

There is a demon that lives in the fry oil of every McDonald's – deep in your heart of hearts you know this to be true. And while it is a vile, loathsome demon, the fruit of its evil is ever so tasty, darlings, and more addictive than heroin.

I refer, of course, to that gloriously greasy golden gift, whose name is whispered in gluttonous growls like Gollum[61] petting his precious ring. Those crispy, potato sticks, which are ceremoniously sacrificed to the demonic oil and assaulted unsparingly with an abundance of salt.

French Fries.

Call them that if you will, and slather them with ketchup if that makes them go down any easier, and consider them a harmless side dish to have with a burger and wash down with an over-sized Coca-Cola if that lets you sleep at night. Go ahead and smother them with cheese curds and gravy and call it poutine if that eases your conscience.

But we all know exactly what those *pommes frites* really are, and that's a delivery system for the demon that lives in the fry oil.

"No one forced you to steal my fries, Helena," the Countess Penelope of Arcadia sighed, interrupting my introduction. You remember the Countess, darlings – my incorrigible niece – dresses like a nightmare version of Alice in Wonderland, suffers from self-inflicted multiple personality disorder, and is cold and heartless when it comes to my suffering.

---

[61] The creepy twisted little creature from Tolkien's *Hobbit/Lord of the Rings*

And I *was* suffering, darlings – make no mistake about it.

The Countess had got it in her head that she really wanted a Big Mac – if for no other reason than the fact that she'd heard Bobby Darin singing *Mack the Knife* and I told her that it had been used in a really creepy McDonald's commercial when I was a kid.[62]

"They had television when you were a kid?"

"Yes," I deadpanned, "and running water, too. How about that?"

"But not the Internet," Penny reminded me. "And aren't you glad that you don't have embarrassing pictures of yourself from high school all over Facebook and whatnot, forever commemorating your awkward youth?"

"Yes, well..."

"So, about that Big Mac?" The Countess Penelope of Arcadia (whose mascot is apparently a giant yellow M) prodded.

I sighed, as I always do when Penny gets insistent on something she knows I don't want to do but will do anyway because I love her and because I'm weak-willed. Sighing is my only form of protest.

"Penny, you know that I can't eat at McDonald's." I reminded her. "Everything there is *loaded* with MSG, and it'll make me sick."

It's true, darlings. There's not a thing on the McDonald's menu that isn't somehow infected by the flavour-enhanced demon that goes, in some circles, by the name Monosodium Glutamate. Well, maybe the cookies.

"What about the cookies?" The Countess countered contemptuously.

"I said *maybe the cookies*," I corrected.

"No, you didn't."

"I'm pretty sure I did," I insisted.

"Whatever," Penny allowed. "But surely the french fries are safe."

"Ha!" I snorted, only, you know, in a very lady-like fashion. "Shows what you know! Did you know that they actually put beef flavouring – pretty much straight MSG – into the fry oil?"

"I thought there was a demon in the fry oil," Penny remarked snidely.

---

[62] A guy in a tuxedo jacket with a giant foam crescent moon head and dark sunglasses, singing Mac Tonight instead of Mack the Knife. Truly, the stuff of nightmares.

"That's another perfectly valid theory," I replied, standing by my aforementioned introductory statement.

"Uh huh," The Countess nodded. "Well, nobody said anything about you having to eat anything. Just take us through a drive-thru and get me my Big Mac and nobody needs to get hurt."

But someone did get hurt, darlings. When you play with the demon, someone always gets hurt. In the end, that someone was me. In the end, the temptation was just too great.

"I told you not to eat my fries," Penny chided, holding my hair as I vomited the next morning; my heartbeat pounding in my head, threatening to explode in my brain.

"YOU... TOLD....ME...." I growled, sounding not entirely dissimilar to a certain Cummerbund Bandersnatch playing a gold-loving dragon.

It was at that point that my head turned around backward, I made certain un-repeatable blasphemous statements involving a crucifix, some Cheez Whiz, and Al Gore's rectum, and then proceeded to crawl, crab-like, up the wall and onto the ceiling.

"The *pain*, Penny!" I cried pathetically. "It's so bad you can't imagine..."

"I'm sorry, Helena," Penny said, stroking my hair. "Is there something I can get you? Anything that will help?"

"LET HARPER FUCK ME!" I screamed, and projectile vomited pea soup all over the wall, and then violated myself violently with a rolled-up copy of Maclean's magazine which featured a story about Canadian Prime Minister Stephen Harper and the ravaging of Alberta's Oil Sands. "HE'S FUCKING THE REST OF CANADA! LET HARPER FUCK ME!"

"Geez, Helena, can a person be both demon-possessed and political at the same time?" Penny interjected.

"I'm not certain," I replied uncertainly. "I believe the correct response would be *I think you can in France*, though, in all fairness, I'm making this up as I go. When you feel like I do, you can do whatever you want, and be as random as you like."

"So what is it you want, Helena?" Penny asked.

"THERE IS NO HELENA, ONLY ZUUL!"[63] I roared, my eyes rolling back in my head until only the whites were showing. Suddenly I was wearing a flowing red dress and floating three feet above my bed.

"Okay, so what is it you want, Zuul?" Penny placated me.

"BRING ME THE HEAD OF JOHN THE BAPTIST!" I growled, and then broke down into a painful sob. "And The Beatles' White Album."

"Well, you know, it's not actually..." Penny began to correct me, an irritating habit of know-it-all-i-ness (yes, it's a word now) that she inherited from yours truly.

"Yes, I know it's not *really* called *The White Album* no more than the Metallica album that features *Enter Sandman* is actually called *The Black Album*, but cut the crap, okay? We both know which album I'm talking about, and which four songs I want to hear in particular, so chop chop."

"*Bungalow Bill, While My Guitar Gently Weeps, Happiness is a Warm Gun*, and..."

"*I'm So Tired*," I finished.

"I know, Helena," Penny said sympathetically. "Is there anything else you want?"

"No, I mean, the fourth song – *I'm So Tired*."

"Yeah, but what about *Martha My Dear*?"

"FUCK MARTHA MY DEAR!" I growled, and fell to the bed, where I writhed and twisted, and lifted the bed off the ground six inches and then dropped it and began laughing maniacally and making lewd gestures and telling knock knock jokes that didn't make any sense.

"So, nothing else, then?" Sister Penny of the Sacred Gushing Chest Wound of the Arcadianites asked, ignoring my pain-induced tantrum.

"A couple of Monster drinks," I requested, burying my head in my pillow. "And some lonelyTylenol."

Penny left and returned twenty minutes later to find me curled up in the fetal position, blankets torn to shreds by my claw-like hands, my head wrapped up in a damp towel. She slowly approached

---

[63] A reference to the demon-possessed Sigourney Weaver in *Ghostbusters*. "There is no Dana, only Zuul."

the bed, fearful of my MSG-possessed rage, and held out a can of Monster energy drink – the demon's only weakness.

"The power of Taurine compels you!" she cried. "The power of Taurine compels you!"

"Very funny," I said weakly, and reached out from under the covers to grab the can. I guzzled the whole thing thirstily and crushed it with demonic fury.

"So the next time I tell you to leave my fries alone?" Penny asked.

I growled in response. Or maybe that was my stomach, which had been emptied of any and all substances. I ignored her smart-ass question.

"Did you bring me anything to eat?"

Penny looked at me like she thought that perhaps an acceptable solution to expelling the demon from me might just be the loss of the host as well, and if she had to be the one to set me free, why, so be it.

"You didn't ask me for anything to eat," she said through calmly clenched teeth.

"I'm starving," I replied. "Let's go get some breakfast. Sometimes it helps to get something in my stomach."

"Well, you know, the perfect cure for a hangover is an Egg McMuffin."

My eyes flared red and my teeth elongated into needle like fangs in order to tear through the silly thick flesh of the Countess' vulnerable throat.

"Kidding!" She wisely amended. "Only kidding! Geez, take a joke. We should get pancakes. Pancakes are good, right?"

"Good," I moaned lustily. "Pancakes... gooooood."

"Right," the Countess smiled. "Pancakes it is. Doesn't Katie owe you pancakes?"

Pancakes are something of a currency in my world, and indeed, I recalled that my friend Katie did owe me pancakes. But Katie was miles away, and virtual pancakes via the Internet were not going to cut it.

"IHOP?" I suggested instead, nursing my second energy drink. I'm well aware that it is inadvisable to drink more than one in a day, but that's the recommendation for mere mortals. It takes more than one to kill the demon.

"Do they have pancakes there?" Penny teased.

"At the International House of Pancakes?" I answered, annoyed. "Yes, I think so."

"Fuck, you're humourless when you're sick," Penny remarked and grabbed my hand and pulled me out from under the covers. "C'mon, let's throw some clothes on you and get you some pancakes."

"Chocolate chip," I mumbled. "Banana chocolate chip."

My sister Cheryl used to make me banana chocolate chip pancakes whenever I was sick. It's all I want when I'm feeling lowest.

"Yeah, Helena," Penny said, suddenly quiet. "I know."

"The power of pancakes compels you," I moaned, stomach lurching as I pulled on random items of clothing from off the floor.

"I cast you out, foul spirit!" Penny chimed in, doing her very best Southern Baptist televangelist, which sounded ah say, which sounded a lot more like Foghorn Leghorn than Ernest Angley.

"Just say CHEESE SAUCE," I added, and we both laughed as best we could.

"Pancakes?" Penny asked, holding the door for me and motioning for us to go.

"Pancakes." I replied. Pancakes always made everything better.

The Hills Are Alive With the Sound Of...

The Countess Penelope of Arcadia singing selections from *Frozen*. Arcadia, it would appear, is somewhere in the frozen heartland of... wherever that movie takes place.

Scandanavia?

Scandinavia's not a country, darling, but thanks for playing.

And speaking of playing, that movie has been playing in our house non-stop for the last three weeks, and I'm beginning to wonder if I'm not secretly a cult leader (secret even to myself, darlings) and this is not some sort of psychological torture to coerce me into turning myself in.

When the Countess (you remember Penny, darlings – bossy thing, gets her good looks from her aunt but her temper from her secret dark father Beelzebub) demanded that I go to the movies to see this bit of cinematic popcorn, I consented – I hadn't any better offers, and besides, I do enjoy her company. Anything can and usually does happen while Penny's around.

What I wasn't counting on was being dragged to the cinema three nights in a row to watch what Penny declared was the best Disney film since *Beauty and the Beast,* and which I couldn't help but enjoy, despite it being full of every fairy tale stereotype in the book. Further, I had no idea that Penny would force me at fist-point to illegally download a bootleg copy of the film, so that she could continue watching it until it came out on Blu-ray (because Penny is truly in denial of the death of physical media, darlings, as you'll recall).

Had I known that Penny would then proceed to play that piece of pre-school pornography in perpetuity, perhaps I would have re-considered my trip to the cinema in favour of a nice pleasant pap smear or maybe a mammogram just for merry amusement.

Such is my displeasure, darlings, at having my entire world taken over, not only by the songs from the film, but references to it throughout the day.

This past weekend, we had a holiday, and Monday morning, I was sitting around the breakfast table, hunched over coffee, humming any random song that I could think of, trying to get the songs from *Frozen* out of my head. They had invaded my consciousness like cuckoos and laid their eggs there, pushing out more favourable information from my memory – I found I'd suddenly lost nearly 1/3 of the songs of Tori Amos and all my fond recollections of seeing *12 Monkeys* at the drive-in with my best friend at the time while stoned out of our minds on mushrooms and red wine.

I had almost succeeded – I had the first few bars of *Still Ill* by The Smiths just queuing up, and then Penny looked at me and cocked her head, as if she could hear my thoughts and couldn't wait to torture me with them.

"What?" I snapped, nearly jumping out of my uneasy skin.

"What do you want to do today?" She asked, slurping her coffee noisily, as if she were six instead of twentysomething.

"Dunno," I replied, looking out the window at what was shaping up to be a beautiful, albeit freezing cold, day.

"Do you wanna build a snowman?" she asked, stepping into the role of one of the little girls from that cursed movie.

"God dammit!" I spat out my coffee.

"C'mon let's go and play," she continued, ignoring me, and then proceeded to launch into the whole song, dancing around the kitchen in her Emily Strange pyjamas, looking like the weirdest contradiction personified.

"How is it that you love a Disney movie this much?" I challenged, and was greeted by the voice of a decidedly Dickensian street urchin.

"Well, iss loik, featricow, ennit? All gran feams an' such," she tried to explain, suddenly holding out her pinky finger in a gesture of poshness that only furthered the inherent contradictions. The posh urchin.

"Yes, darling, it's terribly theatrical, but weren't you just complaining about Disney princesses and their ridiculousness? How you'd just love to see, just once, a Disney prince propose – you know, kind of like... uh..."

"Hans," the Countess Arcade advised in annoyance at my absentmindedness.

"Right, how Hans proposes to Anna within fifteen minutes of meeting him. Didn't you say that you wished that just once, the Princess would laugh in his face and tell him to go fuck himself?"

"I don't fink I said *precisely* that, Helena my love. I fink I'd remember such 'orrible language, I would."

I looked at her with a dubious grin.

"What?" She protested. "I love the music, okay? Good music forgives a multitude of sins – Jesus said that, I'm pretty sure. Right after he said *Stoppest thou being such a wet blanket Helena and letteth Pennyeth enjoyeth her musical. Eth.*"

"Jesus said that, huh?"

"Oh yes," Penny deadpanned. "It's in the book of Cutyourniecesomeslackians, Chapter 2, Verse 6: *Verrily, I say unto thee, Let it go.*"

"Oh, that's it!" I laughed, and grabbed her and put her in a headlock, and began singing *Penny Lane* at full volume, a song that, despite her name, she's not terribly fond of.

"Let it go," Penny sang off key. "Let it go!"

Penny, apparently, wasn't going to let it go, and so I had to pull out the big guns, and began to sing *I Think I Love You* by The Partridge Family at competitive volume as we tried to out-shout each other.

"So what am I so afraid of?"

"A kingdom of isolation, and it looks like I'm the Queen..."

"A love there is no cure for..."

"...Heaven knows I've tried..."

"Believe me, you really don't have to worry..."

"The cold never bothered me anyway!"

Breathless and red in the face, we collapsed on the floor and started giggling until we were holding our bellies in wonderful pain.

Finally Penny sighed and smiled at me.

"Helena?" Penny said sweetly.

"Yes, Penny dear," I replied, equally as sweetly.

"Do you wanna build a snowman?"

I jumped on her again and began tickling her fiercely, eliciting screeches of hoots of protest and laughter. Leaving her red-faced and reeling, I stood up and left her on the floor, suddenly inspired.

I returned wearing my winter coat and gloves, and threw a parka over Penny, still lying on the floor.

"Get up," I said jovially. "We're going to build a snowman."

Return to Arcadia –
Penelope Knows Her Name

My friend Brooke had called me a few months ago to ask for my help – she'd finally kicked her husband out, after several years of being a prisoner in her own home. It was a situation I had been smart enough to escape thus far – but only because I'd watched my mother suffer the same fate, and swore that it would never be me. I didn't actually make it down to see her – I tried, but got pulled over, which led to a whole affair which I won't recap here, but suffice to say I was waylaid and wasn't able to see Brooke until recently. It wasn't the first time she'd called for my help, nor the first time I'd gotten in my car to go rescue her. She was my friend, and I cared about her, but I sometimes thought that she'd been stupid to ever stay in the first place. Me, I'd flown away from all that the first chance I got.

As soon as I was old enough, I ran. I ran, and I didn't look back unless I was forced to. I ran all the way across the ocean, and the day they dragged me back after a botched suicide attempt was one of the hardest days of my life. They didn't send me home. Home was Toronto, with or without my sister who had relocated to a little town in upstate New York where her husband had been transferred. Home was Canada, and I certainly didn't think that my parents' geographical location should have played into it at all, but the decision was out of my hands, and I'd been sent to Arcadia, a town of Mayberry-esque proportions, but with a higher rate of unemployment and alcoholism.

There I stayed for three months, unable to work, unable to go to school, unable to legally drink (not that it stopped me) with only my sister Cheryl for company; and she had her hands full with a newborn

Penelope, future Countess of Arcadia. The town itself wasn't exactly full of friend material. There were maybe a dozen kids of varied high school age – a couple of years younger than me at that point – and another half-dozen post-high school that would have been my age or a couple years older. But there wasn't exactly much opportunity to mingle. Arcadia was where you slept, and then in the morning, you got the hell out of there, bound for school, or work, or whatever you had outside the dull confines of the little town. And if you didn't have any escape, well, then you wore the terms of your confinement all over your face. You were there for life. The only person I ever met in Arcadia that didn't have that look of resignation was Amy LeFevre, and her face bore a haunted look – like a frightened animal that will flinch at you as you pass by and bite you if you get too close.

So when I met Brooke, it had been a welcome fluke. I'd gone to the library to see about getting a library card, and was amazed when the person behind the counter wasn't a hundred and six years old, like I'd expected.

Brooke was a native Arcadian, born and bred, and yet she longed for so much more. She was like Rapunzel trapped in a tower with nothing but books, and all she wanted was to see the world that lived in those books. Sadly, Brooke was also a product of her environment and upbringing in that she'd married the first guy she slept with, convinced that she was special and not just some conquest. She'd gotten pregnant, they'd gotten hitched, and then she lost the baby. Brooke told me this part of the story as if it were a tragedy – that the timing just wasn't right, but that someday...

As I got to know Brooke better, I began to suspect the truth of the matter, and was secretly relieved that they'd never brought a child into their home. Not a year after I'd moved back to Toronto, I started receiving phone calls from her in the middle of the night; phone calls where she practically begged me one moment to come and take her away from the monster she'd married, and then she'd hang up and call me back an hour later, telling me that she'd just been silly, that everything was fine, and that she was okay, and that I shouldn't worry about her.

Then the phone calls would stop – for months at a time, she wouldn't even call me to chat.

So when Cheryl had called me, crying that she was lonely, and that she wanted me to come down to visit – to stay as long as I could, or as long as I wanted – I of course wanted to know why she hadn't heard from Brooke. It had been a long time since I'd visited – too long – but then life has a way of rolling on when you're not paying attention. The last time I'd seen Penny, she was just cutting teeth, but when Cheryl picked me up from the Amtrak station, she was running and smiling and calling my name.

"And you might you be, little girl?" I asked her teasingly.

"I Penny!" she declared. "I Penny, 'elna!"

"Yes you are!" I said, and picked her up and squeezed her tightly.

Cheryl and I took Penny for ice cream, listened to David Bowie on the radio, and enjoyed each other's company for the first time in a long while.

The next day, though, we were visited by our parents, who moved to Arcadia while I was still away in England, and have been there ever since. It's perfectly fine by me, them being far enough away to ignore, but I felt terrible for Cheryl and Ted, who had to constantly entertain them and be subject to their absolute lack of sense when it came to boundaries or proper etiquette. Never mind the fact that there was so much ugly baggage from our childhood that even being in the same room with our parents was like swimming in a pool of toxic waste. I had no idea how Cheryl managed it. I would have exhausted myself by now plotting ways to get away with their murder.

My father knew better than to try to hug me, but my mother, oblivious as always, and with no understanding why I would have any resentment or anger or trauma regarding the two of them, showered me with unwanted affection. In her mind, she saw nothing wrong with the abuses the three of us – that is, my mother, Cheryl and I – had faced at the hands of her husband. After all; she'd forgiven him, and more importantly, God had forgiven him. So why couldn't I? It made me the villain.

I sat beside Cheryl, ignoring my father as best as I could, feeling every muscle in my body tighten when Penny went to crawl up on his lap, instinctively frightened, angry and protective all at once.

My mother kept calling Penny little pet names, which drove me up the bloody wall.

"Come here Penelope Pitstop! Come here my little Penelope cantelope. My little melon ball. Come here Penelope L-M-N-O-P," she sang in a sickly sweet voice with which Cheryl and I were both intimately familiar.

"'top it!" Penny cried, irritated. She wriggled away from her grandmother, who was kissing her all over while calling her pet names. "Doan touch me!"

My mother, ignoring her little grand-daughter, just kept poking her and kissing her and calling her more pet names.

"Oh, don't be like that my little banana-boat! C'mere and give Gramma a kiss, Penelope Potato-head."

And then Penny pulled away, and stomped her feet and rolled her little hands into fists at her side, and glared at her grandmother.

"I Penny, dammit!" she yelled, silencing everyone in the room but me. I began laughing hysterically, and had tears of delight in my eyes. What an amazing woman she was going to be! When I realized that I was the only one laughing, I made myself stop, and when I looked around the room, I found that everyone was staring at me. Mostly scowls, except for Penny, who was beaming at me, smiling with her whole face.

"What?" I said defiantly, and held out my arms, motioning for Penny to come to me. "Her name's Penny, dammit."

Damn, I loved that little girl.

Return to Arcadia - The Radish

After our parents had left (which wasn't soon enough, darlings) I turned and gave my sister a tight hug. Their presence always unsettled me – a doctor these days would probably say I was suffering from Post-Traumatic Stress Disorder, and whatever – putting a name to it or a label on it doesn't make it any easier for me to live with, but if that helps you, then by all means, darlings.

"How can you stand it?" I asked her. "How can you even let him touch Penny?"

Cheryl shrugged, resigned and tired. "What choice do I have? You know how they are; how *he* is. I can't say no."

"Yeah, Cheryl, you can!"

I was upset, and frustrated for my sister. My parents had clung to her like parasites. She never asked them to move to Arcadia when she was pregnant with Penny – they did that on their own. And they did it because they had nothing to hold them back. My mother didn't work while Cheryl and I were little – but then, neither did my father, really, so the government footed the bill for the raising of us girls for the most part. It's not that my father was unable to work, it's that he had such a caustic personality that he was generally unemployable. He had an elevated sense of self-esteem that was basically an overcompensation for how much he hated himself – I can say these things now, darlings, it doesn't make me hate the fucker any less or pity him anymore.

People talk about a sense of entitlement, well, that was my father to the letter. He thought that he deserved better than his lot, but didn't see that he needed any fancy education or degree – or, in fact, to work hard – in order to get it. And so he spent the better part of his life working on a career in complaining and feeling sorry for himself, and taking that frustration out on his wife and kids.

Later, when I was about sixteen, he found Jesus, and just knew that God was calling him to do great things. Even then, he felt that because God had ordained it, that he was just entitled to it. He was going to be a pastor, by God, never mind that other people had to go to seminary, get a degree, learn Greek or Latin, study the Bible under the tutelage of highly educated men and women – he didn't have time for that. Besides, he had books, and he had God's wisdom – that was good enough for him.

(Read: I'm better than everybody else, and the entire world should just get down on their knees and give me whatever I want, or else I'll get mad and throw a temper tantrum.)

You may recall, darlings, that when I was seventeen, I conveniently found Jesus, too. He was hiding in the dreamy eyes of a boy named Andrew, and when I told my father that I wanted to go to England (where Andrew was headed, by the way) to work with an evangelical organization, he was so proud of me. My heart beat fiercely inside my chest that day – not with love, not with pride, but with elation. Every heartbeat screamed *FREE! FREE! FREE!* If my heart had been a civil rights leader from Atlanta, it might have been screaming *Free at last! Free at last! Thank God Almighty, we are free at last!* [64]

"What am I supposed to do, Helena?" Cheryl asked me, her voice coloured with the same frustration I was feeling. "I've got a husband, and a daughter. I can't just take off like you did. I can't run away from my problems like you do."

That stung, and I'm sure that I wanted to say something mean, but I bit my tongue. She was right. In retrospect, I spent most of my life wandering, because when things go bad, as they invariably do, the easiest thing to do is pick up and go.

"Do you remember…" I started, and Cheryl looked at me. We'd played this game before.

"I remember *everything*," she said, and picked up Penny, giving her a squeeze and telling her to go on and play or watch TV or

---

[64] That would be Martin Luther King Jr., darlings.

something. She didn't want her to hear this. This ritual of ours. Remembering. Lest we forget.

"Do you remember the radish?" I asked her.

"Of course," she said. "I nearly choked."

Cheryl hadn't wanted to eat a radish one day – she was maybe eight years old at the time, which would have made me four, and while you might think that this is me being an unreliable narrator, darlings, believe me when I say that these memories were carefully guarded by my sister and I. We popped them into bottles and sent them out on the ocean so that they would never be truly lost; never be forgotten.

We were at the dinner table, eating what was likely a pauper's dinner of egg noodles and gravy with maybe a little ground beef mixed in, and some vegetables. Our father insisted that we have vegetables – because he worked hard to put food on the table. Never mind that the hardest he ever worked was a stint in a steel mill for about three years, but after they laid him off, it was welfare, a bit of cab driving, and god knows what other menial jobs – as I look back, I realize there's a lot that I don't know. I only know that he never seemed to have a job, but he always seemed to have a lot to complain about.

So that meal, it was some raw veggies – carrots, celery, and radishes. And Cheryl didn't like radishes.

"They're too spicy!" She cried.

"No they're not," my father said, agitated but not yet angry. "They taste like peppermints. You like peppermints, Cheryl."

Cheryl shook her head defiantly. She was a kid. She didn't want to eat her vegetables. This is not an uncommon occurrence.

"You like radishes, Cheryl. I know you like them. Eat your radish right now."

There was a feeling like a storm approaching. The air was electric.

"I don't wanna, Daddy, they're yucky."

And my father, a monstrously big man – over six feet tall and 250 lbs, stood up from the table, rattling plates and cutlery as he did, and walked calmly over to where Cheryl was sitting. He picked up a radish from her plate.

"Open your mouth," he ordered firmly. Cheryl began to cry. My mother called his name gently, and he ignored her. Cheryl kept her mouth shut and began shaking her head.

"Open your mouth!" he screamed, like the roar of a demon. His eyes bulged, his face was red, and spittle flew from his incensed lips.

I began to cry, and hugged my knees to my chest.

"Open... your... mouth," he repeated through clenched teeth, and grabbed her face with one hand, squeezing her cheeks to force her mouth open. With the other hand, he shoved the radish in her mouth, pushing it past her teeth. Then he held his hand over my sister's mouth.

My mother called his name again, more insistently this time. She was weak and ineffective.

"Stop it!" She cried. "You're choking her."

My father wheeled around and caught my mother's face with the back of his hand, then turned back to see that Cheryl's face had turned purple – she couldn't breathe.

And here is the worst part, darlings – the part that traumatizes the most. Mr. Hyde disappeared, and my father was again Dr. Jekyll.

"Oh my god, Cheryl, I'm so sorry, honey!" He pounded her back gently until she spat out the radish, and then covered her with hugs and kisses, repeating over and over again that *Daddy was so sorry!*

We heard a lot of apologies.

"Do you remember that poster he used to have hanging in their bedroom?" Cheryl asked me after we'd finished the radish story.

I laughed and nodded. "It was like a poem for abusers. I swear, it was like the Serenity Prayer[65] for people who were absolute assholes. *Sometimes we hurt those closest to us, because they understand. Blah blah blah... I am very sorry. I did not mean to hurt you.* What a load of shit. How many times do you figure he made you read that?"

"Too many," she said. "I remember him picking you up by your hair and throwing you against the wall."

"Because he didn't like my haircut," I finished. "I'd shaved the sides of my head, and left the top. He said I looked like a concentration camp victim."

"Well, you showed him, didn't you?" She teased.

---

[65] The creed of Alcoholics Anonymous. Unfortunately, there is no Assholes Anonymous.

"Yup," I smirked. I'd shaved even more of my hair off, leaving only the bangs in what was known as a Chelsea cut in those days. Then I dyed it indigo blue. Took me forever to grow it back out. I wore a lot of hats for a while. I think when I saw Amy LeFevre, that's how I knew that something was up with her. She'd done the same thing, if for slightly different reasons.

"So, did you take it?" She asked. Apparently we'd reached that part of the conversation. It had at first started as a joke, but it wasn't really funny. She didn't need to say anything more than that – I knew exactly what she was talking about.

"No," I said resolutely. "No, I didn't take it. Did you?"

She shook her head. "No, me neither."

"The mystery remains," I muttered, and Cheryl nodded in agreement.

Return to Arcadia –
The Missing Two Dollars

There are certain stories that are too horrible to tell. If you do tell them, people won't believe you. They'll say you're exaggerating, or stretching the truth, or they'll say things like *Oh, it couldn't possibly have been that bad*, or, *if that really happened to you, somebody would have done something.*

No one wants to believe that those horrible things actually happened to you. So they deny it, sometimes to your face. They do it because they love you, as fucked up as that sounds, and they don't want their image of you tarnished by the terrible story you tell them.

But I'm going to tell my story anyway, darlings, and if I temper it with some humour in a way that is probably not at all funny, well, that's just me, all these years later, trying to tell the story without it being too painful.

We never had much money growing up. And by not much, I mean that we lived in poverty. Now, I've since travelled to places where poverty means so much more, and so I've put things in perspective, but the truth of the matter is, we did go to bed hungry, we were malnourished, and no, I don't remember owning new clothes until I could buy them for myself.

The problem is, looking back, we didn't live in a time of economic depression – or certainly, not any worse than we do now. We just lived with a father who was about as broken as a man could be, and instead of trying to fix himself, or seek help, decided to wallow in self-pity and fear. If I were a removed observer, or a psychologist, I might be able to paint a picture of the man that you might even pity, but I'm not. I was a child, and Cheryl and I weren't removed – we were right in the thick of it.

In trying to understand myself, I've tried, over the years, to understand my father. Again, I'm no psychologist, but the phrase narcissistic sociopath kept coming up in my studies, and it seems to fit.

I've tried hard to retain good memories of my father – and there were periods of calm between storms. But the problem is, those moments of calm were always in the shadow of the previous storm, and were spent in both recovery from the last and dread of the next storm. We were shell-shocked; constantly living in enemy territory.

When Cheryl and I came home from school, we weren't like other kids – we didn't race in the door, fighting each other to the TV to win the right to pick what show to watch, or video game to play. We didn't swing the door open and yell *Hi Mom! Hi Dad! What's for dinner?*

When we got home, we listened for music. If there was music playing, our dad was likely in the basement, working on his book. Yes, my dad is a writer. And here's where you get another big confession from me, darlings. Another big reason I don't use my own last name, is because I don't want to have his name associated with my writing.

If dad was writing, then we were likely safe. We could sneak in and up to our room, where we might find a book to read, or even play a game of cards together or something quiet.

If we didn't hear any music, then maybe we'd hear yelling. If we came home and dad was already screaming at our mother – or worse – then it became a matter of running interference. Cheryl would listen, and try to identify where in the house mom and dad were, and make a decision as to which entrance would be best to use. It was like sneaking through a warzone, complete with avoiding land mines and collateral damage. There was always the possibility that whatever he was raging about could somehow be tracked back to Cheryl or me, in which case, avoiding detection was paramount. Such was the case one day when Cheryl was twelve and I was eight.

On the top of our fridge was an old green tin, with a gold flower pattern. I always thought it was pretty when I was a girl, and imagined that it was some ancient Chinese relic or something – in reality, it was likely a candy tin, or maybe a tobacco tin – for years my dad smoked a pipe in addition to the little cigars he went through by the pack, despite the fact that we were on a severely limited budget.

This old green tin was off limits. Cheryl and I both knew that, and neither of us was stupid enough to touch it. It was where dad kept his cigar money, or his lotto money – another pathetic cliché. Rather than use that $2 for a carton of milk or something extra for his kids – he spent it on what I've come to refer to as the Idiot Tax. Week in and week out, I don't remember ever seeing the fridge without a Lotto 6/49 ticket stuck to the front with a magnet.

That day when we got home, our father was throwing things around in anger. The refrigerator itself was pulled out from the wall, the contents of the top swept off onto the floor.

"Where is it?" His voice roared from somewhere in the house. Cheryl grabbed my hand, and we tiptoed through the debris, careful not to disturb anything. We made it to the foot of the stairs undiscovered, and cringed, hugging each other, as we heard him repeat the question again, punctuated by the sound of his hand hitting flesh in a sharp crack. Our mother cried out that she didn't know, and my sister clenched her teeth in fury. It was clear that she wanted to do something, but I shook my head at her, and she pulled me by the hand up the stairs as quietly as we could. She cursed as one of our feet hit the squeaky board, announcing our presence.

"Girls!" he called. "Girls, come down here, right now!"

We looked at each other. I said I was sorry for hitting the stair, and Cheryl frowned at me, thinking.

Did we hide? Should we run? We couldn't. He'd find us. He'd catch us.

I tried to hide once. It only exacerbated things. The longer he had to build up a temper, the worse it got.

"Go," Cheryl said reluctantly. "Go!"

We hurried back downstairs and stood in the living room, hands behind our backs, feet apart – good little soldiers.

When our father appeared from the hallway leading back to our parents' bedroom, he was already panting and sweaty.

"Yes, Daddy?" we said in unison. We could hardly raise our heads to look at him.

He marched in front of us like an interrogator at a P.O.W. camp. If this had been Germany in the 1940s, he might have been wearing jackboots and brandishing a riding crop, threatening that *Ve haff vays off making you tock*.

"Where is it?" he asked, breathing heavily through flaring nostrils. "Which one of you took it?"

Cheryl and I looked at each other blankly. We had no idea what he was talking about.

"Don't look at each other," he said, "look at me."

"Yes Daddy," we said, and did our best to meet his gaze.

"Now," he continued. "Which one of you took it? Last chance."

I started to twitch uneasily.

"Helena? Was it you?"

I shook my head. Whatever he thought I'd done, I hadn't done it.

"Cheryl?"

She looked at him with as much defiance as she could muster at twelve.

"No, Daddy."

"Liars," he hissed. "The lot of you."

He stepped forward and grabbed Cheryl's arm, dragging her down the hallway to his bedroom, slamming the door behind him.

I didn't dare move. If I ran, he'd just come and get me. I stood trembling and hopping from foot to foot as I heard the slap of my father's belt coming down again and again and again on Cheryl.

Now, whatever your feelings on corporal punishment (or, as I like to call it, using the threat of violence to assert your adult will upon a helpless child, thus reinforcing the idea that if you don't like what someone's doing, the appropriate behaviour is to hit them, thus propagating the cycle of violence) I need to remind you, darlings, that Cheryl and I didn't do anything wrong. In fact, at this point, we weren't even sure what it was he thought we'd done. This was Gestapo tactics, pure and simple.

The bedroom door opened, and Cheryl limped out, whimpering and holding her back. She looked at me with terror in her eyes. She was followed by my father, who took me forcibly by the arm and pulled me down the hall. I tried to plant my feet and resist, but he was so much bigger and stronger than me that I didn't stand a chance.

As he pulled me into the room, I saw my mother collapsed on the floor in the corner of the room, her face red, tears streaming down her swelling cheeks.

My father held his belt in one hand, and grabbed me by my hair. He put his face right in mine.

"Did you take the money from the green tin?"

I started to say no, and his belt came down on my back, stinging and burning. I yelped and jumped, and he held tightly to my hair, preventing my escape as the belt came down again.

"Your mother and I trust you. You know you're not supposed to touch that tin."

"I know, Daddy, I…"

"Don't lie to me!" he growled, and the belt came down on my back, on my bottom, on my thigh. He pushed me away from him, and I crumpled in a heap on the floor. "Get out of my sight. Send your sister back in."

What was I supposed to do? Go out singing and dancing, saying *Lucky you, big sister! You're the next contest on Let's Make 'Em Squeal!*

I crawled down the hallway, unable to stand up, and found my sister slumped against the wall. I motioned for her to go back in. I didn't want to, but what could I do?

"Get back in here, Cheryl," our father warned. "Don't make me come and get you."

Cheryl bravely stood up and hobbled back into the bedroom, where the beating recommenced almost immediately.

I can't tell you how long this went on, or for how many back and forth cycles, but at some point, he brought us both into the room, and he looked at Cheryl, and gave her a choice. The physical torture part was over – or at least, the first round. Now it was to be psychological torture. Many years later, when I was forced to read Orwell's 1984, I recognized the technique that they used to get Winston to betray Julia. After all, it had been used on me.

"Tell me the truth, Cheryl, or I'm going to have to spank Helena."

Now, I've had spankings, darlings. A swat on the bum from my mom for yelling at her – probably when I was three, and diaper clad, and didn't feel it at all – it was more of a prod to *Go on and get to your room.* I've had my fingers slapped when I tried to touch a hot stove –

as a warning, albeit an odd one – that if I touched the stove, I'd get hurt. I suppose that falls under the category of Lesser of Two Evils. But what my father had in mind was by no stretch of the imagination a spanking.

And might I remind you that this wasn't punishment; this was torture.

My father grabbed me by the hair, and I felt my pants go wet as my bladder finally let go. This seemed to incense him more, and he raised his hand to hit me, and was stopped by Cheryl screaming at him to stop.

"Stop it!" she yelled. "I did it! I took it!"

Without asking why, or when, or why she hadn't said anything earlier, our father grabbed her and made to hit her, when I yelled out that it wasn't Cheryl, it was me.

"I did it, Daddy! I took the money."

Had I been older, more culturally aware, and more familiar with the early works of Stanley Kubrick, I might have shouted *I am Spartacus!*

But I was only eight years old. I just didn't want my daddy to hit my big sister anymore.

He let go of Cheryl and sneered at us.

"Liars," he spat, and stormed out of the room. We froze, completely unprepared for the possibility that he might just stop. We listened intently as he stormed through the house, and when the door slammed shut and we knew that he had left, Cheryl and I collapsed on the floor, crawling our way over to our mother, who sat in the corner of the room nearly catatonic. We curled up in her lap and lay there, the three of us, sniffling and twitching with painful spasms.

"Two dollars," I said, shaking my head at the memory. I sat in Cheryl in Ted's living room and watched as Penny played with crayons in the other room.

"You know, he probably spent it on smokes and just forgot," Cheryl suggested, not for the first time. We'd had this conversation a dozen times or more.

"Did you ever get an apology for that one? Even a *read the poster* one?"

She shook her head. "He just pretended it never happened. Which is why I think that at some point – maybe when he was out on his walk – it dawned on him what actually happened, and he realized what he'd done."

"We should have left," I said, and Cheryl laughed. We'd gone through this routine before, too. We were practically Laurel and Hardy.

Who would have taken us in?

Yes.

Who?

That's the guy that would have taken us in.

Who would?

Exactly.

Do you really think he would have let that happen?

Who?

No, Dad.

"Mom should have called the cops. She should have left. Packed us up and left, and way before that, too, but that – that was crossing the fucking Rubicon, Cheryl. No turning back after that."

"Shhh..." she hushed me and motioned toward Penny, who looked up at me and waved. "She repeats everything you say. And then when I give her trouble, she says *Auntie 'Elna says it.*"

I shrugged. "Sorry."

"Don't sweat it," she said, and put me in a friendly headlock. "I miss you. We both do."

"Yeah," I said. "Me, too. But I can't stay, you know that, right?"

She sighed. "I know. I just... I'm all by myself against them here."

I didn't want to ask what I had to ask.

"Cheryl, how is he with Penny?"

"You wouldn't recognize him," she admitted. "But he's still as controlling and coercive as ever."

"But you're not afraid that he'd..."

"I'm never going to leave him alone with her to find out."

That was a good answer. I could breathe a little easier.

"Penny," she called. "Come here, pumpkin."

"Not pumpkin!" she protested. "I Penny, dammit!"

I got a dirty look from Cheryl. For months afterward, when I'd call, I'd ask her how Penny Dammit was doing, and after a while we were able to laugh about it together.

"Come here and give momma a hug, Penny."

The little girl crawled up on her mother's lap and turned and stuck out her tongue at me. She squeezed Cheryl tightly.

"Mommy loves you, baby," she said, holding her protectively. "Mommy loves you so much."

The Countess Penelope of Arcadia's Delayed Reaction

"*I*t's possible... *maggot*," the Countess Penelope of Arcadia (a pastoral community in the beautiful countryside of Florin) admitted, while at the same time managing to both insult me and channel *The Princess Bride*. "You may have been right about Greek life. Sororities are not for me."

Penny had taken some time off between high school and university, due to the untimely death of her parents, and recently, she'd been having some regrets about not really getting involved with some of the more social aspects of university. She'd been doing well with the academic portion, but found that she'd lost touch with the very concept of making new friends.

I had just picked her up from a social function – some sort of alcohol-free affair designed to help off-campus students get involved with campus social life. Having moved down to Hamilton from Toronto to move in with Penny's grandmother had played hell with her already almost non-existent social life, and I was doing my best to encourage her to get out more. What can I say, darlings? If you can't do; teach. (My social life of late left much to be desired.)

"I tried to tell you, darling. There are all kinds of societies you could get involved in – but a *sorority*? Are you going to dye your hair blonde and become a cheerleader, too? Oh, and the line is, *It's possible... pig.*"

"Wow, Judgey McJudgementalstein," Penny said. "Any other college culture stereotypes you'd like to throw out there? Oh, and, bite me. I like my way better."

"Sorry," I said. "It's good that you're trying to..."

"Ooh! McDonalds!" She interrupted, pointing to the golden arches glowing from the side of the highway like a mystical lighthouse. All that was missing were three Sirens sitting at the base of the giant M, singing in hypnotic tones: *Ba ba ba ba baaaaah... I'm lovin' it.*

Sirens or no, we were shipwrecked nonetheless, as Penny insisted we stop for what she constantly referred to as *two all-kangaroo-pouch patties saturated in MSG, questionable sauce, bacteria-laden lettuce, cheese-like plastic, pickles, dehydrated flakes that once belonged to an onion, on a processed bun so high in sugar it would give a diabetic a stroke.*

I know, darlings, it's quite a mouthful – but then, so's a Big Mac. Why does she continue to eat them, you ask? Good question.

"If you hold Big Macs in such low regard, darling, why do you continue to eat them?" I asked her as we got off the highway to head toward the fast food femme fatales drawing us in with the alluring aroma of frying fat.

She looked at me incredulously.

"Because they're delicious, of course!"

"Uh huh," I said, shaking my head. "And not because they put an addictive chemical in them that makes you crave them fortnightly?"

"No, no," she said, shaking a finger at me and slipping into a Scottish brogue not unlike Mike Myers in *So I Married An Axe Murderer.* "That would be The Colonel, *smart ass.*"

I really didn't want to go to McDonald's, darlings. The last time I ate even a few MSG laced french fries, I re-enacted the pea soup vomit scene from *The Exorcist* and may have spoken in tongues, I can't be totally sure. I decided to try another tactic. I began to sing *Meat Is Murder* by The Smiths.

*"And the flesh you so fancifully fry is not succulent, tasty or kind. It's death for no reason, and death for no reason is **murder.**"*

The Countess Penelope of Acadia gasped in utter shock as if I'd slapped her across the face.

"How dare you quote Morrissey at me, Helena?" She feigned offence, though for about two weeks after I introduced her to The Smiths, and she learned that Morrissey was a militant vegetarian, it was Penny who had given me grief if I even put butter on my toast. "You of all people."

"What does that even mean?" I laughed.

"Oh, it's on, Helena," the Countess said, and rolled up her sleeves as if we were suddenly about to engage in fisticuffs. "You want murder? I'll give you murder."

"Cryptic much?" I asked her, putting the car into park in the McDonalds parking lot despite my utter lack of wanting to be there.

Penny looked at me with a devilish grin and began to mu ha ha. Yes, darlings, this is now a verb, conjugated in the present tense thusly: (which is still not a word, by the way) I mu ha , you mu ha, he/she mu ha has, we mu havons, you (plural) mu havez, they mu ha ha ha. Don't ask me about conditional or subjunctive tenses, I've never been very good at those irregular types.

We walked into the McDonalds and for some reason, Penny seemed delighted that the lobby was full of people. As we stood in line waiting our turn to buy our chemically modified foodstuffs, however, she seemed to almost wither. It was like watching a kid crash from a sugar high. I didn't make too much of it, until, when our turn to order came, she stumbled, and I had to catch her arm. She looked up at me and smiled, laughing it off.

"Sorry about that," she said, shaking her head. "Just felt dizzy all of a sudden."

"Welcome to McDonalds," an only barely post-pubescent young man with the unfortunate name of Ronald said unenthusiastically. "Can I take your order?"

I looked at the Countess, who was leaning one hand on the counter and looking up at the menu board for some reason. She didn't need the menu – no one needed the menu at McDonalds. Everyone knows exactly what they want when they walk in the door. Who browses the menu at McDonalds? I mean, really, what are you going to do? Ask if the Filet O' Fish is good today? Ask what the soup of the day is? Say *ooh, the McChicken sounds wonderful! Can I get that with a side of pommes frites and some salsa de tomate? Is it free range chicken?*

"Yes, I'll have the..." Penny said, and stood up straight and shook her head, smiling. "Sorry about that. I'll have a Big Mac, and..."

And then Penny slumped to the floor and started twitching, and then full out convulsing.

"Penny!" I snapped, and looked around the room as people gasped in alarm and stared. "Penny, stop it!"

I was sure that she was pulling some sort of stunt, but then her eyes rolled back in her head and she began frothing at the mouth and making choking noises.

"Penny, no!" I screamed, and dropped to my knees and grabbed a hold of her. People gathered around us to witness the spectacle and pulled out their cell phones to call for the paramedics. Poor Ronald stuttered and stammered and asked what was wrong with her.

Penny shrieked – a high pitched, wheezing cry – and then went still.

One hour earlier...

Penny had been watching the girl in the Paul Frank t-shirt intently, and couldn't figure out what it was about her that she found suspicious. She usually trusted her instincts, but then, there was always a first time to be wrong, and in this situation, she couldn't afford to make a false accusation. It would be social suicide.

No, Penny thought, *I have to be absolutely sure before I say something. Just be cool.*

But she never got the chance. The girl with the monkey shirt and pixie cut walked over to Penny, handed her a drink, and introduced herself.

"Hi," she said, and winked at Penny, who then grimaced. "I'm Laura."

It was the wink, Penny told me later. One wink, and it was all over.

I knelt with my head to her chest, listening to her faint breathing, and screaming for people to get back and leave us alone.

"Oh, Penny," I sobbed in frustration. "Why don't you get up?"

"It's conceivable," Penny suddenly whispered, plainly and clearly. "You miserable, vomitous mass, that I'm only lying here because I lack the strength to stand."

Penny eyes popped open and she put a finger in front of her lips, silencing me. She mouthed the word *maggot*, and I thought in that moment that I might actually strangle her.

She began coughing, faking spasms as if she were recovering. She stood up and acted mortified and embarrassed. She got my nomination for an Academy Award. My performance, however, required no acting.

"Oh, Helena, let's get out of here!" she cried melodramatically, and I indulged her.

We reached the car without me losing my cool, but when we got in the car and closed the door, I swore a blue streak at her.

Penny looked at me, waiting for me to finish.

"Are you done?" she asked, knowing full well that in order to pull off that stunt, she was going to have to face my wrath afterward.

"You went too far," I said, furrowing my brow at her in an attempt to look stern.

"To quote your best buddy, the immortal Ferris Bueller, you can never go too far. Besides, it was funny. In a couple of days, you're going to realize this, and you're going to call me a genius. Because you don't even know what you saw in there; not really. I'm a genius, Helena. A fucking genius."

I sighed. "Okay, genius, tell me what I just saw in there."

"Uh uh," Penny said, crossing her arms across her chest. "You're just patronizing me. Ask nicely."

"Please." I said. "Pretty please with a side of I promise not to kill you in your sleep tonight."

She looked at me sheepishly with a smile that was like looking in a mirror, and I grinned back at her despite my still present desire to push her into traffic.

"Yeah, but what about tomorrow night?"

"No promises," I said, and felt my anger slightly dissipate and my curiosity peaked. "Please. Let's hear the reveal."

An hour and a half earlier...

"So this is just a get to know you exercise," the perky blonde with the sparkling white smile said. "I want you all to go around and introduce yourselves – but be careful – one of you is a murderer. Remember, if someone winks at you, you need to wait an appropriate amount of time before you fake your death – you want to give our would be murderer a chance to get away with it. But if you make a false accusation – well, let's just say the consequences will be dire."

She pointed to a bathtub filled with chocolate pudding. The message was clear.

Penny, it seemed, was an unfortunate victim of the wink murderer.

"So I waited an appropriate amount of time – that is, enough time to get the hell out of there – and when you dropped the murder gauntlet, well... I just seized the opportunity."

"That's the stupidest thing I've ever heard," I said. "And you scared the shit out of me."

"It was funny. Admit it."

"I admit," I admitted, "that it would have been hilarious if I had actually been there and been part of that Wink Murder game. But as it was, I was completely out of the loop, and as such, it wasn't funny at all – it was cruel."

Penny considered this for a minute, and hung her head.

"You're right," she mumbled.

"Oh, I'm sorry," I said, not believing my ears. "What was that?"

"I said you're right," she repeated, and when she raised her head, there was a mischievous look in her eyes that I couldn't help but mistrust. "My genius is wasted on you! You weren't there! Oh, Helena, I could kiss you!"

"Uh oh," I said, worried.

"You promise you won't tell anybody about this?"

I looked at her in disbelief as an idea of what she was thinking began to form in my mind.

"No," I said. "Of course I'm not going to say anything."

"Good," she said, rubbing her hands together like a cartoon villain. "Then I can still use it on those sorority idiots! They'll never know what hit them. Say it, Helena! Say it like you mean it!"

I sighed. "You're a genius."

"Good," she said, grinning maniacally, hands still rubbing together with glee. "Goooooood."

Return to Arcadia –
Arnold Schwarzenegger and the
Chocolate Bunny

It was late August of '98, and Penny was about three years old. Cheryl and Ted were still alive and living in Arcadia, and everybody was talking about whether or not Bill Clinton had sex with Monica Lewinsky in the Oval Office. I mean, everyone was sure he had done it, but in the *Oval Office?* Watching news coverage was like listening to accusations in a game of Clue (that'd be Cluedo for you Brits): *It was Miss Blue Dress with a cigar in the Oval Office!*

I'd just gotten back from a summer in Venezuela – more on that later, darlings – and Cheryl had called me up and asked me to come for a visit. She was going a bit stir crazy being stuck at home with the future Countess of Arcadia who, at three, was a bit of a terror. If you think she's an unpredictable handful as a young adult, just imagine what she must have been like without even an ounce of restraint. If you have forgotten about my adventure in babysitting when she decided not once, but twice, that pulling her own shit out of her diaper and throwing it around like marbles was a good idea, then let me relate another short vignette where I thought for sure I was going to jail.

Imagine all swinging arms and legs with her thrown over my shoulder, wailing like a Banshee as I tried to get her into the car after a trip to the supermarket. We'd gone out to get cream for my coffee, and Penny insisted on going with me. Getting into the car was no problem, and on the drive to the grocery store, we rocked out to Bowie, which would become a favourite pastime for little Penny and me. For the rest of the day, Penny kept yelling *I'm an alligator* - the only words to *Moonage Daydream* [66] she could remember. She doesn't realize that it started here, but sometimes when Penny and I get in each other's faces and things get ramped up (yes, darlings, it happens) in order to diffuse the situation, at some point, one of us will ask the other if they are an alligator. It's sort of a litmus test to see exactly how volatile the situation has become.

For example:

"You slept the whole day away while I was at work, and just look at this place! If you don't have class, the least you could do is pick up the place a little!"

"I'm not your maid, Helena! I was up until 2 o'clock in the morning reading – I have a test tomorrow that I needed to study for."

"You were playing video games when I went to bed."

"I needed a break. I read after that!"

"Uh huh."

"Helena?"

"WHAT?"

"Are you an alligator?"

"Yes! Yes, dammit!"

"Are you a space invader? Will you be a rock 'n' rollin' biznitch for me?"

And then I'll start laughing, because it's impossible to stay mad at someone who's batting their eyes *and* quoting silly Bowie lyrics at you.

"You wanna go for sushi?"

And when the question is sushi, the Countess Penelope of Arcadia (which must be somewhere near Kyoto) invariably answers:

"Hell, yes, Helena-san!"

But I digress, darlings. I do that. I also do a mean Judy Garland impression (old, sad, drunk Judy, not young happy innocent Judy – sorry, darlings, I'm not singing *Somewhere Over the Rainbow* – I bring the house down with *Have Yourself a Merry Little Christmas*) and make a Margarita that will slip you into a coma (hint: it must be all that extra tequila I put in) but none of this is relevant to the story, so I'm going

---

[66] Classic track off of David Bowie's The Rise and Fall of Ziggy Stardust and the Spiders From Mars.

to slip back into the time machine and head back to the late summer of '98 and the parking lot of a Tops Friendly Markets in Arcadia.

Okay. Getting in the time machine now. Hitting some weird buttons. Hey, it's a lot bigger on the inside! There's a guy in here who looks an awful lot like Barty Crouch Jr. from that Harry Potter movie, only more smartly dressed.[67]

Oooh, look! Are those Morlocks?[68]

Easy, Helena – one science fiction reference at a time or you're really going to confuse people.

Shut up, John Connor.[69] All of this is your fault, you know. Skynet, etc...

So Penny and I managed to get the cream for my coffee, and she was picking up things off the shelves, and for the first two minutes it was cute and endearing, and after that it became an exercise in distraction, as I tried to move her along toward the checkout.

"Look, Penny," I said, pointing her toward a bin of chocolate bunnies that were either left over from last Easter or really early for the next one. "Bunnies!"

"Bunnies!" Penny screamed in pure delight, and picked one up.

I patted myself on the back for having defeated a three year old with the oldest weapon in the book. There was an ancient religious order in the 3rd Century that theorized that the apple in the Garden of Eden was actually made of chocolate.

No, really. Look it up. I believe they were called the Ayejustmadethisupians, and they also predicted the rise and fall of a young man from Tupelo, Mississippi who would bring a new commandment to God's people: *Yea, verily I say unto thee, you can do anything that you want to do, but lay off of my blue suede shoes.* [70]

It would turn out that I was premature in my celebration. I never thought I'd be a premature celebrator – I didn't even think it was possible – but I guess it happens to the best of us when we get over-excited.

Wait, are we still talking about chocolate?

---

[67] Try to keep up now... this is a reference to David Tennant, who played both Barty Crouch and Doctor Who. The time machine in question is a TARDIS, then.

[68] Morlocks were the pale, vicious, underground creatures in H.G. Wells' *The Time Machine*

[69] John Connor is from *The Terminator* franchise. He either needs to be killed or saved, depending on the movie.

[70] Elvis Aaron Presley, darlings. I practically gift wrapped that one for you.

What are you still doing here, John Connor? Don't you have to go be your own father or something?

That never happened.

Those movies confused me. Arnie's a bad guy, Arnie's a good guy, Arnie's a pregnant Kindergarten teacher with a brain tumour running from Jesse "The Body" Ventura for the governorship of California. To make things worse (besides the fact that it was not only the worst Batman movie ever made, but possibly the worst movie, period) if he doesn't win, he's going to freeze Gotham City. Who can keep track?[71]

Anyway, we got to the checkout with the cream and Penny's chocolate bunny, at which point, Penny seemed to have an existential crisis as to whether she wanted the bunny or not. She stared at it like it was Yorick's skull and launched into the "I knew him, Horatio" monologue from Hamlet.

Okay, darlings, you may call bullshit on that last little bit of lawn fertilizer.

The checkout girl asked if she was getting it, and I told Penny to give it to the lady; that she would give it right back.

And then Penny did a fairly passable Gollum impression.

"No!" She screamed. "It mine! It came to me! Mine. Filthy Hobbitses!"

(Work with me, darlings.)

"That's fine, Penny, but I need to give it to the lady for a second."

"No, it's okay," the girl behind the checkout said, smiling sympathetically.

"Thanks," I said, foolishly thinking that the crisis had been averted.

"Don't want it!" Penny then said, and threw the bunny into the fires of Mount Doom – or rather, at the face of the nice lady who had offered to ring it in without taking candy from a baby.

I watched as the bunny flew in slow motion past my face and struck the girl right on the nose, and her immediate and instinctive reaction was to say *What the fuck?*

---

[71] If you were keeping track, aside from *The Terminator* movies, there's *Kindergarten Cop, Junior, Predator* and *Batman and Robin.*

The girl slapped a hand over her mouth and started saying sorry, but not before Penny, giggling madly, started repeating the word over and over again.

If you'll recall, I had accidentally taught this word to the young Countess, and she must have picked up on the fact that she shouldn't be saying it – so of course, she said it any chance she got.

"Uck! Uck! Uck!" Penny screamed gleefully, and I turned all kinds of the colour purple, and not the kind starring a young Oprah Winfrey.[72]

Luckily, the bunny seemed to be forgotten, so I paid for the cream and took Penny's hand and quickly exited the store. We weren't two steps out the door when Penny started screaming that she wanted the bunny. And not just screaming – she threw herself down on the pavement and wailed as if she'd just lost a real live bunny, and when I tried to pick her up, she threw up her arms and went limp in the best display of passive resistance since Mahatma Gandhi invented the move in the 1920s. Amid her cries for her chocolate bunny, she'd throw in a line or two demanding that the British quit India, which was, I thought, pretty impressive historical awareness for a three year old, if a bit random and esoteric.

Before she could start into a chorus of *We Shall Not Be Moved,* I picked her up and threw her, kicking and screaming, over my shoulder.

Hey, Helena, how about picking one resistance movement and sticking with it? First Ghandi and now the American civil rights marches?

Um, how about you go back to the resistance against the Terminators, John Connor?

So I made my way through the parking lot toward Cheryl's car, and Penny was still screaming about the bunny and British rule and something about freeing Tibet, and then when I tried to get her into the car and into her car seat, things got really bad.

"Not my mommy!" Penny screamed. "Not my mommy!"

My heart sank into my stomach, and I resisted the urge to put my hand over her little mouth, as that would only make things look worse than they already did. I was pushing an impossibly strong little girl into a car seat, bracing myself against the doorframe for leverage, while she was screaming about being abducted by a strange woman who had offered her candy.

---

[72] See, 'cause Oprah Winfrey was in the movie *The Color Purple....* ah, nevermind.

That's it, I thought. *I'm going to jail. Someone's going to call the police, and I'm going to be wearing a horrible orange jumpsuit for the next 10 to 20 years, with time off for good behaviour.*

A tap on my shoulder pulled me out of my nightmare, and a kindly looking woman stuck a box of candy in my face.

"Here you go, honey," she said sympathetically. "I've been there."

I must have looked like a monster. I felt a little like one at the time, I was so wound up and frustrated. I could practically feel my nostrils flaring and my eyes bulging. I froze like a deer in a vat of liquid nitrogen (fooled you there, didn't I?).

"Oh, I couldn't," I sputtered.

"Please," she insisted, and placed the candy in my hand. "We all have days like this."

Not often do I use the word *hero*. Usually it's reserved for when I'm travelling through certain regions of the United States that refer to a submarine sandwich as a hero. (Otherwise known as a hoagie, a grinder, or a po'boy, depending on where you call home). But in that moment, that anonymous woman was my hero.

"Thank you," I said meekly, in hopes to inherit the earth someday[73] (I'm going to turn it into a giant garden and have Martha Stewart cloned a bunch of times to keep it pretty. I may have to remove her voice box, though. I think that would be a good thing).

I turned and saw that Penny had calmed down and was holding her hands out in anticipation of the candy.

"RAWR!" she roared and giggled. "Ima gator!"

I sighed and laughed, and handed over the candy to my little alligator.

*** Big round of applause for our special guests this week, darlings... Bill, Monica, you've been good sports! Thanks David Tennant for the loan of the TARDIS, and of course Edward Furlong, Nick Stahl, Thomas Dekker and the always professional and never foul-mouthed or verbally abusive Christian Bale for your wonderful turns as John Connor. And hey! Give it up for Gandhi, will you? All right! Let's not forget our musical guest, the Starman himself, Mr. David Bowie! Tune in next time when our guest will be the anthropomorphic representation of that feeling you get when you

---

[73] See, 'cause in the portion of the Sermon on the Mount often called the Beatitudes, Jesus said that the meek.... forget it.

think you forgot something important but you can't remember what it was, and Jack White (but not *that* Jack White — Jack White from the IT department who will demand to know why I've been spending so much time on the Internet.)

Arcadius Interruptus –
The Return of the Revolucionista

*P*enny was fuming as she related to me the events of the past 48 hours. With each passionately produced profanity (in which Penny is preternaturally proficient), she extracted from me an almost religious fervour for her cause.

"We were betrayed," the Countess Penelope of Arcadia cried indignantly, channelling her inner bleeding heart poet. "Someone is going to hang for this, mark my words, Helena. Someone is going to fucking swing."

I watched her pack her bag for school, scrutinizing each item and doing a mental check to see if any could possibly be turned into some sort of incendiary device.

"What are you going to do?" I asked her, the beginnings of a grin on my face.

"It's not funny, Helena," she rebuked; so angry she had tears in her eyes. "It's not fucking funny. You're going to write this as funny and it's not. It's serious. This is... a complete... fucking... breakdown... of the democratic process."

She punctuated each furious word by throwing another item of clothing or paperwork into her book bag.

"It's just the way my mind works, darling," I said, reaching out and stroking her hair. "I want you to storm in there and give them hell – I wish I could come with you, I have a few words for them myself."

"Well, don't exaggerate it, okay?" The Countess begged through trembling lips.

I gave her a lopsided grin, and her smile returned.

"Well, not *too* much, anyway," she conceded. "Believe me, you won't have to. I'm going to let them have it with both barrels."

"Yes, well, just don't burn any bridges with that fiery temper of yours, Penny."

She glared at me, and then became eerily calm.

"This isn't personal, Helena," she said, affecting a passable Al Pacino as Michael Corleone. "It's strictly business. I'm out."

The Countess Penelope of Arcadia (a neighbourhood adjacent to Little Italy, apparently) threw her bag over her shoulder and looked at me with angry resolve.

"Let's do this."

Penny had gotten involved in school politics, because she said it made her feel like a human being again. Throwing herself into the social aspects of university life gave her a life outside of home, which prevented her from sitting at home feeling orphaned and overwhelmed. Being part of the Executive Committee for her student society gave her a voice among her peers – at least, among her fellow students – I'm not sure Penny has peers, which might really come in handy for her someday if she's ever required to be judged by a jury of them.

She'd enjoyed it for the last year or so, until she came home one day looking like her head was going to explode, and I had to talk her down for the rest of the evening.

"It's bullying, plain and simple!" She declared, and then went on to spout a number of profanities, some involving illegal sex acts involving water buffalo. "They didn't get what they wanted, and so now they're going to bully their way to get it."

"Hey, hey," I said, trying to calm her down. "Back up, and tell me what's going on."

And so she did.

Universities have societies – not just fraternities and sororities – but societies based on department, area of study, different campuses, etc... and Penny is on the Executive Committee for one of these societies – I won't say which, darlings, because I'm trying to keep this as confidential as possible. What this means is that she is part of a group of people that makes decisions about, among other things, membership in this society. People have to apply for membership, and because they are going to be representatives of the society, and participate in group events throughout the year, the members of this Executive Committee make their choices very carefully, based on various criteria, one of the foremost is the issue of character and integrity. These decisions aren't made lightly, darlings, and there have been numerous nights when Penny has been gone until the wee hours of the morning because she's been in session voting and discussing these issues.

She often came home disappointed, especially when she saw the sad fact of politics – that sometimes it's a popularity contest. But while she didn't always agree with the choices made, she always respected the democratic process. Whatever was decided as a group was law, and no one person had the power or right to undo those decisions.

Recently, certain applicants, though they had been members of this society the previous year, had been denied re-admittance to the society because of certain accusations brought against them; specifically, their character. There had been accusations of sexual impropriety and underage drinking – things that needed to be taken seriously. The university keeps close watch of these societies, as they are often the public face of the school itself. It is not out of the realm of possibility for the university to order a society disbanded, and its members punished, should they be regarded as an embarrassment to the institution, or in violation of its code of conduct. (In fact, this had happened to another society not that long ago).

The Executive Committee had convened, and after much deliberation, decided not to give these particular students entry into the society. The decision was made as a group, and that should have been the end of it.

Not so, Penny told me that night, trying not to seem as hurt as I could tell she actually was.

"They started a Facebook group," she told me, rolling her eyes at the immaturity of it all. "A *secret* group, and aren't they just oh-so-sneaky?"

She showed me some screenshots she'd been sent by a friend who had been invited to the group, and had joined for the sake of infiltrating their clandestine network and reporting back. Suddenly this was turning into a WWII spy-thriller.

I tried my best to ignore the tears in her eyes as she showed me what people were saying, not just about her, but about the others on the Exec Committee.

Most of it was what you'd expect from this current generation of Internet bullies – cowardly name-calling and mocking, coupled with accusations and threats. I'd been the victim of Internet bullies, or people who hid behind their position to send caustic emails rather than engage in civil conversation, so I knew how much it hurt, and how frustrated and powerless it made you feel.

"Here," she said, pointing to a picture of a smiling blonde, who had just referred to Penny as a *crazy psycho whore who has no business making decisions for anyone.* "I had lunch with her just last week. It's not like we're best friends or anything, Helena, but..."

"Fuckers," I spat.

Fast forward to the revelation of this covert Facebook group, whose goal (other than to gather in the dark and spit venom about their so-called friends) was to overturn the decision to refuse those particular students entry into the society. As if by getting enough members to sign a petition they could force their way in.

The Executive Committee met to discuss how to handle the group – which, by the way, violated so many University codes of conduct that I won't even go into it here – and decided to withdraw membership of anyone that had taken part in this group. There was harsher talk, Penny told me, and real serious discussion about actions that would have gone on the students' permanent transcript.

"Do it!" I said, pumping my fist in the air. "String them all up! Every revolution needs its body count to discourage dissenters!"

At this point, Penny and I had begun referring to each other as Comrade and were blasting The Clash's *Sandanista!* while tying bullets into each other's hair.

(Work with me, darlings).

"It won't stick," Penny sighed. "Claudia's too soft-hearted. She won't see it through."

Claudia is the President of the society, and while she doesn't have the power to make the decision on her own, she can certainly influence the ultimate details of the consequences the students involved will face.

"The talk started at expulsion from the University, then softened to revoking their membership in the society with a life-long ban, and then there was some talk of drawing a line in the sand and giving immunity to anyone who would leave the Facebook group by a certain time – it was like we were the U.N. threatening some crackpot tin soldier regime."

"And did they actually have weapons of mass destruction?" I asked facetiously.

"Exactly," Penny said, ignoring my question. "And by the time the discussion was done, and we had all voted to take their memberships, there was still some feeling that Claudia thought that was too harsh. The very vague word *probation* got tossed around a lot."

"What the hell does that mean?" I asked. "Besides, you all voted to take their memberships, right?"

Penny snorted. "Right."

A couple of weeks passed, and I'd occasionally get an update from Penny that nothing had been done yet, and that while the Facebook group had been shut down, no public apology had been made, nor had any reprisals or consequences been enacted.

Until two nights ago, when she came home shouting about how she was the big bad wolf and that she was going to blow their house down all around them and laugh at the ruin they'd made of themselves.

I, of course, required a bit of elaboration.

"They betrayed us, Helena! Look at this!" She opened her laptop and showed me an email, sent from Claudia, to the members whose memberships had been revoked, inviting them back.

"What?" I asked. "That doesn't seem right. How can she..."

"How can she, indeed!" Penny snapped. "She can't! And what's worse, she lied – not only to me, but to Angela as well!"

"Angela?" I prompted.

"Angela's the VP – she had asked Claudia for an update on what precisely was happening with the dishonourably discharged douchebags – oh, sorry, *couche-tards* – and she was told that by Claudia that the decision was up in the air."

"I thought it was decided that they were losing their memberships?" I said. "At the *very* least."

"It was," Penny said, teeth clenched. "We decided. As a committee. We fought it out. There were tears, Helena. *Tears*. But we came to a decision that we all decided was right."

"And now it seems she's just undoing all that," I said, reading the email. Suddenly all my paranoia came flooding back. "Penny – who knows you have these emails – and who is this Deep Throat that's sending them to you?"

"That's Angela!" Penny shouted at me, as if I were somehow the source of her rage. "Sorry. That's how fucking arrogant and/or stupid Claudia is – these emails are a matter of record, which Angela has access to. Everything I need to nail her ass to the wall is right there in black and white."

"Well, it is right now," I said, throwing Penny my cell phone. "Call Angela. Tell her to print everything up, right now."

I felt like those investigative reporters who busted open the Watergate scandal on Nixon. Rocky and Bullwinkle. Or was it Loggins and Messina? Captain and Tennille? (Insert other '70s reference here).

Woodward and Bernstein, Helena! It was Woodward and Bernstein!

Yes, thank you, darling – I was being facetious.

Penny made the call to Angela on my cell phone, and while she was on the phone, her bag began to play *Spiderwebs* by No Doubt.

Sorry I'm not home right now, I'm walking into spiderwebs, so leave a message and I'll call you back...

I fished her phone out of her bag, and looked at the call display flash the word CLAUDIA at me. I motioned to Penny that I was answering it, and that she should finish up her own call.

"Hello," I said, doing my very best secretarial voice. "Yes, one moment please. Penelope! Oh, Penelope! Phone's for you, darling!"

Penny hung up my phone and grabbed her laptop, where a chat window had popped up.

"You're not going to believe this!" Penny whispered to me, and pointed to her computer.

SHE'S CALLING YOU FROM THE OFFICE, the chat box read. It was Angela. I'M SITTING RIGHT HERE.

"Hello, Claudia," The Countess Penelope of Arcadia, which is just an eloquent hop, skip and a lady-like jump away from Poughkeepsie, home of Vassar – that is to say, Penny can turn on the charm when she wants to. For this to work, she adopts the occasional dilettante-ism as well: "Oh, I was just thinking of you, darling. How are you?

"Yes, I know I'm strange. I quite enjoy being strange. How strange that you take pleasure in being so strangely ordinary.

"Yes, well. What can I do for you? I'm afraid I'm quite busy. Lots of damage control, you know. Lots of gossip to quell, lots of confidence that needs to be restored, that kind of thing. Lots of hurt feelings.

"Oh you have? *You've* made a decision. That's odd. I thought that *we* had made a decision. Together. You, me, the whole Executive Committee.

"Oh I see. So, you want to revisit that decision, then? Discuss it further? And this is what? You inviting me to a meeting so we can discuss this further?

"Oh, okay. Well, that's a relief.

"No, no, I'm fine with discussing it. I just thought that maybe you were going to tell me that you'd already re-instated the memberships, and that you'd already sent emails inviting these people back to the society.

"No, of course you'd never do that – I was just saying.

"Oh, yes, I'll be there. You can count on it."

SHE'S LYING TO YOU, Angela sent. WHY IS SHE LYING TO YOU?

PRINT THOSE EMAILS, Penny replied. PRINT THEM NOW.

"Let's do this," The Countess Penelope of Arcadia (a small but proud democratic nation trying to maintain their autonomy. Major exports - feisty women with a hardline on hypocrisy and Sea Monkeys – little known fact) laced up her Doc Martens and threw her bag over her shoulder.

"Are you sure?" I asked, giving her one last exit, which I knew she wouldn't take. Besides, who was I kidding? I wished I was going with her. This was going to be legendary, and I could only imagine the scene:

Penny sits across the table from the oppressive bourgeois Empress, Claudia the First, and clenches her fists so tightly that she draws blood from eight little crescent moons on her palms. She thinks to herself that there hasn't been such a blatant disregard for the democratic process since Senator Palpatine dissolved the

Imperial Senate and declared himself the first Galactic Emperor. Or perhaps since George W. Bush won the Presidency back in 2000.

"I've been thinking," Empress Claudia declares, and the scribes beside her begin writing down her every syllable with huge feathered pens. Two eunuchs in saffron loincloths stand on either side of her, one holding a tray of chocolate truffles, the other a glass of special wine, made out of the tears of war orphans. "Perhaps we have been too harsh on our fellow classmates."

Penny knows in her heart that she is not referring to the Committee, but rather, that she is using the royal 'we'. Bourgeois bitch, *Penny thinks,* before the end of this day I shall see you locked up in the Château d'If[74] – or hanging from the wall of the Bastille, or poking your pretty corrupt aristo head through La Veuve,[75] if I have my way!

"So I propose that we re-consider our decision to revoke their membership in our society," the Empress Claudia steps forward, her powdered wig sitting flawlessly atop her conniving head.

"Lies!" Penny screams, and stands up atop the table, black leather boots reaching all the way up to her knees. Her tartan kilt lends some to think that she's going to launch into a William Wallace-esque diatribe about how she'll keep fighting until Scotland is free, and how they may take her life, but they'll never take her freedom – but then they see her black t-shirt with the Ramones logo emblazoned on it with the caption GABBA GABBA HEY! *and they start picturing student protests and the summer of '77, and they start worrying that she's going to start singing* Don't Worry About the Government *by the Talking Heads, or perhaps* I'm So Bored With the U.S.A. *by The Clash. Neither song would be recognized in this room full of musical Luddites, though – cookie cutter clones with Pharrell Williams'* Happy *on an infinite loop on their iPods – and so Penny gets right down to business, reaching into her bag and pulling out a red beret and a pile of papers.*

Donning the red beret, she begins to make her speech.

"She's lied to you," she says, looking at her fellow committee members one by one. "She's lied to you. And you. And you. And you, too, Jar Jar."[76]

"Empwess didsa lies to Jar Jar?"

"Yes, Jar Jar, I'm afraid so. Claudia has told you that we are here to discuss this matter in a democratic fashion – but I say to you that you have all been lied to! She's made this decision behind our backs, and I if that's how we are

---

[74] The inescapable prison from *The Count of Monte Cristo*

[75] Literally The Window, this was a term for the guillotine.

[76] Continuing on with the evil Galactic Emperor schtick, Jar Jar Binks was the silly character from the *Star Wars* prequels.

going to be treated, then I for one want no part of this society anymore. I won't wear the colours of this corrupt dictatorship one moment longer!"

I imagine at this point, Penny rips off her shirt and throws it in Claudia's incensed visage. People stare, some blush, poor Jar Jar creams his pants and has to be excused. After a moment or two, Penny remembers that she wasn't wearing her society shirt, and is, in fact, wearing only a purple push up bra from Victoria's Secret, and that the room is quite chilly.

"I would never make this decision behind your backs," The Empress protests, but the Countess, not one to ever be caught with her pants down (her top's another matter, darlings) starts handing out copies of the email where Claudia did indeed invite the disgraced members back to the society.

Fury rises on the Empress' face, and she begins to cry, and then to scream madly, calling for Penny's head, calling for all their heads, and rather than wait for Jaime Lannister (or, you know, some random committee member) to step forward and stab the mad Empress in the back,[77] Penny leaps off the table and grabs the would be dictator by her frilly lace collar and drags her across the room, throwing her on the table in front of the other committee members, all the while screaming Viva La Revolution!

"I want no more part of this, Penny says, and someone throws her back her tattered t-shirt. Instead of using it to cover herself, she holds it high like a flag, looking like Liberty Leading the People from that Eugène Delacroix painting from the French Revolution – you know it, darlings, it's the cover of Coldplay's Viva La Vida.

"I won't be a part of something this weak," Penny continues, more seriously, now. When she's serious, when something means this much to her, she can't help but get teary-eyed. It just ends up adding more credence to her already important words. "We made a decision together – and we made it because we believed in each other, and we stood together and vowed that we weren't going to be bullied."

Around the room, committee members hang on her every word. Years from now they will recount this story to their grandchildren, and teach them the song The Ballad of the Penelope, Countess of Arcadia (a catchy little tune, by the way, that spent an unprecedented 68 consecutive weeks at Number 1 on the College Charts) and they will remember that day as the last time that they truly believed in anything.

"If you do this thing – if you just let her give in, you send a message to everyone out there – to every future couche-tard who doesn't like the way things go for them – that all you have to do is bully the right people, and complain to the

---

[77] A reference to the character from Game of Thrones, and his infamous actions agains the Mad King.

right people — and you can get away with anything. That is the world you will create, if you don't stand up and say that it is not okay. That what they did was wrong; that there are certain inalienable truths that are self-evident; that there is just some shit with which we will not put up!"

At this point, Penny looks around for something, and notices someone spreading Nutella on a piece of bread. She grabs the butter knife out of their hands and holds it to her throat.

"That," she says, and looks to the ceiling, baring her throat to her captive audience, "that is not a world I want to live in."

I don't even want to hazard a guess as to what might happen after that, darlings, but I do hope that Penny speaks her mind. I know that she's made up her mind that one way or the other, she's walking away. I'm proud of her. I know that she doesn't want to be part of something so weak and ineffectual, and if her voice is just going to be ignored or co-opted and vetoed, then it's more frustration than it's worth.

Penny got home that night looking more relieved than I'd seen her in a couple weeks. She actually had a smile on her face.

"So," I asked, "how did it go?"

She shrugged. "About how I expected. The good news is, I now have more spare time to spend with my favourite Aunt."

"I'm your only Aunt," I said, "and don't you have a boyfriend or something?"

She kissed my cheek. "You're still my favourite. And boys are icky — isn't that what you told me?"

"Yeah," I laughed, "when you were seventeen and I was worried about you getting knocked up."

"No boys right now," she confided with a sigh.

"Hey, I'm not complaining, darling," I said, and put my arm around her. "So what do you want to do with all this spare time?"

"Dunno," she said. "I kinda wanna watch a movie. Maybe something with Hugh Jackman in it."

"Have you seen *Les Mis* yet?" I asked.

"No, but if Hugh Jackman's in it, I'm game."

"He is," I said, rubbing my hands together with glee, "and you're going to love it."

The Countess Penelope of Arcadia Ruins Your Childhood (or, Of Monkeys and Professional Wrestling)

"You know," Penny said, crunching on some off-brand cocoa puffs – the breakfast of champions, "if I ever have a kid, I'm not reading her those Curious George books."

"Well, of course not," I agreed. "I mean, it's basically a treatise on Imperialism and slavery. The *monkey* couldn't possibly be happy in his home – he'd be *much* happier taken away from his peaceful jungle and dragged away to a scary new world, dressed in the White Man's clothes, smoking the White Man's pipe..."

"Sniffing the White Man's ether," Penny put in.

"Exactly – which only serves to make him weak and dependent on the White Man to provide him with more ether to sniff, and at the end of the day, George would have been better off if he'd never encountered the poacher in the yellow hat!"

"Well, sure," the Countess Penelope of Arcadia mumbled through a mouthful of mashed muffin, "but thass not it at all, gov."

Penny grinned at me, looking like a Dickensian street urchin, and held up her empty cereal bowl.

"Please, mum," The Countess of Arcadia, late of London circa 1879, pleaded. "Could I 'ave some more?"

"But of course, darling," I said, topping up her bowl with chocolatey goodness. "Now tell me where you're going with this, will you?"

"It's not very much fun, is it? 'E don't get to be 'imself, loik. It's quite sad, really. An' what's wif 'im never flinging 'is own poo about?"

"Well, it is a children's book, darling – we don't want children getting the idea that it's okay to fling their poo about, do we? I mean, *some* people think it's a good idea even if they've never seen it in a book."

"I'm never forgiving you for telling that story, by the way, Helena. You left a mark on my psyche that will never heal."

"I'm sure you'll be fine," I tell her.

"Besides, that's horsepuckey! We have him smoking a pipe, sniffing ether, but never flinging poo? What kind of monkey is this?"

The Countess began to get agitated and animated, throwing her arms around and nearly shrieking, not unlike a monkey.

"Horsepucky?" I ask.

"It's a word, Helena. Look it up."

And so I proceeded to look up horsepucky, only to learn that it is actually an idiom used by people who don't want to say horseshit. Learning this confused the shit out of me because shit is practically the Countess' second favourite word, and she wouldn't hesitate to say shit even if we were in a church with a mouthful of shit for some reason.

"Maybe there were some lost manuscripts, you know?" I suggested, knowing full well that the nice people who wrote Curious George hadn't likely included such scenes as *George throws feces at the Man in the Yellow Hat*, or *George masturbates furiously as a sign of sexual aggression or dominance.* And while it might be funny in retrospect, I seriously doubt that the Reys, even in their darkest moments of inappropriate humour, wrote something to the effect of *Curious George and the Ebola Virus*, or worse, *Curious George and the Man in the Yellow Hat, Who is Revealed to be Gaëtan Dugas.* [78]

Really, Helena?

I warned you it was inappropriate, darlings, and I said that I didn't think they'd write something that awful. Plus, I've no proof that Gaëtan Dugas even owned a yellow hat.

---

[78] Gaëtan Dugas was a French-Canadian flight attendant who was once believed to be Patient Zero for the AIDS epidemic. As it is also believed that AIDS began with monkeys and somehow crossed over to humans, the implication is being made here that... well, you can figure it out.

Well, I still think it's in poor taste.

And you're entitled to think so. Shall we move along? Thank you.

"I'm sure that they didn't publish *everything* they wrote. I'm sure some things ended up on the cutting room floor. Maybe the poo flinging and such got cut out. You should totally remix Curious George, reinserting all the poo flinging scenes."

"What, you mean like the director's cut?" Penny asked, shovelling more sugar-laden cereal into her ravenous maw.

"Sure," I nodded. "Stuff you figure their editor didn't think would work, and got shelved."

"Ooh!" The Countess got a twinkle in her eye. "I can treat it like it's the lost stories – stories too scandalous for the time, and now they've surfaced, and there'll be some big exposé. Picture it, Helena!"

And so I pictured it, darlings:

Sinister voiceover guy: It's the curious secret that he wanted nobody to know.

George was a curious little monkey. You could take him to the park, you could take him to the hospital, you could take him to the fire station – but anywhere you went, it soon became quite clear that you could take the monkey out of the jungle, but you couldn't take the jungle out of the monkey.

"George was a narcissist from day one," said 'Phil' (names fictionalized for privacy), ex NYFD. "He endangered lives that day he called that false alarm to the fire department. And what them books don't show is what he did when we showed up – he was screeching and baring his teeth and puffing out his chest at us. It wasn't cute at all. My cousin got bit by a monkey once at the zoo, and so I wasn't taking any chances. I grabbed my net, and tried to catch the little guy, when all of a sudden he starts flinging his shit at me – caught me right in the eye."

After the incident with the Fire Department, George's home situation came under tight scrutiny. When the contents of the Man in the Yellow Hat's pipe were examined, it soon became evident that the Man had some problems of his own, which would later become George's problems as well.

"George didn't take well to his new living situation at the zoo," Fiona (veterinarian) admitted. "And in those days, we had no idea that he'd already developed a drug habit. We interpreted his withdrawal symptoms as merely the adjustment to life behind bars – you see it a lot with some of the animals; especially the primates. Aggressive sexual behaviour, like compulsive masturbation, or sometimes even rape, is not out of the ordinary. I tell you, the shit I've seen. And speaking of shit..."

George broke free of his captivity one morning, leading to a city wide manhunt. When the police finally cornered the curious little monkey, he had taken a hostage, and kept screaming that he was Ebola positive and that unless he got an entire loaf of Marijuana Banana Bread, he would "Bring down a fiery rain of Outbreak on ALL you motherfuckers!"

Thanks to the bravery of SWAT marksmen, George was subdued that day, but in a cruel twist of fate, broke his leg when he fell, after being hit by a tranquilizer dart. George sued the city and won, and would spend the next several months getting the best care available on the taxpayers' dime. All of this should have been documented in the film that was made, but due to several injunctions by George's lawyers, much of this footage has been destroyed.

It was in the hospital where George began to experiment with other pharmaceuticals. He started with ether, but quickly began branching out into Opiates, eventually becoming so addicted to Morphine that he could barely stand.

"He would shake so badly," Nurse Patty confessed, "I just felt so bad for the little guy."

"Oh he had a monkey on his back, that's for sure," James, a fellow patient, sighed. "I tried to talk him into going to rehab with me, but any time I brought it up, he just got so angry, and started flinging his poop at me."

The tantrums ending in the throwing of feces had gotten so bad, in fact, that George, despite his celebrity, had been banned from all the best restaurants. After the story got out that he'd been working as a dishwasher in an Italian restaurant after having been caught bathing in the spaghetti, he couldn't get served at anywhere that wasn't drive-thru.

From there, things got worse, and George's biographers took pity on the poor little monkey. He'd told the Reys about a trip he'd taken to the moon – a hallucination he'd had from mixing tequila, psilocybin mushrooms, marijuana and peyote buttons. He'd called them from some little town in Southern California – he'd been wandering in the desert for three days, and when they found him, he was emaciated and on the verge of death.

"He just kept mumbling about the moon, the moon," *Ethyl, a family friend, told us. "We just kept feeding him bananas and malt liquor – we could keep him off the drugs, but we knew better than to withhold George's booze. I have the bite scars all up and down my leg from the time I tried to take his bottle of Thunderbird from him."*

After that, it was a series of hallucinations and fantasies for George. He'd promise to get clean, but then relapse. Then he was caught trying to sell his tail on the street and propositioned an undercover cop. No charges were laid because it's not actually against the law to try to sell your actual tail, just to sell sexual services. But it became clear to his friends and family that George wasn't going to change. Eventually, they checked him into the hospital, but even there, George's curiosity got the better of him. Someone had told him that there was a jigsaw puzzle in the game room that had been smuggled in, and that all of the pieces had been soaked in LSD.

He nearly choked to death on that puzzle piece, and this was the final act that broke the hearts of those around him.

Curious George Goes to the Hospital *would be the last book documenting the life of this curious little monkey.*

"I think it was just too painful for them to continue," John, a family friend, confided. "I think they wanted to leave us with hope, that at least George was getting the care he so desperately needed."

"So," I asked Penny, "What do you think?"

"Dunno," she shrugged. "I was picturing more crazy monkey parties and poo flinging, less *Requiem for a Dream*."

"Too heavy?"

The Countess held her fingers up in a tiny pincer shape. "Just a wee bit."

"Care to lighten things up a little?"

"Oh, indubitably!" She cried, and then addressed the studio audience (that'd be *you*, darlings):

"Tune in next time, when we'll discuss what the appeal of Professional Wrestling is!"

"What?" I demanded. "I'm not talking about that – it's ridiculous."

"No, seriously," Penny said. "What is the appeal? It's not a sport, it's not a story - it's just mostly naked men pretending to beat each other up."

"I have no idea, darling," I admitted. "What other ideas do you have?"

"Dunno," she said, scratching her head. "What about a serious discussion on organizing a petition to stop Michael Bay from making movies?

"That, I can get behind," I said, just cringing at the thought of yet another Transformers fiasco, or (shudder) the upcoming Teenage Mutant Ninja Turtles mistake.

"I thought so," Penny nodded, and then put on her very best wrestling announcer voice. "In this corner: the king of schlock, the script-challenged special effects junkie, the master of the explosion, the testosterone terror – Michael (ichael... ichael....) BAY! (ay! ay! ay!) And the challengers, weighing none of your business, the witty, the amazing, Countess and her Dilettante!"

"Um, I think you mean Helena and her Countess," I suggested.

"NO! (oh oh oh)" The Countess Penelope of Arcadia shouted, still sounding like she was talking into a microphone with the reverb turned up to full blast, and echoing herself. "I don't think I do (ooh ooh ooh!)"

"Come now, Penny," I tried reasoning with her. "Helena and the Countess sounds much better. Plus, you need to remember the pecking order around here."

And then she smacked me.

"What the hell, Penny!"

"OOH YEAH!" She grunted, trying to sound as menacing as possible. "IT'S ON!"

"What are you talking about?" I asked, worried that I already knew. Before I could stop her, Penny uttered the five words I was dreading most.

"Let's get ready to RUMBLE!"

After I pinned her posterior to the pavement as it were, having thoroughly trashed the kitchen in the process, we sat panting on the floor, leaning up against the refrigerator and laughing weakly.

"No fair," Penny protested, stuffing a brownie into her mouth. "You started flinging shit like some psycho monkey – that's against the rules."

"Okay – a) it wasn't shit, it was brownies, thank you very much; and b) it's pro wrestling, darling – there are no rules."

"You suck," Penny pouted.

"I rule," I countered, grinning triumphantly.

The Countess Penelope Sells Out

"What's for tea, Mum?" The Countess Penelope of Arcadia asked in the delightfully disarming diction of a late 19th century Dickensian street urchin. "Mum, what's for tea?"

The fact that I am not actually her mother is irrelevant, as is the fact that she is neither a Countess, a street urchin, nor, in fact, British – a sad truth that she laments on a nearly daily basis.

"Mum, what's for tea?" The Countess repeated, and would continue to repeat, I knew, until I gave her the answer she expected.

I couldn't just say, "Lasagna," though I could really go for lasagna. I couldn't say "Cajun Chicken Caesar Salad", which was what we were actually having for dinner. No, thanks to Penny's tendency for fixation and my outrageously large record collection, the only answer that Penny was going to accept was:

"Beans," I sighed, because sometimes it's easier to play along with Penny than to try to re-direct her mostly harmless insanity. "Heinz Baked Beans."

Penny had been thumbing through a thick stack of records I was re-acquainting myself with – a relaxing Sunday morning amusement of mine – and had come across an album called *The Who Sell Out*. The album cover features guitarist Pete Townsend applying a giant deodorant stick on one half, while on the other half of the cover, singer Roger Daltry is literally bathing in a tub of Heinz Baked Beans.

"This!" Penny declared immediately upon seeing it. "This! This! We're listening to this! I don't care if it's an all pedal steel band featuring Yoko Ono on lead vocals – I have to know what this is all about!"

I put the album on and tried to explain to Penny about the history of it – how it was a sort of tribute to pirate radio station Radio London, and how it was kind of The Who's response to The Beatles' *Sgt. Pepper's Lonely Hearts Club Band.* I gave her a primer about how the band used actual radio jingles as well as making up their own, and how it was all supposed to be tongue in cheek irony – the band laughing at themselves because they had been making commercials to promote themselves at the time.

But for all the encyclopaedic knowledge that I was attempting to impart, all that Penny focused on as we listened was the jingle for Heinz Baked Beans. And so, for the rest of the morning, I had been hearing: "Mum, what's for tea? What's for tea, mum?"

The only answer the persistently pertinacious Penelope permitted was, of course:

"Beans, darling. Heinz Baked Beans."

After answering this question in this Penny-approved manner about 37 times (in a row), Penny finally diversified her demands.

"Do we have any?"

Find out if Penny and I actually did have Heinz Baked Beans after this word from our sponsors.

Migraines. They can really ruin your whole day. When I have a migraine, it's like someone's put my head in a vice and is stabbing me repeatedly in the eyes with a rusty screwdriver that's been dipped in iodine while playing Nickelback at full volume on one radio and Skrillex on an infinite loop on another. That's when I turn to Madvil Liqui-gels – and sometimes it even works!

But there are some headaches that even Madvil can't touch. Some headaches are caused by Internet related bullshit – bullying, slacktivism, and the ever-growing illiteracy of the general populous. Symptoms include excessive swearing, nausea, localized pain in the hindquarters, and a growing misanthropic malaise.

When I experience this kind of pain, I turn to Vodka – the deep down, sleepy-headed, fuzzy tummy, drink-til-your-vision's-blurry-and-your-speech-is-slurred, apathy inducing, ah, who gives a flying rat's ass medicine.

Vodka – making bullshit more tolerable.

Even though I had chicken marinating in Frank's Hot Sauce and pepper encrusted bacon fried up nice and crisp and drying out, and even though I'd gone out and bought a wedge of Parmesan cheese for shaving, and fresh Romaine lettuce for breaking up into salad, Penelope insisted (quite insistently, I might add) that we rectify our Heinz Baked Beans shortage immediately. Right away. Post haste, even.

So we found ourselves in the canned goods aisle, looking for the iconic blue Heinz Baked Beans can, which we eventually had to look for in the International Foods aisle, because Penny wasn't satisfied with the Canadian Heinz Baked Beans – it had to be the British can from the album cover.

Not content to buy one can, the Countess began filling our cart with every can on the shelf. When the shelf was empty, she turned to me with a mischievous grin, which I recognized as the one she usually gives me when she's up to what most people would call *no good* but what I had come to refer to as story fodder. Without her saying a word, I knew that we were probably about to do something terribly scandalous, much to the embarrassment of total strangers.

We arrived at the checkout with eighteen cans of Heinz Baked Beans, a package of foot long hot dogs, three boxes of laxatives, half a dozen English Cucumbers, a roll of duct tape, a package of condoms, a box of garbage bags, two tubes of KY jelly, and an old Hannah Montana DVD we picked up in a clearance bin. As the cashier – a girl only a couple of years younger than Penny herself – scanned each item, Penny stared at the girl, making full eye contact and asked her increasingly suggestive questions.

"How long are those cucumbers guaranteed to stay firm?"

"How quickly do those laxatives kick in?"

"How safe are those condoms if they come in contact with hot tomato sauce?"

"Do you know if this is the Hannah Montana episode with the wardrobe malfunction?"

Stay tuned for the answers to these and other questions after these important messages.

'Mmmm... Mum, these tatties ur amazin'! Whit did ye dae differently?"
'Och, it's th' newest hin', Seamus. They caa it salt an' pepper."
'Whit dae ye hink, Dad? Doesnae it taste sae much better?"

"Mebbe sae. But Ah dornt loch it a body bit. Mah mammy ne'er used salt an' pepper, an' we liked it jist braw."

"Och, gie th' pickle it ay yer crease. Ah hink it's brammer, an' we're gonnae use salt an' pepper frae noo oan."

Tired of bland Scottish cuisine? Does the idea of one more tasteless potato and cabbage dish make you want to impale yourself on your own bagpipes? Then try what the rest of the world has already discovered - salt and pepper!

Salt and pepper — now available in finer Scottish markets everywhere!

"Um, I don't know," the confused checkout girl said, looking more uncomfortable by the second. "I'll have to ask my manager."

"Penny," I said through gently clenched teeth so I didn't break into laughter. "Penny darling, maybe we just let the nice lady ring us through so we can get home and untie the boys. We've been gone quite some time now, and you know how hanging them upside down sometimes causes circulation problems."

"Oh, dear, yes," Penny agreed, winking at the cashier. "The last thing you want when you have an evening of debauchery planned is problems with blood flow."

And so we left, sparing the poor girl any further embarrassment or trauma, and went home and cooked up a couple of cans of Heinz Baked Beans and made some toast.

I watched in bewilderment as Penny scraped the actual beans off of her toast, leaving the sauce behind.

"What are you doing?" I asked.

"Yeah, I really don't like the beans all that much. It's really the sauce I was after." She replied sheepishly.

"But I've seen you eat beans a hundred times," I said.

"What can I say?" Penny shrugged. "I'm fickle. And I don't like having the farts. Maybe you should slow down. The last time we had beans, well, you know."

I didn't know.

"What are you talking about?"

"Oh, you know. Beans, beers, and the movie *Good Will Hunting*. You *befouled* our apartment, Helena. *Befouled* it."

"I did no such thing!" I protested.

"Whatever," Penny said dismissively. "I get it. A woman your age needs lots of fibre."

"*A woman my age?* What's that supposed to mean?"

"Oh, Helena," she replied, shaking her head sadly. "It hurts me to watch you lose your mind like this."

"You know, you think you're being funny," I said, "but just wait until you're changing my diapers. I'm going to save these boxes of laxatives and eat nothing but Heinz Baked Beans all the time and brew up something special for you."

Penny cringed in horror, and looked at the sixteen remaining cans of beans sitting on our counter.

"So," she said in sweet supplication, "I feel like I've been a bit evil today. I mean, that poor girl at the checkout, and now I've been ever so cruel to you — what do you say we erase a bit of my karmic debt and take these cans down to a homeless shelter or something?"

I felt a rumbling in my tummy and began rounding up the extra cans.

"Sounds like a plan, darling," I said, and then, as an afterthought, added: "But it doesn't change anything. If I lose my mind, I'm going to shit my pants at every opportunity. Hell, I might even dig it out and throw it around a bit. Maybe play with it like marbles."

"OH MY GOD, Helena, you're disgusting!" Penny shrieked. "I was just a baby! You're never going to let that go, are you?"

"Never," I grinned wickedly. "Not if I live to be a hundred."

Countess Penelope and the Jedi Mind Trick

I walked in on Penny doing something I'll bet she wishes I hadn't seen. But still, we all do it, and there's nothing to be ashamed of. There comes a time in everyone's life when you just need to experiment, to see what your body can do, to learn what you're capable of, and if you do indeed have mental powers.

Yes, darlings, the Countess Penelope of Arcadia (small little moisture farming community just east of Mos Eisley) was trying to use The Force to move her glass of wine to her hand. When I opened the door, she tried to act all cool, as if she were just stretching to reach it, but I caught her with her eyes closed, breathing calmly and legs crossed in a zen-like yoga fashion, hand outstretched and trembling slightly.

"What are you doing?" I asked with a knowing grin.

"Nothing," Penny said, clumsily knocking over her wine glass. "Oh, now look what you've made me do. Dammit, Helena, that's alcohol abuse!"

"Gee, I'm sorry, Darth Penelopecus. Looks like you maybe should have stayed in Dagobah and finished your training instead of running off to the Cloud City to try to rescue your friends."

"Hey, you know what? Maybe that explains it," Penny suggested.

"Explains what?"

"Bear with me, Helena," Penny began.

"I always do, darling."

"Kayso, if you could have Jedi powers, what would you do with them?"

"I already told you, darling – I don't like those movies. And I especially don't like the new episodes. I'd really rather not talk about it."

Penny gave me a look that told me that we were going to talk about it.

"Fine," I sighed in resignation. "Well, as far as Jedi powers go, I mean, you have to give me some guidelines. I mean, are we talking the original trilogy – the ability to move things with my mind if I concentrate enough, or are we talking the ridiculously powerful abilities of the Jedi from the prequels. In those movies, Yoda bounces around like a three year old on a sugar bender, and the Jedi practically fly. But in the original three, Luke Skywalker – supposedly a very powerful Jedi – at *best* leaps out of the carbon-freezing chamber. Now either George Lucas was just drunk on the power of new filming technology and just completely lost his mind, or else…"

"Or else we can only come to the conclusion that in the final analysis, Luke Skywalker was the worst Jedi the universe has ever seen. And *why* would that be?"

"I'm sure you are going to tell me," I said, trying to keep a straight face.

"Because he didn't finish his training!" Penny cried, and pointed to the door. "Now, if you please? I'm trying to concentrate."

"Okay," I said with a sly smile, "but I still say you'd have more luck trying to something-else-ate."

"Wow," the Countess replied. "Sounds like someone really needs-a-date."

"I do," I sighed. "I really do."

I stood in the doorway for a moment, thinking.

"What are you still doing here?" Penny asked snarkily.

"Well, don't you want your answer? What I'd do with Jedi powers?"

"Nope," she replied, and waved her hand at me slowly. "You will bring me more wine now."

"No," I said, turning off her lights and leaving her in the dark and walking away. "No, I don't think I will."

"Helena!" She called after me. "Helena, turn the lights back on! I'm in the dark here!"

"Helena?

"Hey, don't be too proud of your technological terror, Helena! The ability to turn off the lights is insignificant compared to the power of The Force!"

I just laughed diabolically as I continued to walk away. I may not be a Jedi, but I'm the master of the mind trick. Weak-minded fools, beware.

Ten Inch Bamboo Cigarette Holder and Black Patent Leather Gloves

P enny doesn't like Elvis Costello.

Well, that's not entirely true, darlings. Thanks to me, The Countess Arcade has the most exquisite musical taste, and could therefore never utter such a heresy as "I hate Elvis Costello" without good cause. Penny doesn't like Elvis Costello in the same way that someone who once got food poisoning from a bad hot dog doesn't like hot dogs. She obviously likes hot dogs, otherwise she wouldn't have gotten food poisoning in the first place, but now that she's had a bad experience, she just can't even stand the smell of hot dogs.

In the case of Elvis Costello, I'm afraid the fault lies with your favourite dilettante.

Mea culpa, darlings. Mea maxima culpa.

Shortly after Penny and I got our place together, as a sort of christening of the apartment, I set up an office for myself, and built my shrine of music – hundreds – literally hundreds of LPs, cassettes and CDs – certain albums I own on multiple formats because... well, just *because*. Penny laughed at the folly of me trying to organize them, and issued a bold declaration:

"There's no way you could ever listen to all of this music!" she decreed. "Not in a million years!"

Challenge accepted, darlings.

But how to approach it? Well, silly as it seems, some Greeks and Latins (work with me here) and later Anglo-Saxons developed this system called the alphabet, and who am I to argue with a bunch of dead guys? So I decided that I would leave my collection in utter disarray, only shelving an item once I'd listened to it, and that the best way to do that was to listen alphabetically.

We made it through Ryan Adams, Laurie Anderson, Arcade Fire and Joseph Arthur, The Beatles, Bjork, Kate Bush and Bowie, and even the Bangles Greatest Hits (don't judge me – like you aren't right now, as we speak, looking up *Walk Like an Egyptian* on YouTube). Penny cheerfully endured Cake, The Clash, and even the Cocteau Twins – but then we got to Costello, Elvis.

I admit I may be a little obsessive about Elvis Costello. I have every album, every bootleg I could get my hands on – hell, I've even made my own box set of various live recordings, organized by decade. What can I say – other than writing, all I ever really wanted to do was work for a record company.

So after about a week of listening to Elvis Costello and nothing *but* Elvis Costello, Penny finally conceded defeat.

"Enough! No more!" she cried, cringing. "I give up! Listen to something else! Anything else! I can't stand it anymore!"

"How can you not love Elvis Costello?" I asked, aghast. "I mean, listen to the lyrics to *Miracle Man*, and tell me who he's singing about."

"God, Helena, is your personality *completely* manufactured?" Penny asked, as if that were an insult.

I acted wounded for her benefit, and then told her that fictional heroine Lizbeth Salander[79] had called, and said that she needed her look back.

The Countess Penelope of Arcadia, which is apparently located in the heart of London, circa 1977, flipped me the V and spat *Bollocks!* and then pulled the needle off of the record that I was listening to and enjoying, and replaced it with The Sex Pistols' *Never Mind the Bollocks.*

"Did you know that Elvis Costello's infamous appearance on Saturday Night Live only happened because Malcolm McLaren forgot to get the Sex Pistols' visas? It's true. The Pistols were supposed to play, but Elvis filled in at the last minute. It was Elvis &

---

[79] From *The Girl With the Dragon Tattoo*

The Attractions' first big US television appearance. The drummer, Pete Thomas, wore a T-Shirt that said THANKS MALC in reference to Malcolm McLaren's fuck up."

"Gee, Helena, that's really fascinating," Penny said in her most patronizing voice, and then cranked the music up to an intolerable volume and yelled, "If I never hear the name Elvis Costello ever again, I'll die happy!"

Imagine her delight tonight when I tell her who we're going to see at Massey Hall in June.

The Countess Penelope of Arcadia Plays it Cool

"Penny," I whispered at first, and then a little louder: "Penny, wake up!"

WHAP! A hand came out of nowhere and smacked me right in the head.

"Ow! What the hell, Penny?"

"Gimme nine more minutes, please." She moaned. "Just nine little more minutes of snoozy time."

"But Penny," I whispered in her ear, "it's your *birthday*."

Penny rolled over and mumbled something unintelligible. Then she stretched like a cat and rolled over again.

"You know what I'd like for my birthday?" She grumbled.

"Nine more minutes of sleep?" I guessed.

"How well you know me."

Nine minutes later...

"Birthday breakfast is ready," I declared, and then flopped down on her bed and began bouncing up and down repeating, "Breakfast is ready! Breakfast is ready," until Penny finally rolled out of bed onto the floor and crawled her way toward the smell of breakfast.

"So what's for breakfast?" She asked, still moving slug-like along the floor.

"Ah, remember when we stayed with Manuel's mom in Napa, and she made us chorizo and eggs?"

Penny's eyes lit up.

"Well, it's not going to be as good as that – you can't really get proper chorizo here, but..."

"Did you make fresh tortillas?" Penny asked, suddenly awake and excited.

"Hey," I rebuked, "does the name on my shirt say Betty Croquierrez?"

"You don't have a name on your shirt," she replied.

"Yeah, but I was thinking up that Betty Croquierrez line for the last half hour. So, nothing, then?"

"Yes, yes, it was very clever, but I'm just only two-thirds awake and you're expecting what from me, exactly?"

"Never mind," I sighed, feeling greatly unappreciated for my wit and humour. "Come, let us repast, and break the fast, before the time has passed."

"Just loving the sound of your voice this morning, aren't we?" Penny said, not unkindly.

I practically danced to the dining room, and tried to get Penny to join me. I love birthdays. Other people's birthdays, and Penny's in particular. Because I never do what she expects. She's long stopped dropping hints about what she'd like for her birthday, because she knows that the fun for me is not just buying her something she wants, but something she'd never think to ask for but will absolutely love. Now that she's older, I like getting her things that are irreplaceable – like memories, experiences. Things can get lost, stolen or broken, but you'll never lose the memories you make.

You know, Helena, if this writing thing doesn't work out, you could always go to work in the greeting cards business.

You know, voice in my head, if this snarky commentary thing doesn't work out, you could always go and fuck yourself.

Where was I?

Ah yes, Penny was pigging out on breakfast burritos, filled with chorizo, eggs, and fried potatoes with fresh salsa, and washing it all down with hot coffee and cold grapefruit juice.

"So," she said, mouth full of her mostly masticated Mexican meal. "Where's my birthday present, oh favourite aunt of mine?"

"I'm your only aunt," I said.

"And so you're my only favourite," she said without missing a beat.

Without any further flourish, I presented her with an envelope, which I'd doodled all over, putting her name in the middle, surrounded by mosaic-type random shapes and squiggles.

"What's this?" The Countess of Arcadia demanded.

"Open it up! Open it up!" I urged, barely able to contain my excitement.

Penny opened the envelope and pulled out the card, and performed the ritual shaking of the card and finger in the envelope, checking for cash, but instead of cash, she found...

"Tickets to go see Jack White," Penny said, lacking the enthusiasm that I had imagined. "Cool."

"Um, that's not exactly the reaction I was looking for," I said, heart sinking a bit.

"Well," the Countess replied, "Jack White is kind of *your* thing, Helena. I mean, there's even precedent that states that Jack White makes you feel like a seventeen year old girl in a go-go cage."

"Nineteen, darling," I correct her, "I was nineteen."

"Whatever. You bought these tickets so that you could see Jack White."

"I bought these tickets so that *we* could see Jack White. Who's the one who, upon discovering The White Stripes, dyed her hair black and dressed in nothing but red and white for an entire month?"

"That was a fashion challenge," Penny insisted.

"And who wanted to write a stage play based around the song *Carolina Drama* from the second Raconteurs record?" I challenged.

"One has to respect grassroots storytelling abilities when presented in such a stark and harrowing way," Penny countered.

"And who cried like a baby when Jack and Meg announced that The White Stripes were officially finished a couple of years ago?"

"AHA!" Penny said, pointing her finger at me. "That was *you!*"

"True, but you locked yourself in your room and refused to come out," I accused.

Penny sighed. "Okay, it's pretty cool," she allowed. "I guess. If you want me, I'll be in my room trying to figure out how I'm going to salvage my birthday."

"Okay," I said, mocking her melodramatic manner, "you do that."

Penny stormed up the stairs, stomping her feet childishly, and then slammed her door behind her.

I counted to ten, and didn't even get to six before I heard the sound of Penny screaming in sheer joy, followed by the opening drum beat of *Seven Nation Army* being played at full volume.

I smiled and poured myself a cup of coffee.

Mission accomplished.

Postcards from California
Part One

I got a phone call from an old boyfriend for my birthday.
I miss you, you were right, I'm sorry; the west coast just isn't the same without you.

Things didn't work out the way we planned, I think I missed my chance, but did you hear our new song yet?

The record company thinks this might be the one — if we go on tour, will you come and see me?

Happy Birthday, Helena. I wish...

Anyway, Happy Birthday. Wish you were here.

And by the way, did you get those postcards I sent you?

I hung up the phone, not exactly irritated, but not exactly thrilled, either. Ancient history was never one of my best subjects in school.

"Postcards?" I asked no one in particular, and no one in particular answered.

"Penny!" I called out to my lovely niece, the self-styled Countess of Arcadia. "Oh Penny! Did you, perchance, pick from the post a postcard pour moi?"

"Postcard? Pour toi?" Penny pantomimed, "Il n'ya pas possible, parce que pommes de terre parle Portugais, n'est-ce pas?"

I take full responsibility, darlings. Sometimes Penny gets carried away when I start something as silly as a bit of harmless alliteration. In this case, I do fear that she has completely lost the plot in favour of a bit of excessive artifice.

Remembering my grade school French, I cocked my head and said "It's not possible because potatoes speak Portuguese? Really? That's the best you've got?"

"Perhaps there's a package?" Penny offered, rooting through our mail and handing me a manila envelope with a Los Angeles postmark on it. I tore the top open and dumped the contents out on to our table. Several postcards spilled out, addressed to me at the only address this person had for me – some from California, but others from all over the world. England, Brazil, Egypt, Dubai, Thailand, Malaysia, the Philippines.

"Wow," Penny exclaimed, turning postcards over in her hands. "You got a secret admirer or something? Some of these go back a few years, but here, look, Helena!"

Penny showed me a card dated just a month earlier, sent from Manila (home of the envelopes) saying that the sender was going to be in Los Angeles from the 15th to the 30th of April, and that she'd love to see me if I was available.

"Who's Maya?" Penny asked curiously.

I was still a bit stunned. I never thought I'd ever hear that name again.

I remember the first day I met Maya. How could I ever forget?

As usual, I found myself alone in a room full of people.

It's not that I wasn't able to socialize, it's just that all these people were there clamouring for each other's attention, and they belonged to a circle that I was only remotely connected to. I had moved out to L.A. with my would-be rock star boyfriend, and he had promptly forgotten me in favour of, well, everybody else.

I got dragged out to parties, where the free-flowing booze and coke quickly turned everyone into belligerent bi-polar assholes, and I just as quickly grew tired and bored of the whole scene. I hadn't made a friend in L.A. – I'd been offered modelling jobs, jobs in porn, and been solicited by women who ran escort services – but I hadn't met a single person who was just interested in hanging out and having a good time that didn't involve illicit substances or group sex.

I stepped outside to get away from the sleaze of sycophants and so-called friends and lit a cigarette. I remember I was in my Audrey Hepburn phase and so I was using my long black cigarette holder, which completed the little black dress and wide brim hat ensemble so perfectly that I was damn near cosplaying a scene from *Breakfast at Tiffany's.*

I heard the clicking of heels behind me and ignored it. Some stranger coming out to make idle chit chat, maybe try to ask where they know me from, who my stylist is, who I'm fucking – well, they never asked so bluntly, darlings, but eventually, it's where the conversations tended to end up. It's an interview to determine if I'm somebody worth clinging to, or just another wannabe *nobody.*

"Well, look at you," a voice I'd one day try my very best to emulate purred. "All dressed up with nowhere to go."

I turned to give the stranger a polite smile, which was nicer than telling them to fuck off but was understood to mean the same thing, and stopped dead in my tracks and stared at easily the most beautiful woman I'd ever laid eyes on.

"But," the woman said, pulling off her large framed sunglasses, "I think you're missing something."

She put them on me (and I let her, momentarily stunned by this bold intrusion) and took a step back to admire her handiwork.

"Now," she said. "Repeat after me: *I'll tell you one thing, Fred, darling... I'd marry you for your money in a minute.*"

I laughed at her random Audrey Hepburn impression and went to hand her back her sunglasses, when she stopped me.

"Don't be silly, darling," she said, putting a perfectly manicured hand on mine. "They look much better on you, anyhow."

I didn't see how it was even remotely possible that anything could look better on anyone but her.

White people like to use words like 'exotic' when describing Asian girls, as if that completely sums the matter up. This woman didn't look exotic; she looked like she came from a whole other planet. And god help us if the women of her planet ever decided on a full-scale invasion, because if they did, us lowly earth girls would be doomed.

She looked like the design template for every pin-up girl ever drawn, with legs that went on forever, lifted by heels that knew exactly what they were doing, zero gravity boobs, and pursed lips painted the perfect shade of sex. Her skin was pale and pristine – an oddity in L.A., where everyone was bronzed, either naturally or artificially. Her hair seemed to fall perfectly, in a way that everyone knows is just a trick of the movies, and later, when she told me how much her hairstylist charged, I nearly choked on my drink, but had to admit it was worth every penny.

It wasn't just her physical beauty that made me take notice, but her presence. Her aloofness. She should have been the centre of attention, but instead, she, like me, stood on the outside, looking in.

Was she as bored as I was?

It turned out she was, and she told me so.

"I'm Maya," she said, still holding her hand on top of mine and pushing the sunglasses back on my face. "And I'm bored as fuck with this crowd. You wanna get out of here?"

I pulled my hand away slowly and my head turned back to the door of... whoever's house we were at.

"You here with somebody?" she asked.

"Yeah," I said, and then awkwardly added. "And, I'm not, you know..."

She laughed out loud and her whole face lit up, and in that moment, even though I wasn't, you know... I could see how easily I could have been.

"I don't want to *fuck* you, darling, I just want to play! Let's get out of here and live a little! All they seem to want to do in there is sit in the dark putting chemicals into their bodies and jerking each other off. It's so much more fun out here in the sun! Oh look, darling – I'm a poet and I don't know it. Tell me you're not just as bored with those idiots as I am."

I smiled and nodded and sighed.

"Thank god," she said, grabbing my hand and pulling me to the parking lot.

Trailing after her, laughing at the prospect of adventure, I realized something.

"You don't even know my name!" I called after her.

She waved me off.

"Names, names, names! What's in a name? Your name could be Gertrude, Gloria or Guinevere for all I care!"

I giggled at her frivolity.

"And if it's not a G name?" I wondered.

"Well, I suppose I'll just have to live with that, won't I?"

"It's Helena," I offered, and for some reason, I hoped that she approved.

"Outstanding," she replied. "And speaking of standing – Helena, those are terrible shoes. Come, let us remedy the situation. We're young, rich..."

"Uh, I'm not rich," I cut in, suddenly feeling awkward.

"Pity," she said, as if it were a tragedy. "Well, I suppose I shall just have to be rich enough for both of us. After all, I can't let you walk around in those terrible shoes, and we *are* in Los Angeles, darling. What else is there for two fabulous women such as ourselves to do in Los Angeles other than go shopping?"

I looked at my new sunglasses, and noticed for the first time that they were actual Oliver Goldsmiths.[80] They must have cost at least four bills.

I wish that I could tell you that I told Maya that I certainly couldn't accept her generous gifts. I wish that I could report that I gave Maya back her sunglasses, and that I politely thanked her but didn't want to be in her debt. I'd probably look like less of a sponge-like jellyfish if I told you that I didn't, under any circumstances, go shopping on Hollywood Boulevard with this complete stranger and rack up a five-digit bill. And I'd really love not to disclose that upon seeing her car (a Porsche 911 Carrera convertible the very colour of happiness – that would be yellow, darlings) that I didn't drool – not even a bit. It would be my utmost desire to tell you all those things and more, darlings – like how I definitely didn't beg her to let me drive it, and how I positively did *not* scream like a little girl when she let me drive through Topanga Canyon and up on to Mulholland Drive.

But the fact of the matter is, darlings, that each and every one of those things is a lie. I have many character flaws, it's true, but while I may have given in to the moment and allowed myself to be swept away into Maya's whirlwind, I'm not a liar. I'm not sure what it makes me, but whatever it is, it's not a liar.

What I was – how I felt at the time – was special. It was a crazy day, and when it was over, I had no idea what was supposed to happen next. Were we supposed to exchange phone numbers? Were we going to be friends? Lovers? (I thought I'd been clear on that, but...) Would we ever see each other again? My head was dizzy – Maya lived a charmed life, and a girl could definitely get used to that

---

[80] The same brand of expensive glasses Audrey Hepburn wore in *Breakfast at Tiffany's*

— but it wasn't *my* life. The last thing I wanted to do was become one of those parasitic cling-ons, attaching myself to some bright light and feeding off them.

So when Maya gave me her phone number and told me to give her a call sometime, I gave her mine with the same invitation. At the time, it felt like the beginning of a strange but interesting friendship.

It turned out I was a fool.

Postcards from California
Part Two

"Here's one from Santa Monica Pier," Penny said, handing me one of the many postcards that had poured out of the manila envelope. My ex-boyfriend and would-be rock star had been keeping them for me, for years it seems, and I suppose getting a postcard out of the blue a couple of weeks ago prompted him to put them all in a package and send them to me. I honestly hadn't heard from him in years, but a phone call on my birthday brought him back into my life, if only for five minutes.

With that unwelcome re-entry came a flood of memories, not all of them pleasant.

I said that I'd been a fool, but if I was a fool, than it was only because she made me one.

Maya.

I'd long ago stopped being angry with her, but seeing her handwriting, reading the messages in her delicate script sent me spiralling backward through time. Reading the text – so carefree, so oblivious to the hurt she'd caused – just made me feel the pain of being discarded all over again. She had no idea – she was so full of herself; so selfish.

I felt like a little kid again, and part of me experienced a twinge of guilt. Before I'd left for California, I'd promised little Penelope (not yet a Countess, at the age of ten she was always Penny Arcade to me, or, sometimes Penny Dammit when her mom was out of earshot) that I'd someday take her for a ride on the Ferris Wheel at Santa Monica. There I was, on the Ferris Wheel, Maya laughing along with me. Robert was off at some... *wherever* yet again, and I had to fill my time somehow. So I called Maya.

Maya was different from the other fast-moving crowd in L.A. Sure, she attended all the same parties I did, and would stay out all night dancing – but at the same time, she always seemed peripheral – like she was there and not there at the same time. If wanderlust is a communicable disease, I'd say that I contracted a rather nasty case of it from Maya, and I've yet to find a cure. Sometimes I think that the death of my sister and brother-in-law and my subsequent guardianship of Penny is the only thing that slowed me down and kept me in one spot for longer than a year or two at a time. But not unlike with Morphine withdrawal, every once in a while, I still get that *itch*.

Maya must have constantly felt that itch, because she always looked like she was getting ready to leave. I should have noticed that earlier, but frankly, I was having too much fun.

We ate at the best restaurants, danced the night away at the swankiest clubs, went for long drives at high speeds, Maya going on and on about the places she'd been, the things she'd seen, the cars she'd owned, the men she'd dated. I was enraptured. She'd lived a life I could only dream about, been to places I'd only ever read about, had experiences I could never afford.

And yet, for all that glamour, all that luxury, all that opportunity, I just couldn't wrap my head around one thing. She seemed so restless, and often unhappy. I wouldn't have said that at first, but after I'd spent a few weeks with her, I began to see a sadness in her eyes that I hadn't noticed before. In all fairness, I probably didn't want to see it.

One night, over drinks (I had my customary vodka and grapefruit while Maya drank only Guava juice – she never drank, never smoked, never did any drugs) I asked her: "What do you do?"

I had assumed that she was either on vacation, or an actress or model or something. Someone who had an open schedule and a lot of money.

"What do I do?" she asked, with a bit of a sour smile.

"Yeah," I said curiously. "I mean, what do you do when you're not picking up strange girls and spoiling them rotten? Do you have a career? Hey – are you someone famous in disguise? Are you slumming it with me?"

She didn't seem to be amused at my teasing.

"I do anything I want," she smiled at me through pursed lips.

"Yes, but surely you want to *do* something – play music, write, paint, make Lego castles for underprivileged kids, I don't know – *something.*"

"And what do you *do*, Helena?" She asked me.

"I don't know," I admitted. "I haven't figured it out yet. But you have so much opportunity! You could do whatever you wanted!"

"And I do," she replied. The smile was fading from her face. "I do whatever I want. Today, I wanted to eat sushi with you and watch boys play beach volleyball. Who knows what I'll want to do tomorrow?"

"So, *this*, then?" I asked, unaware that I was on very thin ice. "*This* is what you do?"

"Yes," she said, picking up her keys and standing up. "And sometimes I do this. Good-bye, Helena."

And then she left me sitting there, not quite sure what had just happened.

Two days went by and I didn't hear from Maya, which wasn't a big deal, and I wasn't going to call her. I figured that I'd pushed some buttons or something – maybe she had a father or mother who was always asking her what she was going to do with her life – I know how that goes. And part of me knew that it wasn't something that was meant to last. But at the same time I'd gotten used to having her around. Robert and I were all but through. I knew it, and he surely knew it, because every time we were in the same room together I smelled strange perfume on him. I wasn't that big a fool.

So what did I have left, then?

Nothing.

And so, with nothing to lose, or so I thought, I did something very stupid, and made an assumption that I really shouldn't have. In retrospect, I'm probably just as much to blame as Maya in this regard. I had thought about Maya's chosen vocation – that of decadence and self-indulgence – and decided that I could get on board with that. I was young and free and unburdened with responsibilities. I found myself shipwrecked on the shores of Southern California with pretty much only the clothes on my back, and I could either let that be my prison or my opportunity. Maya was my ticket to a world beyond my means, and she had offered it to me freely. In my mind, she was just looking for a partner in crime, and of course that was me.

Of course it was! Wasn't it?

I would call her and suggest we get out of Los Angeles. Go to one of the many places she'd told me about. I'd grab my shit and get on the next plane to Marrakesh or Bangkok or Rio or wherever she wanted to go. After all, why couldn't I go with her?

So I called her. I called her for days. I left messages. I asked her to call me. I begged her to call me. I apologized for imagined slights, and I neurotically agonized and scrutinized every word I ever spoke to her, every gesture. Did I thank her enough? Was I cool enough, was I sufficiently aloof for her liking? What did I do wrong? Why wouldn't she even pick up the phone?

Finally, one night, alone in the apartment, sitting on the bathroom floor crying, the phone rang, and a far-away voice called my name, irritation dripping from the three tiny syllables.

"Hello, darling," Maya said, sounding bored and annoyed at the same time. "I understand you've been trying to get a hold of me."

"Yes," I said, sniffing and trying to hide the fact that I'd been crying. Hearing her voice, any slights were forgiven. I was back in the game. "Where are you?"

"Oh, I don't even know, isn't that ridiculous, darling?" she said with a chuckle. "*Ou sommes-nous?*"

A voice in the background answered in French, and Maya relayed the information.

"It seems we are at the Hotel Raphael," she said.

"Is that up north? Near San Francisco or something?"

"No, darling, I'm afraid not," she sighed. "I'm in Paris. Just felt like a change, you know?"

"Paris?" I asked, feeling my heart sink into my stomach. "As in, *France?*"

"Well, it sure as fuck isn't Texas, darling! Oops, pardon my French," she laughed.

Somehow, I wasn't nearly as amused as she'd hoped.

"But, I thought..." I began. I wasn't sure how to voice exactly what I thought.

A huge sigh came over the telephone.

"Really, darling," Maya cooed, as if talking to a child. "Come now. We had some laughs, you and I, but now you're just being tedious. Quite frankly, this is boring me, so again, good-bye, Helena. I'll drop you a postcard."

Then the phone went dead, and so did I for a good five minutes. I didn't cry, I didn't speak, I don't even remember breathing.

I sat in the dark in the bathroom, still and silent. I have no idea how much time passed when the door to the apartment opened, and I heard Robert's husky breathing, and the fumbling of hands on clothes. I sat perfectly still, nearly outside myself, as I listened as the man I'd moved across the country to be with, the man I barely recognized anymore, assured some stranger that they were alone in the apartment, and that yes, he thought she was beautiful; the most beautiful girl he'd ever seen. I had to listen to their sex noises, had to listen to her scream that she was going to cum. I could tell from her voice that she must be an actress, but not a very good one.

I could have stood up. I could have stopped them. I could have embarrassed him and humiliated her, but I just didn't care. I sat on the floor, my back against the wall, and waited until they were finished, and he sent her away, as I knew he would. I waited until he came into the bathroom to take a piss, and then I asked him:

"Did you at least use a condom?" Which was probably bad timing on my part, because apparently he thought I was a burglar, and in his startled state, turned and pissed all over me while screaming like a ten-year-old boy.

"Jesus!" He cried, spraying the rest of his urine more or less in the direction of the toilet. I had retreated backward into the tub, but had still gotten enough on me to make the scene a great deal less comfortable for me than it already was, if that's possible.

I turned on the shower, and he kept apologizing, but I tuned him out. Everything was far away and out of focus, like a radio station that just won't quite come in, or a photograph so blurred that you can't make out what it is. I peeled my clothes off in the shower and stood with my head in the spray, wet clothes at my feet, until the water went cold and my teeth were chattering. I got out of the shower and wrapped a towel around me. When I came out of the bathroom, my bags were packed, and Robert was holding out a set of keys, offering them to me.

"Take it," he said. His brand new convertible. I'd picked it out, mostly because I liked metallic orange of it.

I grabbed the keys from his hand, avoiding physical contact as best as I could.

"You'll change your mind," I said cautiously. "You'll report it stolen."

"I won't," he promised. "I am sorry, Helena. I..."

"Don't be," I cut him off. "Better now than later. I hope you find whatever it is you're looking for, Robert. And I hope it makes you happy. Just..."

"What?" He asked, trying to make me look him in the eyes. I pulled away from him, cringing at his touch. I needed to leave. I couldn't let him see me cry.

"You're better than this," I said, pushing past him to the door with my bag in hand. "Or at least, you used to be."

He hung his head and let me pass. By the time the morning rolled around, I was gone. Headed north. Headed nowhere. Wandering.

I crumpled a postcard from Paris, a picture of the Arc de Triomphe on the front, all lit up in green and red lights at night.

Penny wrapped her arms around me and let me cry into her shoulder. I had thought that I'd been all cried out, but I guess some wounds never really heal, they just scab over, and it's best to leave them alone.

I picked up what I thought was another postcard, but was instead another, smaller envelope, again with my name on the front, and with a postmark date of maybe six months before.

I opened it up, and pulled out a photograph of a familiar, smiling face, alongside a smaller version of the same face. There was a date on the back, and Maya's name, as well as her daughter's.

Also in the envelope was a stack of folded papers – a letter – a long one, it looked like. At the top was Maya's name, but more importantly, her phone number and email address.

I opened it up and began to read.

Dearest Helena,

I am very sorry...

Postcards From California
Part Three

earest Helena,

I am very sorry for leaving you the way I did. I was a very selfish person — this is the repeated refrain of my life. I look back at the person I was with loathing, and consider her like vomit. I have spent the last few years doing my very best to kill that person, erase her from my memory, and some days I even feel like it has worked, but then I'll remember someone like you, or my ex-husband, and know that I have left bodies in my wake, and the ghost of the old me laughs at me from the mirror.

I'm not here to make excuses, Helena, nor to make amends — it's too late for that and I've learned that empty gestures usually end up being just that — empty. No, I'm just reaching out to you as a way to tell my story, and I thought you would be pleased to know that I'm not just flitting from place to place anymore, just taking anything I want and never giving back.

If you don't ever read this, well, I suppose it is enough that I wrote it down. But I do hope this reaches you, and that someday I can wrap my arms around you and thank you and say good-bye properly. I owe you that, at least.

You may not have realized this, but I was ever so lonely, and I didn't have the time for making real friends — well, of course I had the time, darling, but I just couldn't be bothered. And so I collected... pets... like I collected shoes or cars or purses, and when I was bored with them, or they started getting too close, I tossed them away.

I'm afraid that is what happened to you, Helena, but believe me when I tell you that you are not even close to the worst. I have treated others far worse. Ask my ex-lovers or my ex-husband what it is like to live with someone, to wake up with someone, who is cold and dead and self-consumed.

Of course, you're asking yourself what caused my transformation. Well, I didn't have a near-death experience or join a cult, in case that cynical mind of yours is rolling its eyes right about now.

I can tell you that it wasn't just one thing. I didn't just wake up one day and see things as they really were and do an about face. No, my life was stripped away a bit at a time. What I didn't realize was that while I was busy playing wife and mother and socialite, people around me were tiring of me. I was too self-absorbed to notice it.

I moved back to Malaysia and was actually trying to play at being settled and domestic – can you believe it? But my selfish excess remained, and I drove my friends and family insane with my whimsical choices and erratic behaviour. I had everything every girl ever dreams of – I had the big princess wedding, a handsome prince, a castle and eventually a family.

I almost lost it all. First, the prince got tired of being alternately abused or neglected by me, and left. But not quietly. I don't know if you've ever gone through a divorce, Helena, but they are a particularly ugly experience, especially if a child is involved. Mine was brutal, drawn out, and incredibly painful.

Then my grandmother died, and I shut down. I went inside my room and closed the door behind me, and it was there that I began to change.

Go ahead and make all the butterfly/cocoon jokes that you want, Helena, but it wasn't like that at all. I didn't emerge a better person. I didn't suddenly come out with my mind enlightened and face shining like some sort of prophet or saint. I spent that year depressed and suicidal, and forced to face the real me. And I hated her. I began to plot her murder. I wanted to smash her head in and bury her under some daisies; put up a tombstone, reading HERE LIES A COLD, SELFISH BITCH – GOOD RIDDANCE TO BAD RUBBISH.

So no, I didn't emerge a better person, just an empty, angry person, disappointed in myself – I can honestly say that I am probably the least accomplished person I know – I haven't DONE anything. You were right about that. And so when I opened my door and stepped back into the world, it wasn't as a butterfly, but as a prisoner set free. I had come to realize that I'd been living in a cage of my own making – that it was fear that kept me there. Fear of living. Actually living, and forming relationships, and trying to express myself – my actual thoughts and feelings – and having them be rejected. I was afraid that if anyone knew my desires, my dreams, that they would either laugh at me or hate me – a good Asian girl is not supposed to feel such things, not even supposed to THINK such things.

When I opened the door, the one thing I did have was a new credo — that I was going to be fearless.

What a joke, Helena! As if I could just declare something to be so and it would be so. It would appear that I had some growing up to do; some learning. I had some personal issues to work through, and no idea where to start. So yes, I did seek spiritual guidance. I spoke to a great many spiritual leaders, trying to understand myself, and eventually, discovered that I needed to look outside myself for the answers I was looking for.

Don't get me wrong — a life of asceticism is not for me. I embrace my desires, not shun them — but I needed some sort of balance. I was not prepared, Helena. I fully admit that now, but at the time, I thought that I was ready for anything. I had years of practice showing fake confidence and bravado, and so I charged right in. I began working with non-profit organizations in Malaysia, caring for women and children rescued from the sex-trade. I have seen terrible things, Helena. Things that I can never un-see.

At first I just thought I could throw money at the problem, and that it would go away, thus easing my conscience. I thought I could feel good about myself. But it wasn't enough to expunge my sense of guilt. I kept thinking how my priorities used to be getting my hands on the latest handbag or shoes, and it made me physically ill. I was in a position, or so I thought, to do something about the things I had seen, and not just by throwing money at it. Someone introduced me to an organization called Gawad Kalinga, and so I went to the Philippines to fight the good fight against poverty.

If you can sense the sarcasm and disillusionment dripping off my words, than my writing is not in vain.

I wasn't going to change the world. In many ways, this was still my enormous ego acting up. Directed at a noble cause, to be sure, but still an exercise in vanity. It took me quite some time to come to that realization, though.

Don't get me wrong — Gawad Kalinga is doing great work trying to rebuild a nation — you really can't believe the poverty, Helena. This isn't people without jobs, people with not enough to eat, people living in the streets, sleeping in bus shelters. This is people without clothes, people squatting in the mud, entire cities full of people living and dying in the street. Literally millions of people without regular food or shelter — entire generations living out their short, miserable lives without hope of anything close to what we take for granted.

I am no hero. I never was, and I never will be. But I have met heroes, and so I took it upon myself to try to document their work, going as far as helping start a film company to make a documentary about NGOs working to rebuild communities and eradicate poverty — specifically focusing on Gawad Kalinga. I thought that I could bring attention to the work that they were doing, and by doing so, add hands to the cause. It was a good idea, Helena. I swear it was. But again, it was unsuccessful. It seemed that the more I tried to do, the less I accomplished. I realize now that I was trying to wipe out the great debt that I felt I had amassed after years of selfish decadence with a single grand gesture.

In the end, the film industry brought out the worst in me – my vicious ego came forward to insist that things were done my way or not at all, and eventually I knew I had to walk away or again become consumed by that evil, dead thing that once I was.

So again, I went into self-imposed exile. I clearly still needed work. I needed to conquer my ego, face my fears, and battle my demons.

I know, right? Sounds trite, or cliché, but the fact of the matter is, the old Maya would never stoop to something as common as self-examination or self-improvement. I was my own, perfect, flawless goddess, and the world should change to suit me, not the other way around.

So what does that mean, anyway? Battling demons. Well, I cried. A lot. I stopped wearing makeup, and tried to accept that I would never be movie star or model beautiful. I started writing. I'd always written poetry – sometimes depressing nonsense, sometimes, erotic fantasies – but I'd never taken it too seriously. I was proud of it, but it was just for me. But that year, I started writing, examining myself, taking a sharp blade to the deepest parts of me. I allowed myself to think about things I'd long buried, and to examine my role in the train wreck that my life had become. I came out of that with a renewed sense of purpose and understanding.

I expect that you're waiting for the big Hollywood finish here. The story of how I opened an orphanage and saved the lives of hundreds of starving children, or how I became a motivational speaker, taking my story from stadium to stadium and changing the lives of millions.

Sadly, no. The truth is, neither of those things would be a good idea for me. I know how my ego works now, and how poisonous it is to me. No, I'm still just me. I'm still marginally involved with local relief organizations, and I'm still an avid supporter of Gawad Kalinga, but these days I focus on being a mom – my little girl is not so little anymore, and she needs me more than anyone else in the world. If I can instill better values in her, then maybe, through her, I can find my redemption.

Wow, did I really just write that? Sorry, darling, I fear sometimes my poetic nature gets the best of me.

So I'm taking it from day to day, trying to remain free of that cage I spent years creating. I'm writing a blog, and sharing my thoughts, my experiences, and *even my poetry. I think you'd be glad that I am actually doing something for a change.*

I once told you that I did whatever I wanted – went where I wanted, ate what I wanted, took what I wanted, spent time with who I wanted. That was my definition of freedom.

I know now that I was just wild, unreliable and irresponsible. No wonder I found myself constantly alone, cut off from the people I said I cared about. The truth is, I didn't know how to care for people. When we really care for people, and when we truly learn to care for ourselves, we can never be so wildly careless and casual about our presence and responsibility. To be there – to be really present – for the people we love, and to be reliable for ourselves and for the people that depend on us, we need to rise above our own issues. If I want to be someone who can achieve great things, I have to be able to let go of the pain, the anger, and the baggage of the past.

And how do I do that?

God, I don't know, Helena. One day at a time? Isn't that what the alcoholics say?

Anyway, I don't know if you're reading this, or if I'm just practicing for my writing portfolio. If this does reach you, and you care to get in contact, I've given you my current phone number and email address. I'm actually going to be in Los Angeles in a few weeks – are you still in the area? I really would love to see you, if you don't think it would be too awkward.

I won't hold my breath.

I wrote this as much for me as it was for you (see, I'm still a bit selfish) and so as I close this, I suppose I do feel a sense of accomplishment. I wanted to reach out to you and apologize, and tell you what I have tried to become, and now I have done that, and it will have to be enough.

I wish you true happiness, with the admonition to not look for it in fast cars, fancy clothes, and bright lights.

Much love,

Maya

By the time I finished reading, I was mentally exhausted. Penny was putting postcards in chronological order on the table, sketching out a timeline out of some sense of obsessive compulsion or else just a natural tendency for finding the narrative in things. There were plenty of gaps – some lasting years. I was a bit flattered that I came to mind at all, to be honest. It seems like she was trying to convince me that she was changing.

Look, here I am in the dangerous slums of Mindanao interviewing ex-rebel leaders.

Here I am clothing children rescued from a brothel in Ampang.

This is me making a movie about relief workers in Tanauan.

Postcard portraits of attempts to prove to herself — and me, it seemed — that she could *do* something. There was an insecurity and desperate need for approval in it all that I immediately recognized and related to. I found myself hoping that she was further along the path to self-acceptance than I was, because I could echo the last few lines of her letter to the very word.

I don't know how to let go and move forward.

I just keep trying. One day at a time, like the alcoholics say.

"You should call her," Penny said, reading my mind.

"I know," I agreed, but I wasn't sure that I would.

Leaving Arcadia Part One

"*You* can't keep running, Helena."

That's what my sister Cheryl told me when I finally told her why I'd gone to Venezuela at the beginning of the summer.

We sat in her living room in Arcadia, her daughter, little Penny Arcade running around repeating the word "Bowie" over and over again, and giggling. At three, she was adorably energetic, but the cuteness was often lost on her mother, who was worn down and exhausted.

I'd come down to visit after a tear-filled phone call, and the time was running out on my visit. I was enrolled in classes for September, giving University another go in my continuing on-again off-again fling with higher education.

"You can't just keep running away from your problems," she repeated. "You'll just find other problems."

"And when I do, I'll just put on my best shoes and run in the opposite direction," I grinned, teasing her. I knew she meant well, but I had no intention of sitting down long enough to put down roots and get stuck in some Arcadia of my own.

Arcadia is not a geographical location – not really. I mean, of course it is, darlings, but it's not the geographical Arcadia I'm speaking of. I'm talking of the quicksand trap that's both prison and exile. The slow decay of acceptance and stagnation that makes you weak and vulnerable. A place populated with white picket fences so old and rotten that they would fall apart if the wind blew too strongly. But of course it never does. The wind doesn't blow through

Arcadia, and so time stands still, and people hide behind the same floral drapes that have always hung there, looking out at neighbours they only think they know.

Arcadia is no place for someone with imagination, or a desire for more than potluck dinners, county fairs, and awkward wrestling matches in the backseats of cars.

That my sister ended up in Arcadia was a travesty, darlings. She was trying to make the best of it, but Arcadia was to her like a pair of pants that just didn't fit right. If Cheryl had asked me, "Does this town make my ass look fat?" I would have had to politely lie, which is something I hate to do, and so I'd end up having to tell her the truth, and that was that Arcadia was killing her, and that she needed to get out while she still could.

But she never asked me. She didn't have to – the truth was written all over both of our faces. She would stay. As long as was necessary. She wouldn't run away.

"Some things you can't run away from," she told me, and years later, she would teach me that lesson in the worst possible way.

"Some things you have to run away from, or you'll never get away," I said, suddenly thinking not only of Venezuela, but of how I once ended up across the Atlantic, involved with an evangelical organization as part of my ill-conceived and desperate escape from that particular Arcadia that I had grown up in.

"So did you call the police?" Cheryl asked.

"No," I said, feeling the old familiar shame. "No, I didn't."

I had been seeing a boy, nothing terribly serious, at least not on my part, but he was very intense. He spoke of how I was his destiny, and how we were two souls entwined. He wrote me gloriously romantic poetry, and told me he loved me at least twenty times a day, until I finally felt compelled to say it back, even though what I really felt was smothered and unworthy and insignificant. The girl he described in his poetry and love letters didn't exist – or if she did, she certainly wasn't me. He was trying to create an ideal of me that I couldn't possibly live up to, and as the days went by I began to feel those poems and letters closing in around me like a cage – like I was a pretty bird for him to keep and admire. The problem with being a bird in a cage is that they tend to clip your wings, and a bird that cannot fly is no bird at all (with apologies, of course, to the noble penguin).

So I resolved that I had to distance myself from him. I stopped returning his phone calls, because I'm a coward and didn't think that I needed to spell out with some manifesto or missive that I no longer enjoyed his attention. Unfortunately, the egos of young men often outrank their reasoning ability, and my cold shoulder somehow irreparably injured him. Or, as his poem said: *I cry out your name in the dark and the echoes whisper nothing but cold laughter in return.*

I don't know why he'd been crying out my name in the dark, darlings. We'd never slept together.

I agreed to come to his apartment to talk to him. I suppose I should have thought better and asked to meet at a cafe or something, but I wasn't afraid of him – not at that point. So I went to his apartment and sat with him, and told him that I couldn't really say exactly what it was, but that I didn't feel the same about him as he obviously did me. I didn't want to break the poor boy's heart, but neither could I continue down any sort of path with him by my side.

At first, he seemed to be accepting of what I had to say. Then he just kept telling me how much he loved me, and got all teary-eyed, and of course, I can't stand to see people cry, because it makes me cry, and I couldn't let him see me cry – it would give him the wrong idea. So I went on the defensive, and told me that he didn't love me, that he didn't even know me, which was true. He'd only known me maybe three months, and everything he said about me clearly demonstrated that he wasn't in love with me, but rather in love with being in love. I recognized that tune – I'd sung it myself, and as they say, it takes one to know one.

This didn't go over very well with him, and in the span of a heartbeat, his grief turned to anger, and his anger quickly escalated to rage. I'd grown up with rage, and knew what came next. I stood up and made to leave, and he begged me to stay, pleading that he was sorry that he yelled, that he was just so upset, and that he loved me too much to let me go without a fight.

He said pretty much everything I needed to hear to start me running in the opposite direction, and so that's what I tried to do. I didn't expect him to put me in a headlock, drag me back into the apartment, and throw me on the floor. The animal look of possessive aggression on his face was so horrible. I was a child again, terrified of a father who controlled by fear and coerced with violence. I curled up against his couch and prepared for the blows I was sure I'd receive. I peered through my fingers to see him standing over me, huffing and puffing like the Big Bad Wolf, fists clenched, teeth bared, face flushed red, eyes bulging. I could feel that moment of hesitation, where he was fighting with himself, and I knew from experience that sometimes that moment is all you have – you either run right then or else you're going to get hit.

So I rolled toward him, right into his feet as hard as I could, knocking him over and sending him sprawling over his couch into the wall. I heard him scream, whether in pain or anger I didn't care, but I was up and out of there, running down the stairs of his apartment, down ten flights to the lobby, and out the door, limping and crying in anger and fear.

I didn't go home. He knew where I lived, of course, and that would be the first place he went. Instead, I went to my school. Exams had just finished, and the halls were nearly empty. I wandered around aimlessly, just cooling off and wondering what I was going to do about it. I bumped into a friend – well, a friend of a friend. Actually, the wife of an old friend, who I had pretty much been forced to accept as a friend if I was to remain his, but that's a story for another time, darlings. Anna was cool enough. She was a painter, which was something I was hopeless at, and so I approached her with equal parts envy and admiration, as I do most artistic types.

We started talking about each other's summers, and did we have any plans. I said I needed to get away, and Anna looked at me with a strange look.

"What do you mean, you *need* to get away? Is something wrong?"

I smiled and told her of course not. I told her that I was just bored, and needed a change of scenery. I don't know why I said what I said next, but it ended up being the best thing I could have said.

"I'm thinking of running away to China and teaching English or something."

I hadn't even remembered that Anna was studying Linguistics.

"Oh, that sounds like a great idea," she said. "But most overseas schools want a year or more commitment, you know."

I was young and didn't care at that point. Admittedly, I wasn't likely thinking things through.

"But," she said, "sometimes there are job postings in the Linguistics department. Check the board there, you never know."

You never know. The three most hopeful words in the English language. Followed closely by: Anything can happen, and Two tequilas, please.

It turns out that one of the alumni of my school had married a girl from Venezuela, and the two of them moved back down there and had started language school. And they were hiring. *And yes, of course we'd love to have you come down for the summer.*

Within twenty-four hours, I'd found two friends to sub-let my apartment for the summer, and within forty-eight hours, without even a moment's hesitation, I was on a plane to Caracas, an entire continent away from my most recent problem.

"Have you heard from him since you've been back?" Cheryl asked, concerned.

"Nah," I said. "I'm sure he's madly in love with somebody else by now. Poor girl."

Cheryl sighed. "You can't keep running, Helena."

"I don't mean to," I admitted. "But after that first time..."

I turned away, and called Penny over. She came running over and gave me a great big squeeze, and then tried to get me to come and dance with her.

"Why won't you talk to me about it?" she asked, and I shrugged. I'd never told Cheryl much about my time in England, and certainly not how I'd swallowed a bunch of pills and ended up in the hospital. All that had happened at a time when Cheryl and I weren't talking. She'd gone and gotten married, leaving me alone with our parents. Together, Cheryl and I looked after each other, and with her gone – well, my mother wasn't any use against my father.

"You got out the easy way," I told her. "Ted's nothing like dad. He rescued you, Cheryl. Nobody was coming to rescue me. I mean, look at me. I'm the weird sister – the one people secretly think is a lesbian, the one people laugh about behind her back."

"I'm sorry, Helena," she said. "But I wasn't going to be around forever. Besides, does it look like I escaped? They followed me here! You're the one who broke free."

I thought about the day that I broke free. The story I'd never told her. I had just turned seventeen a couple of months before, and I had discovered love, and routinely fell headfirst in it at least once a week. I tried on different boys like clothes, and I don't mean sexually, I just mean that I didn't know myself, or what I liked. I became a chameleon, becoming a Goth chick one week and a hippie throwback the next, depending on what boy I was chasing.

I have always been impulsive, but at seventeen I was completely unrestrained in my whimsical recklessness, and so one day, to impress a shaven-headed boy in tight black jeans, leather jacket and a Siouxsie & The Banshees shirt, I shaved the sides of my head and dyed the remaining hair black and Manic Panic Shocking Blue. I'd done this in the sink in the art room, convincing the hip young art teacher that it was for a performance art piece, and that of course it was only temporary dye.

That impulse would actually change the course of my life, though for better or worse, I still can't say. The jury's still out. I'm beginning to realize that I have never fully recovered from some old wounds, and that the scars I wear may be invisible to everyone else but when I look in the mirror I relive the pain of each cut.

Other scars are visible. I have a little scar at my hairline. Not much, really, but I'll never forget the day I got it.

"I came home one day with my hair dyed black and blue," I said, and she stifled a laugh. "I ended up with the rest of me matching."

"Oh, very nice, Helena. I'm not laughing at you, I'm just laughing at the thought of you with blue hair. Well, that, and your knack for narrative."

"What?" I said, laughing back at her. "What are you talking about? I'm trying to be serious here."

"I'm sorry," she said. "Please. Continue."

She didn't really want to talk about it. Not because she didn't care, but because it was traumatic and because it would make her angry and upset, and she had to see him on a regular basis.

And so I spared her.

"You know what he was like," I conceded, and changed the subject to Ted's work, to Penny, to anything other than what had happened that day – the last straw that caused me to flee all the way to England.

I continued carrying that burden, which is what I do. Cheryl would have helped me carry it, I know that, but I also don't regret not sharing it with her. Why shouldn't she at least have a chance at being happy, without having to be burdened with my ghosts? She had enough of her own, I knew.

So I didn't tell her how apoplectic with rage our father was when he saw me come home from school that day. I didn't tell her how he grabbed me by the hair, lifted me up, and threw me up against the wall, splitting my head open. I didn't tell her how he called me a slut and a whore, and pulled out the scissors and threatened to cut the rest of my hair off. I didn't tell her how our father had said that I looked like a concentration camp victim, and asked me how many boys I'd let fuck me this week. I didn't tell her about my trip to the Emergency Room, and how I'd lied and told the doctor that I'd taken a spill on my skateboard – which was a laugh, because I'd never ridden a skateboard, though if I ever did, I'd surely end up breaking my neck.

I didn't tell her how I lost all hope that day that I was ever going to escape, and I didn't tell her how I nearly drove our father to murder. When he pulled out the scissors and started screaming at me to get my skinny ass over there so he could chop off my slutty hair, something snapped in me. I had gotten to an age where I realized that part of it – a great deal of his bravado – was just bark and bluff. He just wanted to puff himself up and frighten and terrify and bully, but when pressed, would he follow through, or would he back down? I didn't know, and I didn't care.

I stood up from the hallway where he had thrown me, and I stared him right in his crazy eyes, and I screamed for him to do it. He held the scissors out like a blade, and I stared him down, moving toward him a step at a time and wailing like a Banshee. *Do it!* I screamed. *Just fucking do it already, and stop threatening! Cut my hair, cut my throat, it makes no difference to me!* My mother was screaming and crying, and he seemed to be wavering in his anger and conviction.

I was made of steel that day. He was never going to touch me again after that day. I howled in anger at him – just vowel sounds, nothing intelligible – and ran up to my room and packed a bag. There was a boy at school – Andrew – that I was currently very much in love with, but alas, he was returning with his father back to England, where he ran some church group thing.

I left the house that day, and when I came back three days later, I gave the kind of performance usually reserved for movies where someone is dying of cancer and there's the name of some flower in the title. I told my father that I had found Jesus, and that I begged his forgiveness for being a sinful daughter. I told him that I'd been called to the mission-field, and that I was going to go to England to work with street urchins and prostitutes. (See, in my head, England was eternally Victorian London, and everyone called men gov'ner and ladies mum, and impoverished children sold newspapers or worked as chimney sweeps, or else they went to the workhouses).

He wrapped his arms around me and kissed my forehead, and, though I trembled with anger, I allowed it, because in my mind, I had decided that was the last time he was ever going to touch me.

A month later, I was on a plane to London, where I was delighted to learn that things had considerably improved since Victorian times.

Six months later, I received a letter saying that my parents had moved to Arcadia to be closer to Cheryl, who, they said, was pregnant.

A few scant hours after receiving that letter, I swallowed a bottle of pills and ended up in the hospital.

I wonder now glibly if things might have been different if I'd chosen a different colour hair dye.

Leaving Arcadia Part Two

Brooke didn't belong in Arcadia.

I wanted to steal her away, take her to New York, to Toronto, to Montreal. I wanted to hitchhike across the country with her, show her that there was more to the world than chicken wings, beer and football.

Of course, it didn't hurt that when I first met her, all I'd wanted to do was run away myself. Arcadia was never my home, and yet that's where they sent me when I left England, because that's where my parents were. Never mind that I was technically an adult, I guess they figured that after my actions, I shouldn't be on my own. They were probably right, but at the same time, sending me to Arcadia was like sending me to the Overlook Hotel for the winter with only Jack Torrance for company.[81]

All work and no play make Helena a dull girl...

At that point I didn't have my US citizenship, so I couldn't work, I couldn't go to school, and at 18, I was too young to drink – legally, anyway – and so my options were few. The town did have a library, which is where I met Brooke.

Cheryl and Ted had their hands full. My parents had moved down to be closer to them, but had yet to get a place of their own, and so they were living in the spare bedroom. Having us all under the same roof was like putting a bunch of ex-POWs together and watching a marathon of Vietnam movies. I was constantly on edge, biting my lip at the selfishness of my parents, who didn't seem to

---

[81] Jack Torrance and his family are characters from Stephen King's *The Shining*. A story about a haunted hotel and the ultimate case of cabin fever.

understand the imposition that they were being. My father would walk into a room where we were watching something on TV and just sit down, grab the remote, and start flipping around to something he wanted to watch. My mother would be running around like his personal handmaiden, fetching him tea, or snacks, or whatever his royal highness demanded. I tried appealing to my mother to stop waiting on him and tell him to get off his ass and get his own shit, but she reacted pretty much as I expected – with incredulous disbelief at the mere suggestion. You'd think that I'd asked her to slit his throat in his sleep.

Once I met Brooke, I practically lived at the library. I couldn't stand to be in the same room as my father, and I think he felt the same. Brooke was three years older than me, and already married at twenty-one to her high school sweetheart. It was a small town cliché that I tried my best to ignore, though I often asked her if she hadn't wanted to get out, see the world, and have some adventures of her own before settling down into married life. Her husband wasn't exactly the "let's hop in a car and drive until we run out of gas, and then see where it takes us" type of guy.

The truth is, I didn't know what he was like – not firsthand anyway. She talked about him in terms of him being a great guy, a solid guy, a good husband, but she never spoke about him the way she talked about Margaret Atwood, or her love for 1970s cinema, or The Pixies. I could talk to her for hours, and learned what kind of cake she had at her wedding (chocolate with orange cream), what her favourite subject was in school (English Lit), and what her guilty musical pleasure was (Michael Jackson), but not a thing about her husband other than where he worked, and that they'd known each other since they were kids, and that everyone pretty much knew that they'd end up together.

If she'd seemed happy, it might be considered terribly romantic, but she didn't. At twenty-one, she already seemed so much older, and constantly had that "deer in the headlights" look about her, as if she were in a state of permanent flinching. I slowly began to have my suspicions about her every time I left the library and went back to Cheryl's. I saw the same look on my mother's face – teeth clenched, tension lines around her eyes, unable to relax.

I was trapped in Arcadia for three months that time, and much as Cheryl wanted me to stay, get my citizenship taken care of, and be close to her and Ted and Penny, I just couldn't. I had escaped my parents once, and planned on staying as far away from them as I could. And so, shortly after my nineteenth birthday, I found myself living on my own in Toronto.

The next time I visited, things had taken a turn for the surreal. My father and mother had finally moved out, and had started going to a church in town, and not just going, but getting involved. They were actually living in the parsonage – a house that the church owned and usually let the pastor live in, but since their pastor had a house of his own, they were letting my parents live there. Cheryl had warned me on the phone that Dad had re-discovered Jesus after what he called "his time in the wilderness" and was all about forgiveness and repentance, but she couldn't have prepared me for the greeting I got when I arrived at Cheryl and Ted's that day.

My father wrapped his arms around me and immediately started blubbering, telling me how sorry he was, and asking me to forgive him. He gave me the same old spiel about how we often hurt those closest to us because we know that they understand, and will forgive us. He spoke about how he was a terrible father, and referred to things long past, as if speaking about another person that wasn't him.

My mother added her commentary, saying that "Jesus has forgiven your father, Helena, and so should you."

I'd been there five minutes, and already I wanted to get back on the train and go home. Penny, not quite two, rescued me by clinging to my leg and demanding to be picked up.

I took her out back and stifled a scream by blowing into my little niece's belly, eliciting a peal of pleasure, followed by a gaggle of giggles that served to soften my mood. Penny's always been able to make me feel better, right from the very start. Cheryl joined me on the back porch and put her arm around me.

"Who needs a drink?" I asked, raising my free hand. Little Penny rose her own, mimicking mine, and I laughed and poked her nose.

"Okay, little dumpling – what's your poison?"

She grabbed my finger and stuck it in her mouth, biting down hard enough to hurt.

"Ouch!" I cried, still laughing. "Ouch! Ouch! Ouch! You little monster!"

"Onster!" Penny repeated, and then growled ferociously.

"Ted should be home in another hour," Cheryl offered. "You want me to see if he'll watch Penny and we can go out?"

"Sounds good," I said, "we'll go hit up all the good clubs, maybe catch a band. Is anyone good playing tonight?"

Cheryl looked at me sourly. "Could you not? Please?"

"What?" I said, feigning innocence. Arcadia had no clubs, good or otherwise, and the only band that was playing there would occasionally be the high school marching band for some parade or other. The biggest entertainment in or around Arcadia was probably the high school football games, which held no interest for me.

"It's hard enough being the country mouse to your city mouse without you rubbing it in," Cheryl sighed.

"Well, what is there to do?"

"We have a tavern," she suggested. "They even have pool tables and a jukebox, Helena."

I made my eyes go wide with manufactured amazement.

"Oh my stars and garters! A jukebox! Why didn't you say so? That's a horse of a different colour!"

When Ted got home, I suggested we pick up Brooke from the library – when I'd left I'd promised to keep in touch, and of course I hadn't, so I wanted to surprise her by just showing up.

Sitting outside the library leaning on a bike, smoking a cigarette and reading a Shirley Jackson novel – if I remember correctly, and I always do, darlings, it was *We Have Always Lived in the Castle* [82] – was an Arcadian anomaly. A girl – maybe seventeen or eighteen – wearing short khaki shorts and ripped black stockings, ending in a pair of Doc Martens. The stockings didn't cover up the bruises she wore all up and down her legs, and I felt an instinctive anger fill my head like buzzing bees. Her head was shaved, all except for her bangs, which she'd dyed black. She caught me staring and looked up at me with angry eyes made even angrier by heavy black eyeliner.

"Hi," I said, embarrassed at being caught. "Good book?"

Exhaling smoke, she nodded, and barely audible, she said, "Educational."

---

[82] An amazingly creepy tale about two young women, one of whom poisoned their entire family, but who are acquitted of the crime and continue to live in the same house, and become something of a legend among the townspeople.

Later, I'd have cause to think about that and shiver, but at the time, I just nodded back at her and entered the library without another thought on the matter.

"You know that girl?" I asked Cheryl after we got inside. She shook her head. "Did you see her legs? Someone's hurting that girl, Cheryl. Someone's..."

"I know," she said. "I've seen her around, and she's always covered in fresh bruises. She seems to wear them like a badge of honour or something. She's always getting into fights, getting kicked out of places for mouthing off."

"But you don't know her? Don't know her family?"

Arcadia was a small town, but Cheryl and Ted were relatively new to the community.

"I know her to see her, but I don't even know her name."

Less than a year later, everyone would know Amy LeFevre's name. Her name would be plastered across newspapers, her picture up on posters, with words like *Wanted in connection* and *Police investigation* and most alarmingly, *Murder suspect* attached to them.

But just then, she was just a girl who looked tough and out of place in what was otherwise a slice of day old Rockwellian Americana, and as much as I wanted to do something for her, there wasn't likely much I could have done.

Brooke was happy to see us – I got the feeling that she hadn't seen much of Cheryl, either – which struck me as odd, as they should have been fast friends.

I was in for more surprises when I gave Brooke a hug and she winced, telling me that she'd hurt her stomach falling on one of her bedposts. I tried to make some joke about it being a sexy thing – a bedroom injury – but her fake laugh was unconvincing. The flash of panic in her eyes when we invited her out with us was more authentic.

"Oh, I couldn't," she insisted, shaking her head and smiling. "David's expecting me home, I have to make dinner."

"So he orders a pizza tonight," I laughed. "He's a big boy, Brooke, I'm sure he'll be okay."

"I don't know," Brooke hesitated.

"Look, I'm only in town for a few days, and other than my sister, you're the only good company here over the age of two. And besides

— I'm almost legal — don't you want to take me down to the local watering hole and help me get my drink on?"

"Like you didn't do that before when you weren't almost legal," Cheryl chimed in.

"Yes, but now I'm *almost* legal," I said with a grin. I wasn't quite twenty-one yet myself, but it was close enough by Arcadian standards.

"Okay," Brooke said, and gave a laugh that lit up her face. "Okay I'll go with you. But just for a little while. And I'll have to drop by my house and leave David a note."

I rolled my eyes. I didn't want to believe what was going through my mind.

I didn't know her well enough to make those kinds of leaps or deductions. I lied to myself, saying that I'd just seen a girl with bruises all up and down her legs and was seeing monsters everywhere; jumping at shadows.

But then the next day, when I dropped by to visit her at the library, Brooke wasn't there. The lady covering for her was very sweet.

"Oh, that poor girl," she said. "She's just so clumsy. She said her stomach was still bothering her, and that she might head over to the hospital to make sure she didn't crack a rib or something."

I didn't see her after that.

I tried calling, but just kept getting the machine. I dropped by the library a couple more times, but she wasn't in. On the day I was set to leave I went by her place to say goodbye, but no one answered the door.

It would be nearly three years before I heard the story of what happened to Brooke that night after we'd left the bar.

Leaving Arcadia Part Three

When Cheryl called me and asked me to come down to Arcadia, we'd talked a bit about Brooke. I'd suggested that we try to get her to come out with us, maybe drive to New York, get away for a couple of days, and she'd said that she didn't think that Brooke would be allowed to go. I thought that was a strange choice of words, but then, it also made a sort of perfect sense at the same time. Brooke had married a man like our father, and he kept her on a very short leash.

I didn't see her at all during that visit. I was there for Cheryl, and we needed that time together. Living with my parents constantly looming over her was driving her crazy, and causing all kinds of problems between Ted and her. They had no boundaries, and would come over unannounced, even letting themselves in when no one was home. Our father would make plans in his little black book and just include Cheryl and Ted in them, expecting them to re-arrange their schedule around his, which was suddenly very busy, as he was now training to become a minister. He'd seen the light, and was being called to preach God's message of love to the broken sinners of Arcadia. He still treated my mother like his dog, and maybe he stopped kicking her, but there are more ways to hurt a person than physically, and more ways to hurt a dog than with your foot. By that point, he didn't need to hit my mother – or any of us, really – in order to impose his will upon us. We were so conditioned that all he had to do was growl and we would jump. I hated myself – and him – every time I found myself responding in fear at the tug of his leash.

I couldn't put enough space between us, so understand how desperate I was when I tell you that when Penny was about five years old – just starting school – I went to go live with Cheryl and Ted for almost a year. A year of forced recovery. Moving in with Cheryl was cheaper than rehab, though not less costly.

I'd had my heart broken, darlings. That's the short version.

The long version is just too sad and pathetic, and you don't want to hear it. It involves engagement, wedding plans, miscarriages, lies, infidelity, and a complete mental breakdown.

I lost my mind, I lost two children, I lost my job, I lost my friends, I lost about 20 lbs., along with my self-respect and dignity.

I discovered marijuana and decided I really liked its ability to amputate my emotions.

I flirted with alcoholism, and ended up in bed with it on numerous occasions.

I also ended up in bed with numerous strangers, whose names I don't remember to this day.

I alienated anyone who had any goodwill toward me, spitting in the faces of more than one person who tried to pull me out of the downward spiral that I was spinning into.

I felt shipwrecked.

I didn't trust myself not to complete the job of self-destruction that I seemed to be working on, so I checked myself into the hospital. When I told the shrink that I was having trouble sleeping, and that all I really wanted to do was fall asleep and never wake up again, he gave me a bottle of sleeping pills.

Let's hear it for the health care profession, darlings.

When I got out of the hospital, I went to the very last friend I had, and handed her the bottle of pills, asking her to hold on to them for me, and that if I asked, to only give me one or two at a time. Then I called Cheryl, and cried for about forty-five minutes straight. Cheryl told me she'd come and get me – that very day if I wanted.

I'd been living in a tiny little rattrap bachelor apartment, and the only furniture I owned was a beat-up futon and some folding TV tables that served as both dining table and computer desk. The only possessions I cared about – the things that I dragged with me wherever I went – were a box of my favourite books, a box of CDs, and two milk crates full of records. Sometimes I look back longingly at the days when I could fit everything I owned and cared about into the back seat of a car. There was definitely something romantic about being able to pick up and go at a moment's notice – a life uncomplicated by car payments and credit card bills; by lawn care and home maintenance.

I don't begrudge those that figure out their niche in the world early in life, but it was just never for me, darlings. For many years, if you wanted me to stay in one place, you'd have to nail my feet to the floor. But at that point in my life, I'd run too fast, too recklessly, and when I hit the wall, I hit it hard.

My parents, of course, treated me like the Prodigal Daughter returning from her dalliance with a world of sin. They made a big show of welcoming me with open arms of forgiveness, which I didn't want, didn't need, and resented furiously. They insisted that I come to their church; that I needed healing. My father actually invited me to sing in one of their services. And as much as I would love to tell you that I told him to fuck off; that I yelled at him and screamed all the hurtful things that were constantly boiling in my gut, I cannot. I'd really like nothing more than to be able to tell you that I got up in front of his congregation and exposed him for the hypocritical asshole that he is; that I caused a scene and ruined his reputation. Sometimes, in my darkest moments, I admit that I'd like to be able to tell you I was somehow able to shame him so badly that he took his own life, and if that makes me a monster, then RAAAAAWWR! I'd prefer not to tell you that just being around my father again on a regular basis caused me to regress into a passive, frightened child, even though I was twenty-three years old, and had escaped his influence, or so I thought. I'd desperately like to tell you that I didn't let him control me, but the sad truth is, I did.

I can't say for sure that I will ever escape his influence, and so I try now to keep my distance. But during that year living with Ted and Cheryl, I returned to the nightmare of my childhood, with a strange religious twist. I complied with his requests, and smiled and played nice with his church folks, and even got up and sang. I allowed myself tiny little acts of contemptuous rebellion, choosing obscure songs by Peter Gabriel, U2 or Bob Dylan that could be construed as gospel songs, and watched the churchy Joes and Janes who would likely burn me in effigy if they knew that I was singing (*gasp!*) secular music get their religious freak on, faces orgasmic with holy rapture, hands raised in hallelujahs.

I'd been in Arcadia for three whole months before I ran into Brooke. Cheryl insisted that if I was going to be staying for a while, that I should get my driver's license. So she drove me over to the DMV to fill out the forms and transfer over my Canadian license. Brooke was there renewing her own license, and gave us a lukewarm hello.

I begged her to have coffee with us – it had been forever since we'd spoken, and I really wanted to see someone other than my family or the church people. I desperately needed a friend, and as it was the morning, and her husband was at work, she conceded to have coffee with us.

Never having been one to mince words or shy away from uncomfortable topics, I asked her right away why I hadn't heard from her in nearly three years, and then, in fact, pinpointed the very last day that we'd spoken.

"The night the three of us went out to the bar," I said, and couldn't help but notice her flinch at the recollection. "The next day, I went by your work, and they said you'd taken a fall or something. I tried calling you, I dropped by your house – what happened?"

She sipped her coffee and I could see that her hands were trembling. She looked up and forced a smile.

"I'm sorry," she said to Cheryl. "I know that you tried to talk to me, but I just couldn't."

Bravely, she fought tears, hands and jaw clenched.

Cheryl reached out a hand and put it over hers. Her immediate reaction was to pull away, but then relaxed and let Cheryl touch her.

"It's okay," Cheryl said. "You don't owe me anything."

"David and I," she started, and then looked around the little diner whose claim to fame was that it was the home of *The Best Darn Club Sandwich You'll Ever Have.* Not seeing anyone in earshot, she continued. "David and I were going through a rough spell, that's all. And I just didn't want to see anybody. Things are better now."

"Better than what?" I asked her, trying to get to the truth of the matter.

"Well, he has a temper," she admitted.

I remembered her wincing when I gave her a hug. I didn't see the point of dancing around the subject.

"Did he hit you?" I asked, and then rephrased the question. "*Does* he hit you?"

She nodded slowly, and then, seeing the fire in my eyes, waved her hands and began to make excuses and apologies, all of which I'd heard before and some of which I'd made myself.

"He doesn't mean to," she said, "it's just that's got a hair-trigger of a temper, and sometimes his hand just moves faster than his mind. And he's awfully sorry about it – he just hates himself because of it."

"What happened to you that night?" I asked, afraid to know the answer, but needing to. "The night you went out with us."

She stared at me with wet eyes and went pale and bloodless.

"It was an accident, Helena," she said in a low voice. "I swear it was an accident. He only meant to hit me, and I lost my balance. I shouldn't have been sneaking up the stairs. I should have just come in and slept on the downstairs couch. If I hadn't have been sneaking up the stairs, he wouldn't have woken up, and he wouldn't have gotten angry. It was just an accident. I was stupid. I should have known better than to make him angry."

I wanted to call her an idiot. I was so angry, and that anger was, at first, displaced. Then my compassion kicked in, and my anger found its proper place.

"You need to get out of there, Brooke," I said firmly. "You can't let him break you down like that."

"What?" Brooke said, taken back. "No, no, everything's okay now. David's working through things. He's changing – he hardly even loses his temper anymore, and he hasn't hit me in a long time. I love him, and I have to believe that he can change."

I wanted to tell her that sometimes it wasn't about whether he was hitting her or not. I wanted to tell her how it's about control, and dehumanization, and co-dependence. I wanted to ask her how many friends she had, and if she saw any of them – or if he kept her all to himself, like a bird in a cage.

I wanted to talk to her about Amy LeFevre, and ask her if she'd seen her around town, covered in bruises, full of the rage and vitriol that are the telltale signs of abuse. Part of me wanted to help her plot her husband's murder, removing her tormentor just as Amy LeFevre had done away with hers. At the very least, I wanted to drive her to a courthouse right there and then and file the papers for divorce.

But I knew that she wouldn't listen; wouldn't hear what I was saying. And so I just kept trying to build our friendship, with the hope that I could make baby steps toward trying to open her eyes. Or

– and this was a fairy tale I desperately *wanted* to believe but could not bring myself to be so naïve – the hope that I was wrong, and that David could change, and that if Brooke was willing to forgive him, that they could be happy.

Of course, I was wrong about that.

Leaving Arcadia Part Four

*I*t's come to my attention, darlings, that I haven't told you much about Ted, my late brother-in-law. The truth is, he was a hard person to get to know – he didn't say much. His quiet demeanor, coupled with his size, his tattoos, and his motorcycle, made him kind of intimidating. When I first met him, I was terrified that Cheryl had fallen in with a man like our father, but later discovered that nothing could be further from the truth.

I never heard him raise his voice to Cheryl, and the only thing they ever argued about was our parents, who hated him – which won him points in my book, of course. They looked at him and saw a mindless thug, when in reality, Ted may have been the smartest guy I ever met. He was a mechanical engineer by trade, and could fix any machine known to man, but he was no gear-head or grease monkey, despite what my father thought. He read, and thought about what he read. I've learned more about Ted since he died than I did while he was alive, and the weight of that regret is an almost physical pain, especially when I open up one of his books and see notes in the margins. A battered and well-loved copy of Cormac McCarthy's *All the Pretty Horses* sits on my bookshelf next to a picture of Cheryl and Ted. I caught him crying once while reading it, and he gave it to me when he was finished with it.

He was fiercely protective of my sister and Penny, the future Countess of Arcadia. I'd like to think that he liked me – and though I'm sure he thought I was a screw-up, he tolerated me, and never turned me away when I'd show up on his doorstep. I carried around a lot of guilt – my psychology's fucked up like that – for what happened in Arcadia. But then, that's victim mentality – it must have been my fault. Ted never blamed me, or at least, he never said so. Cheryl was sort of relieved, I think, when the smoke cleared and the dust settled. It was sort of the beginning of the end of their time in Arcadia.

Cheryl didn't like to talk about our childhood, and while I couldn't say what she did or didn't tell Ted about our father, I got the feeling that a lot of that stayed between us girls. Had she told him some of the things our father did, I think Ted might have killed him. As it was, my father was busy building a reputation as a miracle, standing up in church and crying, lamenting what he referred to as a life of vice and sin, calling himself a horrible broken man, saved by grace to do the Lord's work. The people of Arcadia didn't know him like I did, and while he alluded to his horrible temper, saying that he was plagued by demons of anger and rage, he never gave specifics; never told his fellow churchgoers the things that he did to his family. If he had – if he'd told the stories that I could tell – they'd arrest him, not treat him like some miracle or saint.

But people love a good tearjerker, darlings, and so they called his public emotional outbursts "brave" and "courageous". They saw them as a sign of contrition rather than shame – and it was shame, I'm sure of it. He should have been ashamed, but instead of hating him for it, they loved him, and they rewarded him with compassion, friendship, and support. He blamed his actions on demonic oppression, and the prevalence of sin in a fallen world. It was a nice way for him to avoid taking responsibility for his shitty behaviour.

And then he wrote a book.

A quasi-confessional autobiography, pretty much regurgitating all of the same tripe he was spewing as he went from church to church giving his testimony of redemption. Again, all vague, no details, no real sense of acknowledging the irreversible and long lasting damage he'd done. In fact, in his book, he blamed drinking as another of the demons that were really responsible for his actions, though to be honest, I would have never said that my father had a drinking problem, and I certainly never remember smelling it on him.

And everywhere he went, they loved him for it. They saw his public persona – a man grieving for a wasted life, trying to make up for lost time by serving God. They didn't hear him griping about how the people in his church (*his* church, as if it belonged to him) were all blind fools, and that he had a vision for Arcadia, but how they were holding him back because they were afraid. He liked to quote *Butch Cassidy and the Sundance Kid* as if it were the words of a prophet: "I've got vision and the rest of the world wears bi-focals."

They didn't hear him screaming at my mother; didn't see the mad look in his eyes, as if it were taking everything in him not to hit her. When he volunteered to make a trip to some mission in Texas, they saw it as selfless charity – they didn't know of his life-long love of Louis L'Amour and Zane Grey novels, and how a trip to Texas would be like an Elvis Presley fan getting to tour Graceland.

It took me a while, but I gradually regained my senses and removed myself from his influence. He'd ask me to join him to sing at some church he was speaking at, telling me that it was really important to him that I was there, and at first I'd make some excuse, but after a couple of times, I simply just told him that I wasn't interested. I think it was the line about how it was really important to him that did it.

Since I wasn't busy running at my father's beck and call, my time was substantially freed up, and I took it upon myself to try and spend more time with Brooke. At first, I'd take it however she felt comfortable – which usually meant during the day, while her husband was at work. We'd get together for coffee a couple of times a week, and sometimes I'd just drop by the library and loiter, chatting with her all morning until it was time for me to pick up Penny from school. Cheryl was going to school herself, taking college courses to become a nurse, and so I was the full-time live-in nanny for Penny Arcade, who, at five, was a constant barrage of questions and observations. I hardly had time to answer one of her questions before she had three more for me, and often she'd end up answering them herself, which made me wonder why, if she knew the answer already, she asked the question in the first place.

But the minds of children elude me to this day, and so it shouldn't surprise you to know that I may have fucked with Penny just a little bit from time to time, which may explain quite a bit.

"Auntie Helena, why does the road have lines on it?"

"Oh, that's so spaceships overhead can see where to land."

"Auntie Helena, why does that lady have a white stripe in her hair."

"She was bitten by a skunk, silly. You know, like how Spiderman was bitten by a spider, and Batman was bitten by a bat? Well, that lady got bitten by a radioactive skunk, and now she has the proportional stench of a skunk."

"Auntie Helena, what's *radioactive* mean?"

"Oh, it means someone who listens to the radio a lot – see, it's a combination of the Greek *radiogoogooradiogaga* and the Latin.... uh... *activus*."

"Auntie Helena, why aren't you married?"

"I have no idea."

"You wanna marry me?"

"Only if you want to get an operation and move to Arkansas."

"Auntie Helena, you're so crazy!"

"You have no idea, kiddo."

Ted never yelled at Penny. He never struck Penny. I never once saw Penny cringe or shudder in fear. I never saw Penny pee herself upon hearing her father get home from work. In fact, when Penny heard her daddy's big noisy bike come rumbling into the driveway, she'd jump up from whatever I was doing with her and go running to the door, yelling *Daddy! Daddy! Daddy!*

Ted would pull off his helmet and shut off his bike as fast as he could, dismounting and holding his arms wide for his little girl. Penny would run and jump into his arms, squeezing his neck so hard he turned red, his laughter like music in my ears. How I envied Penny her sweet, gentle father, and not a dozen years later, when her Daddy was taken from her, how I wept for her.

"Cheryl's going to be home soon," I told him one afternoon when he put Penny down. "I've got dinner in the oven, but I've got to get going. Brooke and I are going to the city to see a show."

"The city?" Ted asked. "Are you taking the car? Not for nothing, Helena, but you know you haven't paid that speeding ticket yet. You don't want to lose your license."

He may or may not have said that last part, darlings, I don't quite remember – but wouldn't it just be perfect if he had? Let's just say he did, and chalk it up to me being an unreliable narrator. If he had said that, and I'd heeded his advice, I might have avoided all kinds of unpleasantness years later, when that speeding ticket came back to bite me in my decidedly delectable derriere.

"No, we're taking the train – we're going to *the* city – you know – start spreading the news, I'm leaving today, the Big Apple, the city so nice they named it twice."

Ted looked at me and clenched his jaw. He did that when he was trying to think of a delicate way to say something in front of Penny.

"You're not going to get Brooke in any trouble, now, are you?"

"Yeah, Auntie Helena," Penny mimicked. "You're not going to get Brooke in trouble. Daddy, who's Brooke and why's she in trouble?"

"Head inside, Penny Arcade," Ted said firmly.

"Not Penny Arcade," she said, scrunching up her face and furrowing her brow. "I'm Penny, dammit!"

Ted stifled a laugh.

"Don't let me hear you say that again, little girl," he said, sufficiently parental enough to be taken seriously by Penny, but I could see the corners of his mouth fighting to turn up in a grin.

"Yes, Daddy," Penny frowned, but headed inside as she was asked.

Ted looked at me, and like I said, he was a hard guy to know. I usually have a good feel for people, but I never had any idea what Ted was thinking. He furrowed his own brow, and I could see Penny's little face all grown up into his.

"What's going on with you and Brooke?"

I laughed. "God, why does everyone think I'm a lesbian?"

He didn't find it funny.

"Sorry," I said. "Nothing's going on. There's a concert in New York that we both want to go see, and her husband won't take her, so I'm taking her."

Ted nodded. "Does he know she's going?"

Cheryl had told Ted some of what was going on with Brooke. I guess I figured she would, but then, I wasn't privy to their most intimate conversations.

"I don't know *what* she's told him," I admitted, "but she's an adult, and besides, she says he's different; that he's changed."

"Like your father's changed?"

I nearly choked in sick laughter.

"So," I said, "the penny drops."

I'd never spoken to Ted about my father, but my disdain for him was pretty obvious, and it would seem that Cheryl had told him something of the matter.

"I just don't want to see anything bad happen to her," Ted said, and for some reason, I got really angry.

"Nobody worries about anything bad happening to him!" I snapped. "Why should she be afraid of him? She's a grown-ass adult and should be free to do as she pleases – which includes going to New York with me."

"And if he decides to... *punish* her?" Ted asked, and his face twisted in disgust at the word.

I considered it for a moment, and then said something ill-advised.

"Well, then maybe he'll just have to take a trip down some stairs, won't he?"

Ted grimaced. "Don't even say something like that. Not around here."

Of course, I knew exactly what I was saying. Amy LeFevre's father had been found at the foot of his basement stairs, or so the story goes.

"Maybe it's what she needs," I said, not believing the words coming out of my own mouth. Apparently, neither could Ted, because he shot me a confused look.

"That's not what I meant," I corrected. "I mean, maybe she needs to defy him. *Christ,* would you listen to how that sounds? *Defy* him? As if he is in a position of power or authority over her? As if he owns her? What I mean is that she needs to act like an adult, and an adult is free to come and go as they please, and if he does something, then maybe she'll see what a complete asshole he is and finally kick his ass to the curb."

Ted nodded. "Maybe. Or maybe he'll beat her so bad she wishes he killed her. And how are you going to feel, knowing you were the catalyst for that?"

"I'm not responsible for his actions," I insisted.

"No, just yours," Ted agreed. "And you know this isn't going to go well."

I sighed. "So what am I supposed to do, let her remain a prisoner?"

"If she's a prisoner, whether you like it or not, she's a willing prisoner. This isn't a prison break you're talking about – you want to sneak her out for a few hours, after which she has to return to the prison to face the music."

I hung my head. He was right, and I hated it. I hated Brooke's husband, my father, and all the men like them. I hated the women, too weak, frightened or stupid to get up and walk away. The women who think they can change a monstrous beast into a handsome prince.

"Okay," I said, disappointed, and hating the entire world for being the way it was, and my inability to change it. "I'll call her and make up some reason why I can't go."

"Why?" Ted asked.

"Because," I said, "I can't tell her the truth. I can't tell her that I'm afraid her husband's going to spank her for running away with naughty, wild, Helena."

But I didn't get a chance to call her, because at that moment, she pulled up and got out of her car, a huge excited smile on her face, all ready to head to the train station for our weekend adventure in the big city.

I didn't have it in me to crush that smile with the truth, and so I smiled back.

"C'mon! C'mon! Let's go!" she cried, giggling.

I gave Ted a parting glance, trying to convey what I was thinking without words.

I can't take this away from her.

I have to let her escape, if only for a day or two, consequences be damned.

I may need your help when we get back.

I'd like to think he understood.

Leaving Arcadia Part Five

I t was my first time in New York City, darlings, and Brooke's too, but I wasn't worried about the big, bad city.

Pussycat, pussycat, where have you been?

I've been to London to visit the queen.

London didn't faze me at seventeen, though I confess I probably wandered around with my mouth open and my eyes as big as banana and chocolate chip pancakes (scrumptious, darlings, you simply *must* try them) the whole time, especially in Piccadilly Circus. But Piccadilly Circus has nothing on Times Square, and the sheer amount of people in New York City is staggering. It was easy to see how you could get lost in the shuffle; just disappear into a sea of people, swept away by the current of shoppers and stockbrokers, tourists and professional grifters.

We arrived at Penn Station at nearly ten o'clock at night, and went straight to our hotel and straight to bed. We did not pass GO, and we did not collect $200. We were going to see The Flaming Lips at this great club called the Centro-fly the next night, and so we had all day to play in the city before the show. I called Cheryl and let her know we got in all right, and I expected that Brooke would call her husband to do the same. The fact that she didn't should have been my first clue that something was wrong.

We did all the touristy stuff we could fit into one day. We got bagels from a Jewish bakery and stood in front of Tiffany's on 5th Avenue and had our breakfast. We saw the Empire State Building, and posed with miniature versions of the Statue of Liberty outside of a souvenir shop. We bought hot dogs from a street vendor and had lunch in Central Park, both agreeing that even though it was only August, we could forever after sing *Danke Schoen* to each other with impunity.

I recall... Central Park in Fall...

We stood in Battery Park under the shadow of the World Trade Center, which would only stand there for another two years or so before it was gone forever. We posed along the railing in front of the harbour, with the real Statue of Liberty in the background. The pictures turned out horribly, but we had fun. Brooke was smiling and carefree, and it made me smile in return to see her so alive; so unrestrained.

At the concert, Brooke took a hit off of a joint that was being passed around, and then liked it so much she took another. By the time The Flaming Lips started in on *Waitin' for a Superman*, Brooke had a permanent silly grin on her face. She gave me a big hug, which was unusual for her – she wasn't real big on physical contact – and thanked me for bringing her. Then she said the second thing that made me realize that something was definitely wrong.

"Let's stay another day!" she shouted over the music. "They're playing again tomorrow night, we can stay another day, right? I wanna stay, Helena. I don't ever wanna go home."

I didn't answer her. She was a bit intoxicated, and what she felt in that moment she might not feel come morning. But in the morning, with our train tickets in hand, Brooke was pressing the issue again, even more insistently.

"Listen," I suggested, "why don't you call David and let him know you want to stay another day?"

She looked at her feet and mumbled, "Can't."

She was trembling, and I reached out and took her hand, and she let me hold it tightly.

"Does he know where you are?" I asked, already knowing the answer.

"No," she shook her head. "No, I didn't tell him. He would have said no. He wouldn't have let me go."

I thought to myself that this is the kind of conversation you have at twelve, when you sneak out to go to the movies with your friends, or at sixteen when you meet up with your friends to go to a party where there's going to be booze and smoking, and making out. This was not the kind of conversation you had in your twenties, where the *he* in question was your husband.

So of course, we got on the train and headed back to Arcadia. On the five-hour trip I tried to talk her into leaving David. I told her that she could make a new start, leave Arcadia behind and go wherever she wanted. She told me that I had no idea what I was talking about; that it wasn't as easy as I made it sound. She had a house, a mortgage, and car payments. She couldn't just walk away from all that. I thought it was the stupidest argument I'd ever heard for life in captivity, and I told her so. I even pitched the idea of us doing it together – that we could go anywhere she wanted to go together, and make a new start for both of us, just us girls. I didn't give a thought about the logistics of it; I was just being my sweet impulsive self.

We were both young and afraid, the difference was, I suppose, that I'd already broken free once. Not that my emancipation was exactly a stellar success. But I knew that it could be done, and I had to believe that Brooke could make it, too.

By the time we got back to Arcadia and got off the train, Brooke and I had cried ourselves dry. It was mid-afternoon, and it was sweltering. I told Brooke to go ahead to the car and get the A/C running, and that I was going to grab us a couple of Cokes and meet her at the car. When I arrived out in the parking lot, though, Brooke was wandering around with a confused look on her face.

"Where's the car?" I asked her.

"I don't know!"

"Are you sure this is where we parked?"

"Yes," she said, sighing. "Do you think someone stole it?"

I couldn't imagine what would happen to Brooke if her car were stolen. I remember one time when I was a kid my mother lost a twenty-dollar bill out of that famous green tin, and I thought my father was going to kill her.

"No, no," I lied. "I'm sure there's some explanation. But maybe we should call the police, huh?"

We went to a row of payphones, and I called Cheryl and asked if she'd be able to pick us up. She said she'd send Ted, and that I needed to have Brooke call her husband. Apparently the police had come by looking for her – David had reported the car stolen, and her missing. The police had obviously found the car, and now the only thing missing was Brooke.

"Brooke," I said, slamming the receiver down on my phone. "Brooke, hang up the phone."

"I'm on hold with the police," she said, and I shook my head.

"Just hang up the phone. I know where your car is."

We dropped Brooke off at her house. I asked her if she wanted me to come in and explain, and she said no, that it was going to be all right. Then Ted asked her if she wanted *him* to come in with her, and she gave him a smile and said she thought that might just make it worse.

"You give us a call if you need anything, Brooke," Ted offered, and watched her walk slow, steady steps to her door. It felt wrong, letting her go in there alone. Watching the door close behind her was like watching a car crash in slow motion, and being powerless to do anything about it.

The next day I went by Brooke's house around the same time we usually met for coffee – I figured that her husband would be gone to work, but I figured wrong.

David opened the door, standing in the opening with his hand up on the frame, forming a barrier.

"Oh, it's you," he said, standing up straighter, towering over me.

"Yes, it's me," I confessed. "Is Brooke here?"

"She's sleeping." He glared at me as if daring me to contradict him. "We were up late last night, and now she's not feeling well this morning."

"Uh huh," I said, "well, do you think she'll be going to work today? Maybe I'll just catch up with her then."

"No, I don't think she'll be in today. She's pretty sick. All that excitement, I think maybe she got a touch of sunstroke."

"Helena?" I heard Brooke's voice from inside the house. David wheeled his head around.

"Go on and get back in bed, honey."

"Helena, I'm okay..."

But she didn't sound okay. I placed my foot on the first step and moved toward him.

"Could I just see her for a moment? I just wanted to give her the ticket stub from the show."

"You can give it to me," he said with his hand out.

I took another step up, and tried to peer over his shoulder.

"Please, I'd just like to see her for a second," *just to make sure she's okay,* I almost added, but thought better of it.

"Helena, really, I'm fine," Brooke said from behind her husband.

"Okay," I said, locking eyes with David and handing him Brooke's ticket stub. "I'll see you later, then."

I turned as if to leave, and heard David murmur something that sounded suspiciously like *stupid cunt,* and I spun and threw myself into him as hard as I could.

Now, David had been a high school football player, and was probably about 250 lbs. of still pretty solid muscle, so when I hit him with my shoulder, I pretty much bounced right off of him. If it weren't for the element of surprise, my gambit would have been completely in vain. As it was, I was able to knock him off balance enough for me to catch a glimpse of Brooke, who was sitting at the bottom of the stairs with her head in her hands.

"You sonofabitch!" I screamed at him, and began beating his chest with my useless, flailing fists. Brooke's face was a map of bruises, with one eye swollen shut. Her lips looked like they'd been mashed against her teeth, and she had scratches and bruises on her neck, as if he'd been choking her. I fought as hard as I could to get past him, but he kept pushing me toward the door, and finally out. Foolishly, I tried once more to lunge at him, and was met by a backhand across my face.

"Get out of my house, you interfering bitch!" he roared. "And stay the hell away from me and my wife."

Leaving Arcadia Part Six

When I got home, I locked myself in the bathroom and iced my face. I cried until I couldn't breathe, not because I was in that much pain, or because I felt sorry for myself, but because I was so angry that I thought I could murder David. At the same time, I felt that same sense of being powerless that I always had as a child.

I called the police, only to learn that they'd been at David and Brooke's the night before. They wouldn't tell me anything of course, but since David was still free, I could only assume that Brooke hadn't pressed charges.

I was supposed to pick Penny up from school in less than an hour. I didn't want her to see me like that – my face was already turning purple. I looked at my face in the mirror and realized that no amount of powder or concealer was going to make me look normal. I love Penny like she is my own daughter, and I didn't want her to worry about me.

Then I remembered a really horrible shirt that Cheryl owned – a silk, multicoloured harlequin pattern that looked like it belonged on a jester in a production of King Lear. So I decided that I would become Pocket, the King's Fool. I'd rather Penny think me a little eccentric than worry about me being hurt.

I found some white greasepaint in a box marked Hallowe'en Supplies as well as a simple colour palette with a little paint left in the red and yellow. I painted my face white, laying it on thicker over the tender bruises across my cheek, and gave myself rosy red cheeks and lips drawn into a big friendly smile. Lacking a proper harlequin hat, I stapled three different coloured socks to a New York Mets ball cap, and borrowed a pair of Cheryl's green denim pants to complete the motley ensemble.

Penny thought it was hysterical. The other mothers and such picking up their kids looked at me like I was John Wayne Gacy,[83] and I was worried that I was going to have the cops called on me, but Penny's teacher saved me from indictment as a creepy kidnapper by asking me if I was doing children's birthday parties. I think she was trying to hire me, and so I went with it and told her to call me. Well, it was either that she wanted to hire me, or that she had a creepy clown fetish, and I had an evening of balloon handcuffs and seltzer water to look forward to.

As it was, I spent the afternoon giving Penny horsey-back rides, during which she called me her cow – I think the poor girl had her animals mixed up – and doing my best balloon animals, most of which just looked like DNA twists, which is all I could manage to figure out how to do.

Cheryl got home first, and looked at me in wonder.

"Are you and Auntie Helena playing circus?" she asked Penny.

"Uh huh," Penny nodded excitedly. "Helena's a clown. She does birthday parties."

"I see."

I smiled. "I'm a clown."

What was I going to say?

"Penny, dear, get off of your Aunt Helena's back and let her get cleaned up. Clown time is over, sweetie."

"MOMMY!" Penny yelled. "Clown time is not over!"

I may have started randomly singing an Elvis Costello tune about clown time being over, which really wasn't helping, so I stopped.

Cheryl looked at me, and then at her sternly, and asked her if she felt like spending the rest of the day in her room, to which Penny pouted and growled, and then stomped off to her room and slammed the door.

"She's such a sweet, demure child," I sighed.

"So?" Cheryl asked, referring to my get up.

"We were playing circus," I replied. "I'll go wash up."

"Just put my clothes in the wash, please."

---

[83] Chicago area serial killer who dressed up like a clown to lure his child victims.

"Um, actually, the real circus called and wanted to know if they could buy this shirt."

"Ha ha. That's real silk, I hope you didn't get any makeup on it."

"How would you tell?" I asked with a wink, and went to go get cleaned up. The make up was going to have to come off at some point, but until it did, I didn't have to say anything just yet.

Washing my face, I looked in the mirror at the effect the white paint made as it came off in wet smears. I appeared to be melting, and the lines from Hamlet came to mind as terribly appropriate.

Oh, that this too, too solid flesh might melt, thaw, and resolve itself into a dew...

I wanted to disappear. I didn't want to admit what had happened, not to Cheryl, not to Ted, not even to myself. I'd been hiding all my life from the violence done to me and to those close to me.

Ted got home and Cheryl called me to come downstairs for dinner – and did I want to order a pizza or maybe go out? When I came down the stairs, head held high, it became obvious that I didn't want to go out. Cheryl's eyes watered with tears, and she picked up Penny and took her out back to play, leaving me to face Ted, who put two and two together without me having to say a word. His face twisted into a ferocious mask of anger, and his hands clenched the back of a chair so tightly his knuckles were as white as pearls.

He didn't say anything, which I thought was strange. If Cheryl would have stayed, she would have been asking all kinds of questions, and getting upset and yelling about what kind of shithead would do this, but then, Cheryl was intimately familiar with what kind of shithead would hit a woman – or a child. Ted couldn't countenance the very concept. Without a word, he turned and grabbed his spare helmet and tossed it to me.

"Come on."

David didn't even have a chance to say hello before Ted grabbed him through the open door and pulled him across the threshold, tossing him like a bag of dirt down his own front steps and on to his yard. My brother-in-law had made me promise to stay by his bike, and as much as I wanted to, I restrained myself from going and kicking Brooke's asshole husband in the head.

Instead, I just watched, in admitted pleasure, as Ted kicked the living shit out of David in his own front yard. I lived vicariously through my him, remembering every fantasy beating I ever wanted to give my father. I had tears clouding my vision and streaming down my face, so I didn't see Brooke come out her door with an empty wine bottle, cocked to knock Ted over the head.

"Stop it!" she cried. "Just stop it, please!"

Ted got up, again, not saying a word, and spit on David who lay motionless on the ground, his face bloody and his crotch wet where he'd pissed himself. Ted wiped David's blood off of his hands and shot Brooke a stern look.

"If you don't do something about this, he's going to kill you, you know."

Then he pointed at me, and didn't need to say anything else. Brooke fell to her knees and started to cry.

"You tell him," Ted said, lip quivering and near tears, "that if he touches you again, that I will kill him. I'm not your guardian angel, but I will be your avenging angel if he ever hurts you again."

"Get out!" she screamed through her tears. "Just get out of here! I didn't ask you for this!"

Ted shook his head and walked back to his bike and me.

"Can you drive?" he asked me, and I laughed at the notion.

"Okay," he said, hands trembling, "just hold on then. I'll go slowly."

I didn't see Brooke again after that. It's not that I didn't want to, it's that I didn't know what to say. I looked in on her once or twice over the next couple of weeks; more to make sure that David didn't retaliate than anything else. I poked my head into the library long enough to see she was there, but never said a word, or let her see me there.

I couldn't stay in Arcadia after that, so I moved back to Toronto. I suppose I could have gone anywhere, like I'd told Brooke, but I always seem to come back to the same city, the same streets, the same familiar shops and faces. It's not home in the sense that some people have home, but it's as close a thing as I have.

A little over a year later, Cheryl and Ted left Arcadia for good. She'd finished a two-year associate's degree in nursing, and so she'd convinced Ted that they didn't need to stick around Arcadia, in fact, they'd both have a better chance at careers in a larger city. They'd moved to Arcadia in desperation – they were young, pregnant, and Ted was going to lose his job if they didn't move. But now they had more options.

My father had also gone full out wacky by that point (and you wonder why I use a pseudonym) and had embarked on a tour of the northeast, speaking at revival meetings and preaching hellfire and damnation with the same condescending fury that he used to use when telling us to eat our vegetables or he was going to shove them down our throats (which was, of course, not an idle threat, and was enacted upon on more than one occasion).

Arcadia had soured for Cheryl and Ted like a piece of fruit left out in the sun, and everywhere seemed rotten and covered in carrion flies. So they packed up their house, wiped the dirt of Arcadia from their shoes, and moved into the house that Penny and I would end up in after they died. Our parents stayed behind in Arcadia, and for an entire decade, Cheryl and I lived free, out from under their shadow.

Brooke kept in touch with me, calling from time to time, usually when she wanted out. She'd call me and beg me to rescue her, and I'd tell her that I would come and get her in a heartbeat. Then I'd hang up the phone and start to get ready to go get her, and the phone would ring again and she'd tell me not to come, that she'd changed her mind, and that everything was going to be okay. I'd tell her that everything was *not* going to be okay, but that I'd respect her wishes. I'd tell her to call me any time, day or night, and that I was only a few hours away. The closest she ever came to seriously asking me to come and get her, I was living in California, and I nearly got on a plane right then – I would have, but she wouldn't let me.

After a while, the calls became few and far between, until about a year ago, just over twenty years since I'd first met her, she called me to tell me that she'd finally ended it with David. He'd been having an affair with someone in Syracuse – even had a little love shack there – and she'd kicked him out. She wanted me to come down to be with her while he moved his shit out, and so I got in my car and started to drive down.

Alas, I was stopped for speeding, and learned that I'd had my license suspended because of a fifteen-year-old speeding ticket from my time in Arcadia, and had to call off my trip. I then spent the next few months going to court to avoid charges of Aggravated Operation of a Motor Vehicle (seriously, darlings, the only thing aggravated was me, I assure you) and it was nearly nine months before everything got settled to the point where I could legally drive and travel in the States again.

So, after far too long, I finally went back to Arcadia one last time, to visit my newly emancipated old friend.

Leaving Arcadia Part Seven

rooke looked about ten years older than she should have. Not to be unkind, but she looked like she'd spent the past ten years in jail, in a state of constant fear. Her face looked worn out, her hair had started to go white, and if it weren't for her smile, and the easy laugh she'd suddenly re-discovered, I wouldn't have recognized my old friend.

We didn't talk about the bad old days — the past was gone and best forgotten.

We talked instead about what we were going to do now.

"Well," Brooke said dryly, "I was thinking I'd open up a chain of women's shelters called *Ye Olde Friar's Shelter* to serve hand-battered women with fresh cut fries and salt and malt vinegar."

I looked at her and salivated, trying not to laugh, and failing miserably.

We continued the next part of our conversation at Jill's Diner, where we had passably edible fish and chips, with homemade coleslaw.

"And what about you?" she asked between mouthfuls. "How is it that you've stayed in one place so long?"

"I had to stop running sometime," I replied. "And then when Cheryl and Ted..."

She reached out and put her hand on mine.

"I'm so sorry I wasn't there for the funeral," she said, the first of many apologies. "It's just — "

"Don't worry about it," I said. "It doesn't matter."

"I should have been there," she insisted. "After what Ted did..."

"You were a prisoner, Brooke. I don't hold it against you."

She sighed. "I wish I could tell you he never hit me again after that, but..."

She shrugged, as if talking about something that happened to someone else, so long ago that even the memory was hazy.

"Have you seen him or heard from him since he moved out?"

"No," she said, shaking her head and smiling. "And I won't have to until the divorce goes through and we go to court. I got a restraining order against him on the same day I filed for divorce."

"Good for you!" I laughed.

We were quiet for a moment.

"How's Penny?"

I pulled out my phone and showed her a picture of the grown up Countess of Arcadia, tongue out, eyes crossed, flipping the camera the bird. Brooke laughed so loud she snorted.

"Oh my god, she looks just like you when I first met you!"

"You think so?" I asked, looking at the picture again. "Every time she smiles, she looks just like Cheryl, and every time she scowls I see Ted's face. Sometimes it breaks my heart just to look at her. Other times, I'm not sure what I'd do without her."

"How long has it been now?"

"Five years," I said. "Well, almost five years now."

Penny was seventeen years old, and hardly needed a babysitter, but she'd gotten in trouble for ditching class and so was sort of under house arrest. She'd heard a rumour that Marilyn Manson was going to be appearing at the Hard Rock Cafe downtown, so she'd cut class and caught the subway into the city, only to be disappointed when the rumour turned out to be false. Cheryl and Ted had to go out, and I was nominated as the Countess' warden for the evening. I thought it was pretty funny, them painting me as the responsible adult, when I probably would have done the same thing if I'd been in Penny's shoes, and it was, say, Morrissey and not Marilyn Manson (not that Morrissey would set foot in Canada, darlings, what with our continued barbaric practice of seal hunting, but I digress. I do that, darlings. I also make strange abstract macaroni art and do a passable Tom Waits – for a woman, anyway).

But Penny didn't mind – while she resented the implication that she couldn't be trusted, she and I have always been and always will be the very best of friends, and an evening with her favourite aunt (never mind that I'm her only aunt, darlings) was hardly punishment. We made huge bucket-loads of popcorn and blasted Brian Eno's *Here Come the Warm Jets* so loudly the windows shook, and danced around in our pyjamas and had popcorn fights while bouncing around on the furniture.

Penny and I were in the midst of glamming it up to *Baby's on Fire* when the doorbell rang and changed our lives forever.

Looking back, Penny will tell you that she knew something was wrong as soon as the doorbell rang, but then, I think that's just Penny's way of trying to make sense of the senseless, as if by giving the story some sort of narrative thread, she could somehow control it. The truth is, none of it made any sense. The police officers at the door said something about an accident, and there was some semblance of sympathy and a surprisingly sincere apology, which, when my mind wandered and began trying to protect itself with sarcasm and humour, I found terribly funny for some reason. Why was the officer apologizing? Were they the one driving the car that slammed into my sister's car? Were they somehow responsible for my brother-in-law being nearly decapitated, and so brutally disfigured that we chose to have a closed casket funeral? Why would he apologize?

Later, at the funeral, I would think the same thing, and when some well-meaning person would come up to me and tell me how sorry they were, I would hug them and whisper *you should be*, and then break into hysterics. I spent most of the time at the visitation laughing, and how strange is that?

I don't know the details, and if I ever did, I've since forgotten them. I know the driver of the car was drunk, and I know that he survived the accident with very few injuries. They say that being drunk is the best way to be in an accident – your body doesn't tense up and so the opportunity for injury is lessened. Ted was killed instantly, they said, and they had to use the Jaws of Life to get Cheryl out of the wreck. She never woke up again. I never got to say goodbye – not that she heard, anyway.

When I did see her, she was attached to machines; a tube inserted down her throat breathing for her, and half of her face was completely covered up. She didn't stay that way for very long – the doctors were fairly clear with Penny and I that there was really nothing they could do. She wasn't going to recover.

It took me nearly two days to track my parents down, and when I did, I learned that they were somewhere in Maine at some Holiness Camp or something, and when I told them about Cheryl's condition, they told me that they'd pray for her.

"I think it's a little beyond that, now," I said. "But you go ahead and pray if it makes you feel better."

"Please don't mock my faith, Helena," my mother said.

"If you want to do something, then *do* something. Your prayers aren't helping anyone."

"Please, Helena," she cried.

"Look, I don't think you understand," I said, trying my best to be patient and less antagonizing. "She's dead. There's nothing you can do for her."

"Don't say that!" she screamed at me from far away.

"I'm sorry, but it's true. The reason I was calling was to tell you to come right away if you want to be here when they take her off the machines."

There was silence on the phone for what seemed like ten minutes, and then finally, a small, timid, voice – a voice of a woman that had been beaten down for over thirty years – said two words, and those two words nearly made me vomit with rage. My head spun, the world went bright and I thought that maybe I was having a stroke or something.

"We can't," she said, and then waited for my response.

When I finally regained equilibrium, I spoke evenly but firmly. "What do you mean, you can't?"

"Your father..."

I didn't need to hear anymore.

"Mom," I said through clenched teeth.

"Helena, please, you don't understand," she pleaded. "We're in the middle of a revival. Tickets have all been sold."

"What am I supposed to do?" I asked, not really speaking to my mother.

"We'll be there as soon as we can. You'll do as you must. You always have."

So again, it was left to me. I would be the one to stand by my sister's side while the nurses turned off the machine that was breathing for her. I would be the one holding Penny's hand while we watched her mother's face turn purple, and I would be there when she died less than a minute later.

"Will you be up for the funeral?" I was barely able to ask the question.

"We have one more meeting tomorrow and then yes, I think we'll be able to come up."

"If you can't be here by the weekend, don't bother coming at all," I said, resisting the urge to tell her that I never wanted to see either of them ever again. I'm sure that somehow, she was grieving, and that at some point it would hit her.

She started to say something else and I just hung up the phone and fell to the floor of the hospital, and sat under the payphone and wept.

"Does it get any easier?" Brooke asked, finishing up the last of her coleslaw and pushing bits of over-fried batter around her plate absent-mindedly.

"I don't know yet," I said with a forced smile. "I'll let you know."

"Still, you got away," she said, almost a question. "You're a born survivor."

I laughed at that, thinking of how I'd survived, and how successful I'd been at survival.

But then again...

"Yeah, but not without my scars. And hey, now you've gotten away. What are you going to do now?"

"I told you... some sort of shelter-slash-fish and chips place with a terribly inappropriate pun about battered women in the title."

I grinned. "Yeah, but after that?"

She shrugged. "Well, I tell you what I'm *not* going to do. I'm not dating anyone. *Ever.*"

"So you say," I said with a smirk.

"No, I'm serious," she said seriously, "I don't trust my own judgment."

"Yeah, I've been there," I admitted, "but don't rule it out. I'm not saying you should go out and start dating after being married to a psycho for twenty years. In fact, I'd say quite the opposite – take time for yourself – as long as you need. But if you can find happiness with someone else someday, I say go for it."

"What about you?" she asked, giving me a curious look as I tried vainly not to blush.

"I've actually met someone," I said.

"*Really?*"

"Yeah," I admitted. I'd only seen Spenser a couple of times, but I had a good feeling about it. "Would you believe he's almost ten years younger than me?"

"Holy shit!" Brooke laughed, and slapped a hand over her mouth as a couple of little old ladies gave her a dirty look from two tables away. "You got yourself a sugar daddy!"

"Hardly," I said, a bit embarrassed. "Penny introduced him to me – can you believe it? He works at the bar on her campus, and is going back to school for – are you ready for this? Jazz Studies."

"What?"

"He's a pianist – a classically trained pianist, and oh, my god, he plays like fucking Bill Evans."

Brooke gave me a blank look.

"Oscar Peterson?"

"Uh uh. Sorry. Oh wait, was he the guy who did the Charlie Brown music?"

"No," I said. "That was Vince Guaraldi. Do you know Ben Folds?"

"Yes!" she said excitedly. "Yes, I think so."

"Doesn't matter," I sighed. "He plays like a lounge act. I close my eyes and I can almost smell the olives from the martinis, the smoke from the cigarettes. I could listen to him play forever."

"And you're happy?"

"It's too soon to tell, but yeah, he seems nice. He's the first man I've been interested in since... well, in a long time."

"You made it, then," she said, and lifted her glass of water to me to toast. "At least one of us did."

"You will, too," I said. "You'll see."

"Sure," she said. "I know. But did you hear they found Amy LeFevre?"

"What? No! When?"

"A few months ago," she replied. "It was big news around here."

"Well, sure," I said. "But what do you mean, they found her? Did they arrest her?"

Brooke shook her head.

"What?"

"She killed herself. They found her in some hotel room, overdosed on heroin or coke or something – I'm not sure."

"Shit," I said, feeling the gravity of it. There, but by the grace of whoever…

"You're not her," I reminded her. "And if you can't handle things, you're smart enough to reach out to a friend. You know. Like *me*, for example."

"I know," she said with a smile, and gave my hand a squeeze. "Thank you, Helena."

"I've been waiting a very long time to hear that," I told her. "I'm just glad I did get to hear it."

"Well, the next time you hear it, I'll be far away from here," she said.

"What do you mean?"

"I'm selling the house," she said. "I'm leaving Arcadia, and I'm never coming back."

I couldn't help it. I started smiling so big that my eyes welled up with tears, and I started bawling like a baby right there at the table of Jill's Diner. I reached across the table and awkwardly wrapped my arms around her.

"Good for you, darling," I said.

And with that, I went home. I didn't see my parents; in fact, I haven't seen them since the funeral. That's all part of escaping that Arcadia of the mind; that small-minded prison that I found myself born into, and which I lived in, until even the stone walls became comfortable, and I felt afraid and unsafe without them. Walking out the door and closing it on the past requires locking it behind you, unless you want to relive all that horror again. Sometimes you run, and you never really get away. Amy LeFevre never really escaped, it seems, but I had to believe that Brooke could, because if she couldn't, then what chance did I have?

Before I left, I helped Brooke put the FOR SALE sign out on her front lawn, and it all felt real. She's leaving Arcadia, and so am I.

I Know Very Well How
I Got My Name Part One

*T*his is a love story. But not a Hollywood love story, darlings, so I can't in good conscience offer you any promises of a happy ending. Or at least not in the "they rode off into the sunset together and lived happily ever after" way.

It's a story about honesty – about being true to yourself – about loving enough to let go.

I met Adam at a particularly low time in my life. My sister Cheryl and her husband had died not six months before, and I had (is inherited the wrong word to use here?) my niece Penny. I was suddenly no longer just fun Aunt Helena; I had to look after her. Not that Penny, already technically an adult – though just technically – needed diapers changing (well, not very often, anyway) or to have her every need provided for. For that I could be thankful – that in a way, we were a support for each other.

Adam was a fixer-upper. Not the first project I've taken on, and – give me strength – probably not the last. He was an actor, or at least, he wanted to be, at any rate. He worked through the agency I work for, taking jobs as a background actor – an extra. You know, the crowd of people that fill out the scenery in movies and television shows.

It's not exactly a full-time gig, and it's all Adam did for a living. The rest of his time he spent painting – but I'm getting ahead of myself, darlings.

The end of the year was approaching, and I had been invited to a very important party for New Year's Eve. Not the type of party with celebrities and directors – I wasn't there yet, darlings – but with a lot of casting agents and other industry contacts. If I ever wanted to get out from behind my desk and in front of a camera (sigh – yes, I, too, dreamed of the silver screen) then I had better drag myself out of my mourning funk for one night only, and show off my dazzling... wits.

I didn't want a date. Really, I didn't – but much as one does not simply *walk into Mordor*,[84] one does not show up at the biggest to-do of the year on one's own. No, like it or not, I needed some arm candy. Adam just happened to walk in my door – the most beautiful man I'd ever laid eyes on. It didn't hurt that he was wearing a tuxedo – a pinstriped suit that the wardrobe department had provided for him for a shoot of some ballroom scene set in the 1930s.

I really hadn't said more than a dozen words to Adam before that day. Just business – *can you be here at such and such a time, etc...*

When I asked him if he would be my date for New Year's Eve, it felt strangely like a similar business transaction.

I don't think I spoke to him at all between that day and New Year's Eve, when I called him to make sure we were still on, and did he have a tuxedo, and blah blah blah...

He meant nothing to me. For all intents and purposes, I might as well have hired an escort, except that the advantage of being a woman – and a beautiful, charming one at that, darlings – is that I can always find someone willing to be seen with me, even if for just an evening.

The night itself was nothing to write about. We had fun. We danced, we drank, we had a few laughs. It's not that he wasn't a nice guy, it's just that it was all fake for me. I was just going through the motions, trying to put on a happy face when I was anything but. By the end of the evening, I was drunk enough to invite him back to my place, and even drunk enough to let him get a bit frisky with me, but not *so* drunk that I turned into a complete slut.

No, darlings, I'm happy to say that we fell asleep with our clothes on, and in the morning, I kicked him out after a polite thank you and a cup of coffee. We did the ever-popular I'll Call You Two-

---

[84] Yet another *Lord of the Rings* reference that has come to mean understanding the true gravitas of a task.

Step (cha cha cha) and said good-bye, both expecting that would be the last of it.

But a month later, I got invited by a friend to go out on the town for Valentine's Day. She'd won some prize package that involved a limousine, fancy dinner, nightclubbing, and Niagara Falls, and she insisted that I join her, and was I seeing anybody? I don't know why, but for some reason, I told her that yes; yes, I had started seeing someone on New Year's Eve, and yes, Adam and I would love to join her.

Adam and I never made it to the Valentine's Day party, though.

"How come you haven't called me?" I asked, feigning disappointment. He saw right through me.

"What do you need from me now, Helena?" he laughed.

"That obvious, huh?"

"I knew what New Year's was. I had fun. But I got the feeling you didn't, so I let it go."

I couldn't see him over the phone, but in my head, he shrugged, and it was adorable.

"I need a date for Valentine's Day," I blurted, and he burst out laughing. He had an amazing, deep chuckle that made me grin sheepishly in return.

"Why do you assume I've got nothing planned for Valentine's Day? What if I already have a date?"

"Oh, you can't!" I declared decidedly. "You simply can't. You have plans with me. You'll just have to break that poor other girl's heart!"

"Actually, my best friend is flying in from Vancouver on the 12th, and staying with me for a few days. I'll tell you what – if you have room for two more – assuming you can find him a date – then I'm in."

"I'm going to need to know more about your friend if I'm going to set him up on a date with someone on Valentine's Day. And he's going to have to buy roses. Lots of roses." I insisted, negotiating the contract.

"Roses on Valentine's Day?" he laughed. "Do you have any idea how much they cost on Valentine's Day?"

"Oh, and chocolates," I added. "And not some drug store heart-shaped box of waxy $2.99 specials. Truffles. From an actual chocolatier."

"Wait, aren't you the one who asked me for a favour?" he asked, amused.

"I am offering you the pleasure of my company for the most romantic evening of the year. If you insist on bringing your friend – whose charm and character have yet to be proven, along with us – then I think it only fair that you sweeten the pot a little."

"Oh I see," he said. "Well, why don't you come pick me up for a drink, and I can fill you in on the details about my friend?"

By the time Valentine's Day rolled around, we'd spent nearly every waking moment outside of work with each other, talking over coffee – those long auto-biographical conversations you have at the start of a new relationship. A sort of unpacking of your heart for the purposes of barter and exchange. You show me yours and I'll show you mine. For him, he played his cards one at a time, insisting that he was hiding nothing back. But of course, this is another familiar dance. Only a fool would lay all their cards on the table all at once. Ordinarily, I came to the table with armour firmly fastened to my fine frame, prepared to protect my past. Maybe it was vulnerability, or exhaustion. Maybe it was just an honest, deep longing to connect with another person; to wash away my sorrow and bury myself in the comfort of love. For whatever reason, this time I came to the table with both my weapons and my defences down. For good or ill, the game had begun.

He played the King of Diamonds - a wealthy, successful father in Vancouver who had all but disowned him when he refused to go work for him in his construction company.

I countered with the King of Clubs - an angry, abusive, controlling father who created an atmosphere of terror for me and my sister growing up.

He laid the Jack of Spades, and explained about his trek across the country, totally broke and hungry, running as far away as he possibly could, living in his car and busking on the street; painting stylized portraits for gas and food money.

I countered with the Queen of Hearts, and confessed my passion for life, love and the arts. I spilled all the relevant details of my dalliances with love, up to and including the painful tale that ended with me miscarrying on my sister's front porch.

He returned with the King of Hearts, declaring that didn't think he'd ever been in love, but that he thought he'd know it when he saw it.

I played the Queen of Spades, and told him about Cheryl and Ted's fatal car accident, speaking honestly of the grief that had been eating away at me.

He showed me the Jack of Hearts, and told me about his best friend Paul, who he'd grown up with and for whom he'd do anything. Paul's mother had just died, after the doctors discovered an inoperable brain tumour not three months prior. He was coming out to Toronto to stay with Adam for a few days just to get away from all the people in his life that were hanging all around him, doting over him and trying to help him and constantly asking him if he was all right; if there was anything they could do.

I dropped the Queen of Clubs, and proudly described my brief stint as the singer of a band out in California, and how it had ignited a desire to perform, to create, to show the world what I could do. I told him how I'd tried to show my writing to people – little short stories and poems; the makings of a novel – but how I'd gotten a lot of blank stares from people, or polite nods and smiles. I had no idea what to make of that – was my writing any good? Or were they just placating me?

He slapped a pair of Jacks down – Diamonds and Clubs, and told me that he didn't *really* want to be an actor; that all he really wanted to do was paint – that if he could ever make anything as incredibly cool as his hero Jean-Michel Basquiat,[85] he could die a happy man. He wanted to be famous for his paintings; to have his own gallery and studio. He gravitated toward little artist communities, and loved meeting and collaborating with other artists, and he fantasized about opening up a collective studio, like Andy Warhol's Factory; just opening the door to all the freaks and artists and musicians and creating something amazing.

I held the King of Spades and the Queen of Diamonds in my hand, and wondered if this was supposed to be us. Him, the black sheep of his family. Me, the glamorous pseudo-orphan – equal parts castaway and self-imposed exile. Neither of us having any idea how to love properly, what with our model upbringing.

---

[85] Basquiat was an artist in the late '70s and '80s who started as a graffiti artist and found international acclaim with his Primitivist paintings.

At some point, the game must have become strip poker, because we ended up in bed together, desperately devouring each other, exploring each other's hard and soft places, guiding each other around the labyrinth of our bodies. He was nervous at first, but willing to learn, and we spent hours in session, with Professor Helena providing PowerPoint presentations on the proper procedure for pleasurable foreplay preceding penetration.

We shut out the world for days, ignoring the phone, me calling in sick to work, emerging only for necessities like food and water. We had been in a state of coital bliss for three days when it dawned on us that we had completely missed our Valentine's Day date, and Adam had missed picking his friend Paul up from the airport. Adam had several angry messages on his cell phone from Paul, saying eventually that he was going to stay at a hotel, and that he didn't know where Adam was or what was going on, but that he'd wait for his phone call.

Feeling guilty, I offered to go with him to pick up his friend, to sort of kill two birds with one stone. I'd heard so much about Paul, and knew that if he was important to Adam, that I'd have to meet him and make a good impression. Considering the circumstances, I was pretty nervous.

I shouldn't have worried. We loved each other immediately, and from that day on, the three of us were inseparable.

In retrospect, I should have seen right away that Adam and I weren't meant for each other.

I Know Very Well How
I Got My Name Part Two

"*H*elena, I think I just want to sell the house," Penny said, holding me tightly and crying into my shoulder. "Let's just sell the house and get a place that's just yours and mine."

After everything that had happened in the past two and a half years – from Penny's parents – my sister and brother-in-law – dying, to Adam moving in, to the whole thing with Paul – I was inclined to agree with her.

"A fresh start," I agreed, wiping tears from my own eyes, and looking around at the house that had been left to Penny in her parents' wills. "Are you sure?"

Penny nodded, and I held her tightly.

Two months later, we were moving into the third floor of a gorgeous Victorian, a place we both immediately loved, and could imagine us staying for some time.

As I was hanging up a poster Adam had given me, I had a rare moment of breakdowniness (it's a word, trust me) and Penny came to my aid, as she is wont to do.

"I miss him," I said, emotionally exhausted.

"Me, too," Penny agreed. "I miss them *both*."

Paul had only meant to stay for a few days, but being around Adam seemed to be incredibly therapeutic for him. A few days turned into a few weeks, and as Adam was spending so much time with me, that meant that Paul was hanging out, too. Adam's place was a loft studio the size of a broom closet, so that meant that the two of them were hanging out at our place – that is, mine and Penny's.

Penny was still grieving terribly – we both were – and having them around was at first difficult, but then Penny started coming out of her shell, and started talking and laughing again. When Paul finally had to go back to Vancouver, she was devastated. He was an instantly likable guy, and he'd quickly become the big brother Penny never had. I knew I was going to miss him, too.

So when he called up a couple of months later and said that he was thinking of moving out to Toronto – that he needed a change – it just made sense that he'd come and stay with us. Adam got rid of his apartment and moved in with us officially, and when Paul arrived, he took an empty downstairs bedroom. We had more than enough room, and having them around made a big lonely house less empty; less lonely.

Our house never wanted for laughter. Paul got a job as a waiter at an Italian restaurant and was constantly bringing home the most amazing pasta for us. Adam worked extra gigs and painted, claiming a corner of the basement as his studio space. I'd sneak home in the middle of the day to make love, distracting him in the nicest possible way from his artistic endeavours. Penny was applying to universities – she'd deferred her acceptance when her parents died, but too much time had passed and her deadlines lapsed. But she'd started showing an interest in life again since the boys moved in, and I was hopeful that we'd be able to get through this.

There was only one small problem with the whole situation – as much as I loved Adam, I couldn't help but be developing feelings for Paul. He was attractive, and funny, and he was always around. He lived with us, and as much as I'd love to say that I didn't have naughty thoughts about him, darlings, that would be less than honest. I mean, I'd very much like to tell you that I never once fantasized about Paul instead of Adam whilst in the throes of self-abuse in the bath, but then again, that, too, would be less than 100 percent truthful, darlings, and if there's one thing I am not, it's a liar. And so I won't tell you that I once came in late and, finding him asleep on the couch, sat down beside him and stroked his handsome, exquisitely featured face, stroking his magnificent jawline with one lustful finger. I won't tell you that I buried my face in his hair and breathed in his scent. Further, I'll conveniently neglect to mention that when he stirred, I ran in guilty terror up to bed, where I immediately jumped on Adam and gave him the fuck of his life.

But we both know who I was fucking, darlings – let's not kid ourselves.

After that, things started to get a little weird between Adam and I – or maybe it started before that, and I just hadn't noticed. It was just little things. I'd make excuses to avoid him, and he didn't really object. I'd start pushing it – like I was testing him; trying to piss him off – and nothing really bothered him. It was like he didn't mind; didn't even care, really. He was never mean or upset about it when I didn't come to bed when invited – I stayed up watching a lot of television, because Paul was watching television. I enjoyed his company, I liked hearing him talk, I just liked being around him.

I couldn't keep up the emotional charade – I knew that I was going to have to say something to Adam. It wasn't fair to him – if I had these feelings for Paul, then it wasn't fair to either of us. I wasn't going to let anything happen between Paul and I – I had made that decision – but I at least had to be honest with Adam. I owed him that.

Making a decision to do something feels wonderful, darlings – it really does. You pat yourself on the back and feel really good about yourself as a human being, just for having thought about doing the right thing. But thinking about doing something and actually doing it are two different things, and so while I thought about telling Adam about the way I was feeling about Paul, three months went by, and Adam and I were both miserable, though neither of us could say why.

Until Paul got hit by a car, and everything changed.

It was November, I remember, because it was the beginning of the end – the end that came so fast that it left us all whip-lashed and traumatized. One minute we were all living a strange sort of domesticity, sharing a roof together, eating meals together – a patchwork family, that, like any family, had its problems, but functioned nonetheless. The next minute we were gathered around Paul's hospital bed, each of us questioning if we knew each other at all.

When I arrived at the hospital, Adam was already there. Paul was unconscious but stable, and was hooked up to a breathing tube. One of his lungs had collapsed, he had broken some ribs and one arm, and had a concussion, but he was going to be okay. You wouldn't know that from the scene I walked in on.

Adam was holding Paul's hand, and had his head to his friend's forehead, weeping so hard he was hyperventilating. He kept saying how scared he was, how he thought he'd lost him, and how he never got to tell him how much he meant to him. Just on a frantic, terrified loop.

I stood outside the room, watching this; giving Adam his privacy. There were tears in my own eyes, but I knew to wait my turn. Those boys had known each other since they were practically babies.

I watched Adam stroke Paul's hair lovingly, looking at him with fear and worry. And then I watched, as Adam bent down and kissed Paul, at first nervously, and then more firmly, full on the mouth.

I inhaled sharply in surprise, and Adam turned to see me in the doorway and hung his head.

"Come on in, Helena," he said quietly. "Come see him if you want."

I froze, unable to move. I felt like such a fool for not seeing it before, and I felt like an idiot for being there then and interrupting him.

"I'm going to leave now," Adam said, sounding exhausted and all cried out. "I'll meet you down in the cafeteria. We can grab a coffee and talk. We... we have a lot to talk about."

I stared at him, not knowing what to say. I forced my feet to take a couple of steps forward.

"Does he...?" I asked, motioning toward the bed where Paul lay oblivious to the conversation.

"No," Adam said, shaking his head sadly. "And if for some reason he wakes up, please don't say anything."

I nodded. I could give him that.

I sat across from Adam, unable to catch my breath. I waited for him to talk, but he could hardly meet my eyes. I just wanted to understand.

"But... but..." I stammered, trying to think of what to say. "But you're not gay."

Adam looked up at me and laughed. Laughed until he started turning red in the face and I was sure he was going to pass out. I couldn't help but laugh with him – and there was a degree of relief in the laughter, as if we had both been holding something in for months.

"Well, that's a relief," he finally said. "It's a good thing I'm not gay, because then all these feelings I'm having would be really strange. They must just be figments of my imagination."

He smiled sadly at me, eager for understanding, acceptance, and forgiveness. And here I thought that I'd be begging the same from him.

I wish I could tell you that I used that opportunity to confess what I'd been feeling myself, darlings. I'd certainly come across as a much better person if I could tell you that I used that moment to break the tension by saying something like "Well, I don't blame you, darling – I've been wanting to get my hands on him for months now," but sadly, that would also entail the telling of tall tales, and as has been previously established and well-documented, darlings, I am no teller of tall tales. I may have been accused of being not exactly the most reliable narrator from time to time, and I admit to the occasional bit of revisionist history in order to direct my narrative in the direction I'd like it to go – but outright lies?

Moving right along, I did the only thing I knew how to do. I stood up, I walked around the table, stood Adam up and gave him a great big hug, holding him and telling him that I loved him. If I could play the hero in this scenario, I would. I certainly didn't want the role of the faithless hussy set to step out on her man. And I didn't really relish the role of competition for Paul's affections. Would that make me the other woman, or the other man?

"You should tell him," I said, holding him tight. "He needs to know."

"You don't think that's going to confuse the hell out of him?" Adam asked. "We've known each other for nearly our whole lives."

"Adam," I said, looking him in the face. "Don't you think maybe he already knows?"

Adam gave a bit of a sick moaning laugh.

"Helena, I didn't even know," he said. "I didn't think it was possible. I've only ever been with girls, and it's not like I don't enjoy that."

"You certainly seemed to be enjoying yourself," I agreed with a smile.

"But having Paul around this past year, seeing him every day... I'm sorry. You don't want to hear this."

I knew what it was to have feelings for someone you're not supposed to have feelings for.

"No, it's okay," I said. "I meant what I said. I do love you, Adam, and I want you to be happy."

He looked at me and began to cry again, more gently this time.

"Then when I saw him in the hospital bed, and thought that he might have died – well I knew then what love was. I knew that I loved him, and not in the way I thought I did, and I couldn't help myself. I couldn't stop feeling it."

"You can't help who you love, Adam," I said, and held him again.

When we returned to Paul's room, we found Penny sitting by his side, holding his hand. He'd woken up and was weakly laughing at something Penny had said. We must have looked a fright, because he looked up at us and coughed in alarm.

"Jeez, you guys," he wheezed, "who died?"

Adam smiled and let out a relieved sigh.

I motioned for Penny, giving her the universal sign for "Hey, let's leave these two alone, they really need to talk about some life-changing things, and hey, do you want to maybe get a bagel? On the way in I smelled the intoxicating smell of fresh bagels from this bakery we passed and I just realized I haven't eaten anything practically all day, and I'm starving. Also, I could go for a coffee."

You know that sign, right?

Penny looked at me with a blank stare, and so I had to resort to words.

"Hey Penny, let's go grab a coffee? What do you say?"

"Are you going to make me cry, too?" She asked, nodding her head toward Adam, whose eyes were all puffy and red.

I grabbed her hand and pulled her out of the room.

The next time I spoke to Adam, he was nearly catatonic with grief. Penny and I had gone out for dinner, and when we arrived home, we heard Adam making sick noises from the bathroom. He was throwing up, but not just vomit – in between bouts of actual physical sickness, he was wailing and howling – the most awful sounds of loss and misery I've ever been unfortunate enough to hear.

I tried to talk to him, to tell him I was sorry that things didn't go the way he wanted them to; that Paul would come around; that the important thing was that he had been honest, and that his feelings were out in the open. I lied to him and told him that everything was going to be all right.

When Paul got out of the hospital, he packed his things and moved back to Vancouver, hardly saying a word to any of us before he left.

Adam moved out a week later, and Penny wouldn't stop crying for days. We were losing our family all over again.

"What do you think?" I asked, positioning the poster of Andy Warhol and Jean-Michel Basquiat over our new fireplace.

Penny nodded, and went to say something, but was interrupted by the doorbell.

When she returned, she had Adam in tow, carrying a canvas with four strange, beautiful figures painted on it.

He presented to me awkwardly, and gave me a kiss on my cheek.

"I call it *Home*," he said. "It's for the two of you, really. The time we all spent together, it was..."

"It was the best," Penny said, and glared at the both of us. "And you ruined it. Both of you."

Penny stormed off to her room to sulk.

"She'll come around," I said sadly.

"I've heard that before," he replied.

"Have you heard from him at all?"

He shook his head and wiped a tear away.

"No, but I've got good news."

"Yeah?" I asked, welcoming some good news.

"Yeah, I'm going to have a show of my art," he said, excited.

"That's great, Adam," I said. "I'm really happy for you."

"And what about you, Helena?" he pried. "When are you going to start writing again? You have so much to say."

"Yes, but no one's listening," I sighed. "We've been through this before."

I'd told Adam all about my forays into writing, how I'd even tried showing my writing around, but I couldn't get anyone interested. Or else, the people reading my stuff were friends and family, whose objectivity couldn't be trusted.

"Besides," I said, "I'm all out of stories. I'm done. Which is fine. These pills the doctor gave me pretty much kill any creativity I might have had anyway."

"Oh, I think you have plenty of stories to tell," he laughed. "Why don't you tell our story?"

I looked at him with tears in my eyes, and shook my head.

"I'm not ready to tell that story yet," I replied. "I'm not strong enough. All the stories I need to tell, they're too much – I don't know if I have the strength to tell them."

And then Adam looked at me and told me what I needed to do.

"Hide," he said. "Hide behind someone stronger than you are. Use that sharp wit of yours and dream up someone stronger than you to tell those stories. Someone who's you, but amplified to the nearly unbelievable – someone bold and sassy and so completely you, but without the fear and reservations. Someone with a fuck you attitude and a killer smile, who borders on caricature but has feet planted firmly in reality."

"And what's this fantasy girl's name?" I demanded to know.

"Helena," he replied without hesitation. "My fantasy girl's called Helena."

I pulled away from him, realizing for the first time that I had actually been hurt by the whole situation.

"Don't," I said. "Please don't do that."

"Sorry," he said, "but it's true. I never felt about any woman the way I did you. I'm sorry we weren't better suited for each other."

"I know," I admitted. "Everything just went to hell in a handbasket once Paul moved in."

I may or may not have phrased it exactly like that, darlings, but let's just for the sake of narrative assume that I did.

"Don't be angry with him," Adam pleaded. "It's not his fault."

"I know," I admitted again, wanting so badly to be angry at someone but not finding it in me.

We shared an awkward silence, gave each other a hug, and said good-bye.

The next couple of weeks, I couldn't stop thinking about what Adam had said, about re-inventing myself as someone else – a character I could hide behind, pouring as much, or as little of myself into her as I wanted.

One day in early March, Penny came home and threw a new CD at me.

"Hey, Helena, I was just at Starbucks and saw this – did you know there was a new Bowie album?"

"What?" I said, excited. "No way!"

Penny and I both shared an unnaturally overenthusiastic love for David Bowie. His music had practically been the cradle songs of Penny's earliest years. She'd been ostracized by her little classmates, who just didn't get it when she'd say things like *bully for you; chilly for me*, or *Ooh baby, just you shut your mouth.*

The new album, *The Next Day*, became the soundtrack to my life for the next week or so, and I thought I finally had the catalyst to my creativity.

I'd spoken to my doctor about coming off of the medication I'd been on – the medication that had been turning me into a zombie – and over the past weeks I'd been weaning myself off of them. The emotional turmoil was intense, and I hope to never go through that kind of withdrawal ever again.

One day after eavesdropping on conversations at Starbucks (careful what you say in public, you never know when I might be listening), I came home and started thinking about what this imaginary persona I'd begun to conceive of might have to say about what I'd heard.

I wrote something up, pouring all my sarcasm and quasi-harmless misanthropy into it, and showed it to Penny.

She shrugged, and said it was not bad, but it was missing something. I asked her what she thought it was missing, and she struck a pose.

"Why, *me*, of course. Everything is better with a little bit of *me* in it."

I laughed at her boldness, and realized that it's exactly what I needed. I needed to borrow a little of Penny's brashness.

"Okay," I said, playing along. "And what shall I call myself?"

The answer sat right in front of us, and we didn't even know it.

"What if you just change your last name – I dunno – take grandma's last name or something?"

"Helena Hann?" I asked, shaking my head dubiously. "Sounds awful. Why not Helena Hann-Job, it can be a whole other type of blog."

"Oh dear," Penny smirked. "Oh! Oh! I know! What about Helena Mauvaise? It's French, it's a bad pun – it's perfect!"

"Helena Mauvaise... you mean, like *haleine mauvaise* – French for bad breath? What, should I invent an imaginary boyfriend named Hal I. Tosis?"

We both considered it for a moment... I mean, actually considered it for a moment, darlings. I came *this close* to being your favourite dilettante, Helena Mauvaise.

"Did you know that one of Andy Warhol's Factory Girls was named Helena Handbasket?" Penny asked, searching the name Helena on Google. "Look, I found a picture."

And there she was. Bored looking, fuzzy and out of focus, smoking a cigarette and projecting an image that said she didn't give a flying rat's ass. (Later I would discover that "Helena Handbasket" was actually a transvestite, but the less said about that right now the better).

"That's perfect," I said, unable to take my eyes off the screen.

"Yeah, but it's been done," Penny said. "You're, like, nearly forty years too late."

I stared at the picture of Warhol and Basquiat, and smiled.

I ran to my laptop and typed: Being the Memoirs of Helena Hann-Basquiat, Dilettante.

Penny, looking over my shoulder, smiled.

"Yup," she said. "That'll work."

"Should I post that story?" I asked.

"Sure," she shrugged. "Whatever you like. It's a start. I still say you need to work me in somehow. You're ever so dull without me, darling."

She affected a very aristocratic tone, part posh British and part Cruella de Vil. I loved it immediately.

"I'm taking that!" I declared, and she gave me a blank stare.

"Why, whatever are you talking about, darling?"

****

A week went by and I hadn't written anything else. I was beginning to think Penny was right – that first post was missing something.

Then I got a notice in my email about a once in a lifetime concert opportunity. A band you've never heard of (and really, that's your loss) was playing one of my favourite albums beginning to end. I wasn't going to let the fact that it was a seven-hour drive away dissuade me from seeing them.

"Penny!" I yelled, excited beyond belief. "We're going to Montreal! Grab your coat!"[86]

---

[86] Back to where it all began – see *Memoirs of a Dilettante Volume One*

Acknowledgements

Two long years not only writing these stories, but being Helena, and that in itself was its own task. It did not go unaided, and I have so many people to thank.

First, as always, I thank Penny. And Penny. And Penny. And Penny. For putting up with my and for allowing me to steal bits of her life as inspiration – it was ever flattery, darling, I assure you.

Second, those goodly souls who graciously allowed me to confide in them along the way. Hannah and Scott and Jennie and Marie and Katie. As the list grew to include Selena and Jex and Michelle and Hayley and Sandy and Freya, the road to my eventual unmasking became more clear.

Of course, I have to mention Lizzi, who has taken me on almost as a cause – rather, my writing. Me, she has taken simply as friend, and should I stop writing tomorrow, I know she'd never stop scolding me but I also know it wouldn't change her friendship.

Thank you Hasty for your keen eye, your artistic bravery, and your kind heart.

Thank you to Shirley Maya Tan, to whom Postcards from California is dedicated with love.

And to REDdog, who has always had Helena's back.

Thank you to Dawn and Andra and Katie C. for your time and effort.

Thank you Jim – how awfully embarrassing and dull my life would be without you.

Lastly, thank you to Katherine, for tolerating this and so much more. I love you.

About the Author

The enigmatic Helena Hann-Basquiat dabbles in whatever she can get her hands into just to say that she has.

She's written cookbooks, ten volumes of horrible poetry that she then bound herself in leather she tanned poorly from cows she raised herself and then slaughtered because she was bored with farming.

She has an entire portfolio of macaroni art that she's never shown anyone, because she doesn't think that the general populace or, "the great unwashed masses" as she calls them, would understand the statement she was trying to make with them.

Some people attribute the invention of the Ampersand to her, but she has never made that claim herself.

In 2014, she published Memoirs of a Dilettante Volume One, several e-books which now make up the book in your hands, as well as a multimedia collaborative piece of meta-fictional horror entitled JESSICA. Her most recent project is a Shakespearean-style play titled *Penelope, Countess of Arcadia.*

Helena writes strange, dark fiction under the name Jessica B. Bell, and her first collection of stories, entitled *VISCERA* is set for publication in 2015 by Sirens Call Publications.

Find more of her writing at www.helenahb.com or www.whoisjessica.com or connect with her via Twitter @HHBasquiat.